BLOOM OF LOVE

A BBW INTERRACIAL WESTERN ROMANCE

COWBOYS OF LONG VALLEY ROMANCE
BOOK ONE

ERIN WRIGHT

Copyright © 2021 by Erin Wright

ISBN (Regular Print, Paperback): 978-1-950570-13-3

ISBN (Regular Print, Hard Cover): 978-1-950570-59-1

ISBN (Large Print, Paperback): 978-1-950570-39-3

ISBN (Large Print, Hard Cover): 978-1-950570-91-1

This book is a work of fiction. The names, characters, places and incidents are products of the writer's imagination or have been used fictitiously and are not to be constructed as real. Any resemblance to persons, living or dead, actual events, locales or organizations is entirely coincidental.

All rights reserved. No part of this book may be reproduced, scanned, or distributed in any manner whatsoever without written permission from the author except in the case of brief quotation embodied in critical articles and reviews.

Richard Rodgers & Oscar Hammerstein II © 1943 – *Oh, What a Beautiful Morning*

Carrie Underwood © 2009 – *Mama's Song*

Mark Knopfler & Willy DeVille © 1987 – *Storybook Love*

Cover Designed by Sunset Rose Books

This one's for all of my fans who waited patiently (whether they wanted to or not), as the release date of "Bloom of Love" was pushed back again and again.

I hope it's worth the wait.

PS To my hubby – I'm so glad you loved The Princess Bride. It would've been sad if I would've been forced to turn down your proposal.

CHAPTER ONE

CHRISTIAN

As you wish.
~Westley in *The Princess Bride*

END OF MAY, 2020

"WE HAVE TO GET *EL TRONO*, *Mamá*," Nieves Palacios said, the whine in her voice grating on her brother's nerves. "Everyone at school will make fun of me if we book *Café Rubio* instead. They're just a bunch of old men. I told all my friends we're gonna have *El Trono*. We can't change it now."

Christian Palacios flicked through Instagram mindlessly, his irritation growing by the second with his youngest sister.

It was bad enough that she was spoiled rotten. It was even worse that he had to sit through yet another *quinceañera* planning meeting.

Yesenia, his second youngest sister and the complete opposite of Nieves in every way, caught his eye and grimaced. She was just as unhappy as he was to be there, but yet, there they were. Him, to be ordered around and told what heavy stuff needed to go where. Her...well, because she was single and still lived at home between semesters at college, so she always got sucked into Nieves' World.

"I'll talk to them," Autumn said calmingly, patting Nieves' arm. "Maybe they can change their bookings around."

Autumn, friends with yet another sister – Rosa, this time – had somehow been roped into actually planning this party. How that had happened, Christian wasn't sure. Maybe she was masochistic and loved nothing more than helping a spoiled brat plan a *quinceañera* that was more extravagant than most weddings.

"Okay," *Mamá* said in her heavily accented English. She very rarely spoke that, instead preferring to stick to her native tongue of Spanish, but with Autumn there, she was doing her best. "We do that. *El Trono*, just for you. Now, we not talk about flowers yet. Joyful Flowers is good."

The whole room paused for a moment, everyone scrambling to figure out who or what Joyful Flowers was. Autumn beat them all to the punch. "Oh, you mean Happy Petals?" she asked with a sincere smile at *Mamá*.

Christian had never had much reason to hang around Autumn up to this point in his life, but her tact and lack of snottiness about his *mamá's* English was endearing him to her more by the moment. She was gorgeous, to boot. It was too damn bad she was so young. She had to be, what, 26, 27 years old? Compared to him at 38, she seemed like a child.

And then, the full force of what Autumn said actually hit him and his thumb stopped scrolling and his mouth dropped open. "I'll go!" he practically shouted. "To go pick up the flowers," he added.

The room stopped.

Every eyeball was pinned on him.

Even Yesenia, who'd also been glued to her phone – no doubt scrolling through Facebook, hoping that the agony of this meeting would actually end someday – was staring at him, mouth agape.

"You guys are busy. With planning the—" he almost said The Party from Hell, which was what he'd been calling it in his mind for weeks now, "the *quinceañera*. Lots to do and still figure out. Music, and…and stuff. Carla always knows what to do when it comes to flowers, right?"

They still just stared.

He felt the sweat beading on his brow. He shouldn't have been so eager. So obvious. But the chance to see Carla again…

"Are you sure…?" Autumn asked slowly, the skepticism obvious in her voice. She and Nieves exchanged quick glances. "Flowers aren't really your specialty."

"Like you said, Carla always knows best." Actually, it was him who said that, but he didn't slow down long enough to let them remember that fact. "I'll just bring the fabric samples down, show them to her, and let her spin her magic."

"Right…" Autumn said, her dark green eyes narrowed as she stared at him, clearly trying to figure out what his game plan was. "Carla is good, though," she said begrudgingly. "Just let her know what the budget is and give her these." She held out a few fluorescent-colored strips of fabric. "Do you have any flower preferences, Nieves?"

His youngest sister shook her head, staring just as hard at him as Autumn was. "I only care about the colors. *No* pastels."

"Well," Autumn said with a forced cheerfulness, "we have the music maybe figured out and the flowers for sure figured out. Let's talk food."

Christian pocketed the strips of fabric, trying to hide the ridiculously giddy smile threatening to spread across his face. Yesenia caught his eye and cocked one eyebrow.

He shrugged nonchalantly and began flicking through his Instagram feed again. Yesenia may be his favorite sister, but that didn't mean he was gonna say a word to her about Carla.

Carla.

He was gonna see her again.

He only barely kept himself from whistling.

CHAPTER
TWO
CARLA

Isn't that a wonderful beginning?
~Grandfather in *The Princess Bride*

S tart of J une, 2020

"O h, what a beautiful morning," Carla Grahame sang from one of her favorite Roger & Hammerstein movies, *Oklahoma*, as she threw together a quick rose bouquet. Perfect for those times when a guy really shoved his boot into his mouth. "Oh, what a beautiful day."

It was her Monday – Tuesday to the rest of the world – and although she hadn't had much of a weekend, what with Mr. Ziebarth's funeral and all, she was still happy to be at work. Who wouldn't be happy, surrounded by beauty all day long like she was?

A thorn sliced through the hard callous on her thumb and with a moan of pain, Carla popped her thumb into her mouth, automatically turning to pull out her ever-present box of bandaids. She really should just wear gloves while she worked like every other florist out there with two brain cells to rub together, but she never seemed to remember to put them on—

The doorbell jangled and Carla looked up automatically, her professional smile sliding into place even as she quickly pulled her thumb out of her mouth.

Whoa.

Christian Palacios. She hadn't seen him in ages. He was standing by the glass front door, the bright sunshine streaming in around him, making it hard to see his face, especially under the brim of his baseball cap. But she'd recognize him anywhere.

A guy like Christian Palacios didn't just walk into a store without a girl noticing. That simply didn't happen.

She quickly wrapped up her still-bleeding thumb in the bandaid, throwing away the wrapper even as she rounded the counter. "Hello!" she said warmly. "How are you today?"

He moved a little further into the shop, edging in like he was afraid he was going to somehow breathe wrong and destroy the whole place.

This was the way guys *always* felt in her shop. More than one guy had told her that he felt like a bull in a china shop. She figured that it was just nerves. They didn't know what they were looking for, and they were nervous they were going to pick the wrong thing.

Which was why she was there. She'd never lead anyone astray.

He shot her a smile so brief, if she hadn't been watching closely, she would've missed it, and began looking at the bouquets in the buckets, studying them as if his life depended upon it.

And thus began the game that she *always* played when a nervous guy came into the store – the "What Did He Screw Up?" game.

He cheated on his wife. Oh. Never mind. No ring. So, maybe his girlfriend. Or! He forgot her birthday. Maybe their anniversary. Poor woman.

He'd moved on and was now looking at the most expensive bouquets in the store.

Oh my God, he called her the wrong name during sex!

Now that she'd hit upon it, she was *sure* that was it. Funny – she couldn't remember ever hearing that he'd gotten married, but maybe it happened while she was gone to college, or while she was working at the Toadstool Flower Shop in Boise. She certainly hadn't done the flowers for his wedding. Somehow, she was just sure that with the bouquet sizes he was eyeballing, it had to be for a wife. Girlfriends didn't merit bouquets *that* big.

Poor woman. I can only imagine how hard she's taking this. I wonder if she kicked him out. I would kick him out.

She admired the long, sleek muscles of his arms as he picked up and put down some of the figurines in the window display.

Huh. It'd have to be really *obvious he'd called me the wrong name, though. Not just a grunt that could be misunderstood or something.*

How long had it been since she'd had arms like that wrapped around her in bed?

She let out a long sigh. If she could have arms wrapped around her like those, she might just put up with him singing another woman's name during sex.

"I'm here to order the flowers for my youngest sister's *quinceañera*," Christian rumbled suddenly, breaking the silence of the store, and her wandering thoughts.

Her mouth gaped open for the barest of moments – *quinceañera? The last time a guy was sent in to pick out flowers for that was...oh that's right, NEVER* – and then she regained her composure. "How nice of you to help out," she said with her warmest smile, immediately flipping the script in her head. No wife in bed, eh? Maybe...

Maybe their parents died in a car wreck, and that's why his mother isn't in here, ordering the flowers for the party. And his sister was in the car too, and now she's paralyzed, and this is a big party to commemorate her parents' passing, combined with her 15th birthday party.

Yes, that's it.

She was quite proud of herself for figuring that one out with only the *barest* of clues. She only just restrained from physically patting herself on the back, but she made sure to give herself a hearty mental pat. Sherlock Holmes didn't hold a candle to her and the clients in her shop.

"Did your sister give you any ideas on what she's wanting?" she continued.

Christian had moved from the figurines back to the flower section again, this time gently stroking the petals of the deep red roses bouquet that she'd been sure just minutes before he was going to be buying for his girlfriend / wife.

But...maybe he doesn't have a girlfriend. Or a wife.

She tried to squelch the excitement just that mere thought flamed up inside of her. Christian Palacios would be interested in her – a big, fat lump of a girl like her – about the same time he'd be interested in stabbing himself in the eyeball with a fork.

"She...uhhhh...didn't mention which kind of flower she wanted," he finally said, almost like he was embarrassed to admit that. Carla was busy trying to figure out why *that* would be embarrassing when he pulled some silky strips of fabric out of his pocket.

"These are her colors," he said, holding the fluorescent-colored strips out to her. "She said any flower is fine, but no pastels."

Carla took the strips in hand with a little laugh. Construction orange, bright purple, and eye-popping pink.

No, pastels wouldn't work at all.

"You know," she said thoughtfully, running her calloused thumb over the fabric mindlessly, the bandaid keeping her from bleeding all over them, "I think I might have just the thing for your sister. Something she's never seen before. What's her name?"

"Nieves."

"Oh, that's right!" Carla said, attempting to snap her fingers and failing because of the ribbons she was holding. Flushing, she ignored this flub and hoped he'd follow her lead. "And you said she's the youngest of the family, right?"

"The baby."

There was a wealth of meaning behind those two words that Carla was both dying to know, and happy she wasn't a part of. Christian's tone…there was drama happening in the Palacios family, she was sure of it.

Well, of course there is, Carla! You silly goose. After all, their parents are dead and Nieves is now in a wheelchair. Huh. Funny, I never heard about the car wreck. Poor guy. Doing so much to help his baby sister.

"Well," she said with a bright smile, "tell her that I'll make sure she's taken care of. There's a form you need to fill out with budget and date of delivery and such on it; you'll need to answer that while I take some pics of these ribbons. That way, you can have them back."

He scribbled a few answers on the paper – true to form, since guys were never as detailed and thorough as women – and then pocketed the ribbons once she'd taken a few photos with her phone.

"I can deliver the flowers out to this address," she murmured, pulling her reading glasses off the top of her head and settling them on her nose as she scanned over the form to make sure that nothing stuck out as needing extra attention. "Everything looks fine," she said, pulling her glasses back off and settling them back into her hair. "Since the party doesn't start until the afternoon, I'll drop the flowers off in the morning so they'll be as fresh as possible. Does that work?"

"Sure," he said, and flashed her a quick smile, again so quickly that if she hadn't been watching him closely, she never would've seen it. He was one she really had to pay attention to

– just brief glimpses of emotions or thoughts and then it was hidden away again.

Instead of heading for the door, though, he just stood there, shuffling his feet and mindlessly rotating his baseball cap in his hands.

"Is there…something else?" Carla asked politely. Every one of her spidey senses was going off – there was something going on here. Something she hadn't figured out yet.

The only thing she loved more than a mystery was solving a mystery.

"No, no," he mumbled, pulling his cap back on his head firmly. "Have a goo – is this your cat?"

Carla blinked twice, completely confused by the change in topic, and then saw him leaning over to pet Leo, and she laughed. "Oh yes, he's mine. He's our shop cat. He loves everyone. He'll let you pet him until the cows come home, and then still complain that you haven't petted him long enough."

"Nice kitty," Christian crooned, and Carla smiled to herself. He sure was a damn nice guy, which squared up with what she remembered about him from high school. He'd been a year ahead of her and they'd never really run in the same circles, but she'd never heard a bad word about him.

He straightened up and pulled on his cap in one swift motion. "Have a good one," Christian said, pulling on the brim of his cap, and then he was disappearing through the front door, the jingle of the bell co-mingling with Carla's lusty sigh.

That *ass*.

Those *eyes*.

She had about as much chance of dating him as she had flying to the moon next week, but that didn't mean she couldn't appreciate a good-lookin' man when she saw one.

And there was a *lot* about Christian Palacios to appreciate.

CHAPTER
THREE
CHRISTIAN

I myself am often surprised by life's little quirks.
~Westley in *The Princess Bride*

CHRISTIAN SCRATCHED AT THE RASH AGAIN, cursing fluently under his breath. The best thing about being bilingual was, he knew all of the best swear words in *two* languages.

"What's up with the rash?" Stetson Miller asked, jerking his head towards the swollen red bumps on Christian's arm.

"Nothin'," Christian said automatically, dropping his arm by his side and flashing his boss a quick grin. "An allergic reaction. I just took a Benadryl. It'll calm down here in a minute. Must've gotten into something."

Stetson nodded, unconcerned, already having mentally moved on. "Good. Look, I need to head over to Declan's place for a minute. He's fighting his new combine and needs me to take a look at it. You guys got this handled?"

"Of course. We'll be fine."

Stetson headed out, his pickup leaving a cloud of dust in its wake, as Christian turned back to the fence they'd been fixing, wiping at the sweat trickling down his brow. Two more farm hands were further down, fixing another weak spot, but after this, they could probably call it for the day.

Which was damn good. Because petting Carla's shop cat was quickly turning into an incredibly stupid thing for Christian to have done, and he was officially miserable. Fixing fence was never fun at the best of times, but doing it while wanting to tear at his skin was making the project just that much worse.

He realized he was scratching the rash again and forced himself to stop. Picking up his wire pliers, he knelt down in the lush summer grass and grabbed the thin metal strand, pulling on it and tightening it up. Cows used any excuse in the world to go wandering out where they weren't supposed to be, and a loose fence was *more* than enough of an invitation for them to take a stroll into the neighbor's field.

The rash on his arm was distracting as all hell, though, pulsing with each beat of his heart, and he had to grit his teeth to avoid the temptation to tear at the skin.

So yeah. He was allergic to cats. He should've petted Carla's shop cat like he should've eaten glass for breakfast. But he'd wanted some reason – *any* reason – not to leave the shop, and had been desperate enough to do something he damn well knew he shouldn't.

Desperation. It was a thing.

And after causing one of the biggest flare-ups to his allergies that he'd had in years, he'd gotten what out of it again?

That's right, nothing at all.

Carla had been so damn sweet, promising him that she'd drop the flowers off herself the morning of the party. It'd been the one thing he'd held onto after he'd left sans a date or a promise to chat later or even her phone number. He could've asked – he should've asked – but he had just as much experience asking girls out on dates as he did riding bucking bulls.

He did both of those things a couple of times when he was young and dumb and full of cum, but hadn't in years.

In this moment, a bucking bull seemed a lot less scary than Carla Grahame. Her, with her thick, long brunette hair, and her big hazel eyes that could change from blue to green and back again in the space of a heartbeat, and her even bigger tits.

She was gorgeous.

She was way too good for him.

Her straight, white teeth flashed through his mind, her natural cheeriness omnipresent even in his memory, when *snap*! The strand of wire broke, his pliers flew out of his hand, and the roll of wire zinged back onto the spool, the end slicing across his left forearm, leaving a thin red line in its wake, already oozing blood.

He let loose with a few of his choicest swear words and Dave looked up from his work. "You okay, boss?" he called.

"Yeah, yeah," Christian said, waving the farm hand's concern away. It was what he deserved for concentrating on Carla's smile instead of the damn fencepost.

Grumbling, he pulled the spool of wire back into place and began wrapping it around the T-post again. Between the bleeding cut across his left forearm and the rashy bumps across his right forearm, though, he was having a damn hard time paying attention to what he was supposed to be doing. His temper wasn't much improved by the fact that his mother had been downright pissed with him when he'd visited his parents' place after ordering the flowers from Carla. Didn't he know he was supposed to ask her what kinds of flowers she was going to use? Didn't he know that he was supposed to get all of these stupid details that only women cared about?

Christian yanked the wire into place with a little more savagery than he probably needed to.

Women.

How was he supposed to know he was in charge of asking

Carla all of these questions? No one had said a word to him about it.

Show her the fabric samples and give her the budget, they'd said.

Not *Reenact the Spanish Inquisition on her ass.*

Pissy, his mom had huffed that she'd go and pick up the flowers the morning of the party to make sure that they'd work. He'd tried to tell her that Carla had offered to drop them off, but his mother had dismissed that suggestion angrily. No, she had to go check on them herself. She shouldn't have let him order them to begin with.

With a grunt, Christian clipped the wire and then looked critically at the fence repair. It looked good, which meant he could call it a day. Finally.

He waved to the farm hands further down the fence to let them know he was heading out, and then grabbed his tool bag to head for the farm truck.

So what if his mom was going to pick the flowers up for Nieves' *quinceañera*. That didn't mean Christian couldn't trump up some other excuse to go back to the flower shop. He could...

Dammit. He was drawing a complete blank. Yesenia, his favorite sister, didn't have a birthday until February. It was the start of June. He wasn't willing to sit around for another eight months.

There was Mother's Day, but that was even further away – almost a full year. Mother's Day this year was why he'd crossed paths with Carla to begin with.

Weeks ago, he'd been heading home from the morning chores when he'd remembered that it was Mother's Day, and he hadn't bought his mom a damn thing yet. Happy Petals had been right there, so he'd taken a left into the parking lot, intent on grabbing a small bouquet in under five minutes to save himself from the guilt trip that would've otherwise happened.

Except...

Well, he didn't think the heavens had opened and the angels had actually sang, but he'd be willing to go so far as to say that they should have. There she'd been, behind the counter, working and smiling and chatting easily with customers, always moving, efficient but warm and friendly. He'd watched her for a bit, the stream of customers seeming to be neverending, and was just trying to decide if he had the guts to ask her out, when a kid – she had to be in high school – came over and asked him if he was going to buy something or not. Christian had flushed red; he hadn't even realized that there was another employee in the store, and to be caught standing in the back and spying on Carla was mortifying.

He blindly grabbed the bouquet nearest to him and thrust it at the high schooler. It wasn't until she'd rang him up and he'd headed out the door that he'd realized that there was a Congratulations! balloon sticking out of the bouquet, with a pink baby rattle tied to the neck of the vase. Embarrassed, he pulled out the balloon and baby rattle, and had thrown them out in a trash can at the city park on the way home. He could only imagine what his mother would've thought if he'd presented her with *that* bouquet for Mother's Day.

No, waiting for Mother's Day almost a full year to go back and see Carla again was even less tenable than waiting for Yesenia's birthday.

Surely he had an aunt or a cousin who had a birthday coming up. He'd ask Yesenia. She'd know, and might even tell him without forcing him to tell her why he suddenly cared.

He felt his mood grow cheerier already. He'd get the birthdate of the next female relative of his – God only knew, he was related to so many, this wouldn't be hard – and then with that in hand, could go back and order flowers from Carla again.

And not pet the cat this time.

And ask Carla out on a date.

He could totally do that.

CHAPTER
FOUR

CARLA

Who said life was fair?
~Grandfather in *The Princess Bride*

CARLA PICKED UP another red rose and snipped it short, plucked the baby's breath from its pile, and wrapped it all up quickly with florist tape, her fingers conducting the dance without missing a beat.

She could probably make boutonnières in her sleep.

She probably had at least once, come to think of it, during a late-night push. Boutonnières never had the good graces to come in gentle waves, but were rather like tsunamis, burying unsuspecting florists beneath their onslaught.

"Aunt Carla, we want to play Go Fish," whined Noah, her adorable 7-year-old nephew.

Or, at least he was adorable when he wasn't whining and complaining.

So, not so adorable right now.

"I know, dear," she said, setting a third finished boutonnière down. Only 61 more to go. "I have to finish these first, and then we will, I promise."

"She's busy," Maggie said officiously. Carla opened up her

mouth to thank her 10-year-old niece for her understanding, when she added, "She always is. She's not going to play with us. C'mon, let's go build a fort in your bedroom."

Carla snapped her mouth closed, her cheeks flushing with embarrassment. She didn't think she was *that* awful of an aunt, was she?

A fourth boutonnière was added to the growing pile and already, she was working on a fifth one as she watched her niece and nephew tear down the hallway to rip Noah's room to pieces. She should probably tell them not to make it too big of a mess, but Maggie's words stung, and she couldn't bring herself to say anything at all.

Honestly, this was all Sammy's fault. If he'd given her more than two hour's notice that she was in charge of watching her niece and nephew overnight, she would've asked her high school assistant, Valrea, to come into the shop for a few extra hours of work this afternoon. Valrea could've knocked these out and Carla would've been free to actually play with Noah and Maggie this evening instead of dragging buckets of flowers, snips, floral tape, and pins to her brother's house.

A thorn sliced through her middle finger and Carla quietly let out a curse, popping the offended digit into her mouth.

"Sammy," she muttered around her finger, fishing through her bag with her other hand for the always-present box of bandaids, "you owe me big time."

Instantly, she felt the guilt wash over her. Of course Sammy didn't owe her anything for the privilege of watching her beautiful niece and handsome nephew. Why, she was downright blessed to be able to watch them.

A couple day's notice wouldn't kill him, though.

She shoved the thought down into the depths of her soul. How could she think such a thing of her younger brother? He'd had a babysitter arranged for tonight. He'd told her so when he'd called to ask her if she could step in instead. The babysitter had flaked on him, though, and so he'd had to ask her at the very last moment. Totally not his fault.

Funny how his babysitters are always so flaky. The same thing happened the last two times he took his wife on an overnight trip. It's almost like—

Just then, Noah let out a blood-curdling scream as Maggie began yelling too, the cacophony reverberating through the house. Carla let out a sigh as she shoved herself to her feet, setting #27 boutonnière off to the side. Despite the fact that they sounded like someone was dying – or perhaps more than one someone – Carla knew better. They were fighting over something stupid, no doubt.

Noah went quiet for just a moment and Carla winced inwardly as she headed to his bedroom door. Some people might be lulled into thinking that the sudden silence was him quieting down, but Carla knew better. It was just him sucking in a deeper breath so he could really—

"Aahhhhhhhhhh!!!"

And there he went.

As she pushed the bedroom door open, revealing a wrecked room and two very petulant children, Carla promised herself that after she finished the boutonnières, they'd watch *The Princess Bride* as her reward for getting her work done, and not even killing any small children in the process.

She wanted her own Westley – oh, how she wanted – but in the meanwhile, she'd just have to content herself with Movie Westley.

CHAPTER
FIVE
CHRISTIAN

Anything you want.
~Count Rugen in *The Princess Bride*

CHRISTIAN FINISHED UP his morning chores out at the farm as quickly as he could, practically chucking the hay at a few of the slower moving cows. "C'mon, you guys," he muttered under his breath. "My *mamá* is already pissy. I can't be late."

Finally, cutting a few corners he could only hope wouldn't come back to bite him in the ass later, he hollered a quick goodbye to Stetson and headed out for his parents' house.

Today was the Big Day. A person could be forgiven for thinking that Nieves was getting married, based on the size of this damn party, but considering Nieves was turning 15, Christian could only hope that marriage wasn't anywhere close to being on the horizon.

He was also quite sure that his mother had gone completely 'round the bend. He had six sisters. He knew what a *quinceañera* should look like. He'd lived through five others.

Today's party was nothing like anything he'd ever seen before.

Was it because Nieves was spoiled rotten?

Probably. She was the baby of the family, in every possible meaning of that word.

But his parents had managed to raise six other children who weren't spoiled rotten. Somehow, with Nieves, they'd completely lost their minds and had decided that giving her whatever she wanted was exactly the right path to take.

His mom had never said as much, but he wondered if it was because when the older six children had been growing up, they'd struggled for money. Oh, how they'd struggled. Moving from farm to farm, migrant workers without stability or guarantees that they'd even have a home the following week.

Then Wyatt Miller hired Christian's father, and things slowly got better. They had a place to live, even if it was a double-wide trailer. His dad was the foreman, so he wasn't being laid off at the end of each season. They weren't moving every couple of months, following the produce around the country.

Of course, things got *much* better after Wyatt met and married Abby. If there was ever a case for a woman changing a man, it was Abby changing Wyatt. Christian would've swore that nothing on the planet could change Wyatt, but he would've been wrong.

Abby Connelly did the impossible. Personally, Christian figured that Abby should wear a cape everywhere she went, because there was nothing closer to Superwoman than her.

But not only did falling in love with Abby change Wyatt from the inside out, it also meant that he wanted to build a bigger and grander house than the old Connelly homestead. When Wyatt approached Christian's dad about buying the old home and moving into it (and out of the drafty double-wide where the Palacios' family had been stuffed for years…)

Well, everything had changed again. Eighteen years after Christian'd graduated from high school and left his parents' house, they were finally financially stable. They were finally the middle-class family that his mom had always wanted to be.

And in her mind, that meant throwing the Party of the Year for her youngest daughter's *quinceañera*.

Christian pulled up in front of the old Connelly-homestead-turned-Palacios house, and let out a deep sigh. He had hours yet to go, a stressed-out mom who was going to be barking orders at him all night, and no chance of seeing Carla, thanks to his mother's belief that he'd incompetently ordered flowers.

How he could possibly have screwed up ordering flowers, he couldn't begin to guess. Was Carla going to bring over beautiful flowers that matched his sister's color choices? Yes.

What else was there to worry about?

Women.

Which was when he saw Carla's delicious ass sticking out of the back end of the bright turquoise Happy Petals van. There was a van no one ever missed – it was bright and cheerful and eye-catching.

Just like its owner.

Suddenly feeling about a thousand times better, Christian hopped out of his truck and hurried over to her side. She was there. She wasn't supposed to be, but she was.

He sent up a silent *thank you* to the heavens for this excellent bit of luck.

She spotted him and smiled broadly in greeting, and then picked up an oversized cardboard box with a swirl of bright colors poking out of the top.

"I thought my mom was going to pick this stuff up from you," he said as he reached her side, and then took the box out of her arms, ignoring her protests. No woman was going to carry a heavy box while he was around.

He breathed in deep. The flowers smelled good; Carla smelled amazing.

"Your sister frantically called me just a little bit ago and told me they didn't have time to come pick them up, and asked if I minded bringing them over after all. I told her of course not. She also asked if I had bright orange fabric – I'm hoping this will work." She gestured towards a box filled to overflowing with construction orange fabric. It was ugly as sin, so of course Nieves would love it.

The flowers in the box Christian was holding had been outshone by Carla's beauty, but something about them now caught his eye. He did a double-take and stared down into the box.

"What…what happened?" he whispered, in awe.

He'd never seen anything like these roses before. Swirls of brilliant pink and orange and purple – all of his sister's colors, but tie-dyed across the petals. "Do they grow like this?!"

"Oh no," she said with a small laugh. "I had to pull some fancy florist-ninja moves to make them come out this way."

"Has Nieves seen these yet?" he asked, hoping the answer would be no. Even spoiled and much-too-cool-for-everything Nieves would think these were amazing.

"Not yet," she said, reaching back into the van to grab something else, but before she could, Christian spotted his youngest sister heading towards them.

"She's here," he said, and Carla straightened up, looking around eagerly. She wanted to know if Nieves would appreciate all of her hard work, and he didn't blame her one bit for it. If he'd made roses look like this, he'd want a shit ton of appreciation too.

He swore he heard her mutter, "And not a wheelchair in sight," but when he turned back to her and asked, "What?" she said "Nothing," but much too innocently.

He was busy trying to figure out if he should push it further or just stare at her ruby-red lips and imagine kissing them, when Nieves started hollering at his elbow.

"Wow! *Mamá*, look at these!" Their mom showed up and the two of them started chattering away in Spanish, delighted by the gorgeous flowers.

Christian turned back to Carla, half laughing. "I think they're happy with the roses," he said dryly.

"Is that what they're saying? My Spanish isn't great," she said, gnawing on her lower lip with worry.

"Oh yeah, they're in love. *Mamá*," he interrupted them, "where should this go?"

She pointed him over to a table and Christian was happy to see that Carla was trailing along behind him. He wasn't as happy to see that she had a box in her hands. He really wanted to tell her to leave it all behind and he'd carry it for her, but he knew a lost cause when he saw one. At least this box was smaller than the first one she'd picked up.

After a few more trips, the van was finally empty, and Carla shot Christian a smile that caused his heart to beat erratically in his chest. "Well," she said, pushing a few of the stray tendrils out of her face Christian had to keep himself from tucking behind her ear, "that's it. I hope your sister loves it! I haven't done a party this big in…sheesh, forever. It's kinda fun to go all out like this."

With one last happy smile at him that had his knees watery with lust, she turned for the van door, keys already jangling in her hand.

"You should stay."

Christian didn't know where the words came from. Certainly not out of his mouth. He didn't ask women to attend family parties.

Ever.

He was just supposed to ask her on a date. A normal date. Not a huge-family-party date. It must've been the perfume from all of the roses going to his head. Or the sight of that bright turquoise shirt, straining against Carla's generous breasts as she'd reached into the van again and again.

Whatever the cause for his insanity, he found himself holding his breath. He wanted her to say yes so damn badly, it scared him.

Carla turned back to him, a stunned look on her face. "What? Are you...are you sure? I don't normally attend the parties of my clients. I just deliver the flowers and let them have the fun." She grinned a little at that, and somehow managed *not* to look bitter at this state of affairs.

Let them have the fun.

Christian wanted Carla to be the one having the fun, and he wanted to be the one to help her have that fun. He opened up his mouth to argue his case, when Autumn showed up.

"Carla," Autumn said, slightly out of breath, her curls bouncing around her face in wild abandon, "what do I need to be putting into the water to keep these flowers fresh? I've never seen anything like them before! Nieves is over the moon. But we can't have them wilting before tonight. What's the secret?"

Carla stared at Autumn blankly for a moment. "Why are you here?" she finally asked. "And why are you asking about the flowers?"

"Oh, shit! They didn't tell you? Nieves' mom hired me to plan this party. I went to school with Rosa – do you remember her? I think she was several grades younger than you – and she was telling me about this super elaborate party that her mom wanted to throw for Nieves, and...well, one thing led to another. Here I am." She shrugged. "Now, what should I be adding to the water?"

Christian slipped away to find his mom. The sooner he helped her arrange the tables and chairs (and then rearrange – he knew her), the sooner he'd be free to do what he wanted.

If Carla did stay for the party, he didn't want to spend it moving furniture around when he could be talking to her.

He found himself whistling under his breath. Suddenly, the Party From Hell wasn't so bad after all.

CHAPTER
SIX
CARLA

Are you certain he still wants you?
~Prince Humperdinck in *The Princess Bride*

As Carla arranged the monthly bouquet for Iris Miller from her husband, Declan, her heart hurt. Based on the bouquets that Declan'd been sending to Iris every month, they were trying for a baby…and they weren't succeeding.

She was sure neither of them had contemplated the fact that Carla was "in the know" about their personal lives to such a degree, but the truth of the matter was, Carla was "in the know" about a lot of people's lives in the valley. It came with the territory, and respecting that privacy was part of the sacred duty of being a florist.

Along with other important tasks, such as remembering what each client's favorite flower was. It wasn't hard to remember Iris' – hers were blue irises, of course. With a name like Iris Blue Miller, she would either love 'em or hate 'em. Carla liked to add in stargazer lilies to the bouquets too, a bright white flower that added a lovely contrast to the blues and purples of the irises.

Maybe she couldn't help with the Miller's fertility problems, but she could give Iris something beautiful to cheer her up. She was careful to always have a high schooler deliver the flowers out to the Miller farm, so Iris could retain the illusion that her good friend didn't know a damn thing about her struggles with fertility. It was better that way.

As Carla went along, placing a flower here, moving a flower there, she began to feel herself get a little more cheerful. Yes, it was true that she'd gotten grumpy after the whole Palacios party fiasco, but she never stayed in that mindset long. As always, her natural optimism on life had reasserted itself.

So what if Christian had invited her to stay for the party and then didn't say a single word to her from there forward? Things like that just happened sometimes.

She didn't have a clue of why he'd asked her to stay anyway. By all rights, he shouldn't have.

He was handsome.

She was...well, fat.

Chunky. Lumpy. Rolly-polly.

All of those ugly words with an even uglier meaning.

Sure, she had a pretty face – God knew she'd been told that often enough – but there was no denying that she was *way* too thick in the waist to be desirable by a guy like Christian.

Him asking her to stay for the party had been a weird slip of the tongue, nothing more. Crying herself to sleep that night was just a case of her being overly dramatic. Of *course* Christian hadn't asked her to stay because he'd wanted to flirt with her. That was just plain crazy talk, and she knew better.

The doorbell over the front door jangled and Carla's head shot up, hopeful—

"Hi, Autumn," she said with a forced cheerfulness, and then sent the gorgeous woman a genuine smile. It wasn't Autumn's fault that she wasn't Christian.

"Hey, Carla!" she called back over cascades of tulle. Her gorgeous curls were bouncing with every step – oh, to have naturally curly hair! – and she had a triumphant smile on her face that belied the dark circles under her eyes. She dropped the fluorescent orange tulle on the counter with a shake of the head. "I never knew they made tulle in this color until Nieves' party. Thanks again for letting her borrow it. Too bad Sarah's party next weekend isn't also going to use the color scheme of a princess palace decorated by a 12 year old." She laughed. "Otherwise, I could've just kept all of the items you lent to the Palacios family. Give me a sec – I'll be right back with your vases."

The doorbell tinkled as Autumn swished back out the door, leaving Carla to stare after her, chewing on her bottom lip. Another party? Autumn was in charge of yet another party? How many friends from high school were roping her into helping them out?

When Autumn came back through the door, vases tinkling as they clinked against each other in the cardboard box, Carla asked, "So, another party, eh? Are you wanting to keep doing parties? Like, as a job?"

Autumn shrugged, pulling the drooping shoulder of her sweater back up her arm. "I mean, yeah, of course," she said with a laugh. "This is one of those things that I'd do for free because I love it so much, but electricity companies don't keep the lights on out of the generosity of their hearts. They keep wanting to get paid every month. Bastards." She snorted. "With Johnny not working much right now, it's all up to me to make rent, you know? Doing a few parties is a great way to make a little extra income on the weekends, but the books at ED&J aren't going to do themselves. And the start-up costs! Have you ever looked at what it takes to become a party planner? Rentals and shop overhead and—"

"You should set up shop here," Carla interrupted. It was rude to interrupt, of course, but she couldn't hold the words back any longer.

Autumn stared at her.

"Set up shop here?" she echoed.

"Yeah, of course," Carla said, the words feeling more right by the moment. "We could be business partners, or whatever. Ask Jennifer and Bonnie from Miller & Nash to help us set it up. I've been getting dragged into party planning kicking and screaming for a couple of years now. I just don't have the time for it on top of everything else, but there wasn't anyone else to foist it off onto. I have this closet that I just don't use – you could make it your office!"

"Business partners? You want me to work in a *closet*?" Autumn asked skeptically, but she followed Carla around the counter and into the back. Carla ignored the griping – it was a lot to take in, but she was sure Autumn would want to do this, just as soon as she realized what the plan was.

Just as soon as Carla figured that out.

She flung the door open to the closet triumphantly, and then pulled on the cord dangling from the ceiling so the single naked light bulb could light up the corners.

"I know it's not much," she said apologetically, "but we can pretty it up, and anyway, this would just be where you'd put your paperwork and make phone calls. Party planners spend most of their time out in the field."

Autumn's dark green eyes went wide as she looked around the bare, dusty closet, only a few stray rolls of florist tape to be found on the neglected shelves.

"Business partners?" she repeated, but this time she didn't sound disgruntled or overwhelmed. She sounded excited.

"It works on, like, every level!" Carla said, clapping with excitement. "I'm here all the time, so you don't have to hire someone to man the shop while you're at ED&J or with a client. Instead of a flat fee for rent and power and phone, you can just pay me a percentage of your profits. That way, you don't get in over your head!"

Autumn turned to her, a grin spreading from ear to ear.

"And to think that I just came in here to return some vases," she said, and started laughing.

"I myself am often surprised by life's little quirks," Carla intoned and then flashed Autumn a quick grin. "Westley. *Princess Bride*. Okay, so, you want to talk shop, literally?"

"Yes, *please*!" Autumn exclaimed. "I need to be upfront with you: I can't quit my job at ED&J. Johnny isn't leaving the house much—well anyway, I really would need you to talk to clients when I couldn't be here. Which would be a lot. Are you sure you're okay with that?"

They settled down at the worktop counter. "We might need to see how things go," Carla allowed, trying not to let her natural starry-eyed optimism win by her saying what her gut wanted her to – that there was absolutely no way this could ever become a problem. "But honestly, being a secretary and taking messages so you can return the phone calls isn't going to be a big deal. If you're doing the actual hard work – meeting with clients, planning the parties, putting the parties together, making it all happen – then answering the phone or talking to people when they come into the shop is easy. I'm here anyway." She shrugged. "Plus, foot traffic into the shop might increase, and that might mean more flower sales. I've always thought that planning parties would be a blast, but I just don't have the time to do it. Music, food, chair and table rentals, decorations, drinks, invitations, photography…I mean, I can provide the flowers, of course, but people have been asking for so much more lately, and I'm simply not equipped for it."

Autumn chewed on her full bottom lip. "But what about Belly Bliss Catering? They're out of Franklin, not Sawyer of course, but they've been hired for parties here quite a bit. Remember that huge party the McLains threw a couple of years ago for their wedding anniversary? Belly was in charge of that, and then they've also done some big parties for Zane and Louisa."

"Oh yes, Zane," Carla sighed, staring dreamily off into space for a moment. The day she'd decorated the steakhouse up in Franklin had been the best day of her career. Having a multi-millionaire call her up – or, rather, his secretary but close enough – and ask for her help in creating a night to remember…

It had been magical. She'd helped those two fall in love.

Sure, Louisa and Zane's relationship had had its ups and downs since then, and even worse, those issues had been broadcast to the whole world – just one of the downsides to dating a super star – but still. Who *wouldn't* want to be Cinderella? Swept off their feet and carried away by the prince on a white horse?

Or better yet, be Princess Buttercup, and be carried away by Westley?

"Anyway," she said with another sigh, waving away the daydream, "Belly Bliss Catering does amazing food and they do have *some* equipment rentals, but their choices are sparse, and they tend to run more towards the stodgy. If Nieves had asked them to decorate with those eye-popping colors she liked, they wouldn't have had a clue of what to do. You made it look good. I don't think you'd be in competition with Belly Bliss. It isn't like you'd want to start catering the food, right? Or am I wrong about that?"

"No," Autumn said slowly, thinking it through. "I'm definitely not a cook. I'd much rather eat something that someone else has prepared, then go through all of that work myself."

"Food is only part of what people need," Carla said, pressing on, "just like flowers are only part of it. The whole package? No one out there does it. This is something that Long Valley *needs*."

Autumn sucked in a breath, and Carla could almost smell the rubber burning as she watched her friend think through all of the different angles.

"All right, let's talk turkey, then," she finally said. "You got a piece of paper? I think we oughta write all of this down, and then have a meeting with Jennifer and Bonnie. They'll tell us if we need to hire a lawyer for the paperwork or not."

Carla grabbed a sheet of copy paper off the seldom-used fax machine and together, they began scribbling down all of the details – who was in charge of what, how much was owed, what hours Autumn would work, and so much more.

"Oh Lordy," Autumn finally said, pushing at the curls falling down into her face. "I feel like we've figured out *soooo* much, and I bet we haven't even scratched the surface."

"Jenn and Bon will be a lot of help," Carla said confidently, pulling her reading glasses and settling them on top of her head. "They'll help us avoid any major screw-ups. I'll call them and set up an appointment for us to go over together. Does that work for you?"

"That would be terrific. Work is busy right now at ED&J with summer in full swing, so having you take that off my plate would be helpful."

"Of course," Carla said, and patted Autumn on the hand. "Is work why you look a little…tired?" Her friend looked like she was nearing the end of her rope, honestly, but Carla would never say that out loud.

"Johnny's going through…a rough patch." Autumn's gaze slid past Carla's searching eyes and landed somewhere in the distance. "You know how he is. Johnny is…Johnny. So," and her voice brightened and she sent Carla a sly smile, "what happened between you and Christian at the party? Tell me everything!"

Carla just stared at her.

Sure, she'd gotten all excited because he'd asked her to stay, but then he'd promptly ignored her for a good hour before she finally gave up and left.

In no universe would that be considered something exciting to report.

"You can't fool me," Autumn said with a glower, crossing her arms across her chest. "I know better. Christian practically demanded that he be the one to come in here and order the flowers from you. Didn't you wonder why a guy who is definitely *not* into decorating was the one who came in here?"

Carla shrugged. She was not about to cop to her Sherlock Holmes moment where she was sure she'd figured out that Nieves was in a wheelchair and her parents were dead. There was no reason to share that…tidbit of information.

"C'mon," Autumn said with a laugh, poking Carla in the side, "you can tell me. How many times has a guy come in to order flowers for his sister's *quinceañera*?"

"Never," Carla admitted begrudgingly. "But that doesn't mean he likes me. Maybe he was just bored that day. Or something."

Autumn shook her head in mock disapproval. "You can see it for everyone else but yourself. Christian wanted to order those flowers from you. He asked you to stay that evening. He *likes* you."

Carla's brain felt like it couldn't quite keep up with the conversation. There was a part of her – admittedly, a very large part of her – that wanted to believe that Autumn had it right. Hadn't she had exactly this thought when Christian had invited her to stay?

But that had gone absolutely nowhere. Surely Autumn was just making this up. Wishful thinking and all that.

Just then, the front door swung open and the bell jingled merrily as Christian came walking in.

Autumn let out an audible gasp that had Carla wanting to strangle her on the spot and then she announced loudly, "Okay, business partner, we'll have to discuss the deets later!" With that, Autumn practically sprinted for the door.

Carla was sure that Autumn could not have been more obvious if she'd run out the door holding up a sign that said, "I'll leave you two to make out!"

As the door tinkled closed behind her traitorous friend, Carla was left to imagine all of the ways to slowly kill her (or at least make her really, really miserable – even in her daydreams, she couldn't be *too* violent) as Christian picked up and put down the figurines up in the front display.

Huh. These were the kinds of kitschy items that a person would give to their elderly aunt on her 90th birthday.

In other words, not something she would've expected Christian to be interested in.

"Can I help you with anything?" she asked into the deafening silence as she walked around the front counter and out onto the floor of the store. She didn't want to hover over him while he browsed, but she couldn't help wanting to get a little closer. The night of the party, he'd been wearing cologne, and maybe he was wearing it again tonight.

She sniffed discreetly but couldn't pick it out. She'd long ago gone nose-blind to the smell of flowers, and wondered if that also kept her from picking out other scents when masses of flowers were present.

He didn't respond, instead staring at the ugliest and kitschiest figurine of all, turning it over and over in his hands. *Ugh.* She'd always hated that one. It'd been a lot cuter in the sales magazine. When it'd arrived and she'd gone to stock it on the shelf, she'd thought it was so ugly, she'd shoved it to the back, hoping no one ever saw it again.

Why oh why oh why was he obsessed with *that* one?

Maybe…

Maybe he was acting like this because he liked her, and he was nervous to be around her.

Maybe Autumn was right.

That absolutely insane idea grew like a dandelion weed given a huge heaping dose of Miracle Grow, until it was all she could think about.

It was nuts, of course. But maybe…

What if she talked about how she wasn't busy that weekend? Just in case. Just so he knew she wasn't busy. It…it couldn't hurt, right?

"What a quiet weekend I have coming up!" she said, twisting her fingers around and around each other, feeling her heartbeat take off like she'd just sprinted around the block. "Not a darn thing going on! Just as quiet and lonely as can be."

She was the world's biggest loser. She could not believe she was doing this.

She also couldn't seem to stop herself.

"Too bad I have nothing to do all weekend. Just quiet. And by myself," she added. In case that hadn't been blazingly obvious from everything else she'd said.

"Uh-huh," he mumbled, turning the figurine over and over in his hands. She was sure he was paying *no* attention whatsoever to what she was saying. She could start spouting Irish limericks and he wouldn't notice.

"I'll get this one," he finally announced, avoiding eye contact as he headed to the cash register up at the front counter. She trailed behind him miserably, noticing even in the depths of her misery just how trim and tight his ass was. He walked with that loose gait that every cowboy seemed to have from birth.

As she scanned the barcode on the bottom of the piece of junk, she died a little more inside.

This thing? Out of all of the beautiful items in the shop, and he has to pick out this thing?!

She stuffed it into a bag along with his receipt and with it, threw the last of her pride to the wind.

"I hope you have a great upcoming weekend!"

It was only Tuesday.

She plowed on.

"I can't believe how open my schedule is, myself."

She was officially pathetic. This was *the* most embarrassing convo she'd ever had, and even worse, he didn't even seem to realize that she was practically throwing herself at him.

Whatever had possessed him to ask her to stay for the party last weekend, it was obviously a flash in the pan. Her cheeks burned with embarrassment.

The next time she was tempted to believe a word out of Autumn's mouth, she was going to remember this moment.

Christian began heading for the door, the bag clutched tightly in his hand, and she rounded the counter behind him, intent on flipping the lock, turning off the open sign, and popping down to the Muffin Man to eat a giant donut. With sprinkles. And icing.

And hey, why not – drool over Gage.

Maybe he and Cady were a thing now, but that didn't mean she couldn't at least *look* at him. She was surely never going to get anyone of her own, so drooling over taken men could be her new hobby. After all, she'd spent most of her life drooling over Westley, and he was taken by Buttercup. Why not continue the tradition. Moving to men who existed in the real world could only make her less pathetic, right?

Just then, Christian stopped, one foot out the door, and turned back to her. She managed to stop *just* short of barreling into him.

Wouldn't *that* be the icing on the cake.

"You're…you're free this weekend?" he asked, as if the last ten minutes of her very one-sided conversation had only now registered in his mind.

"Ummm…yes?"

"Want to go out on Friday night?"

"Ummm…yes?" Now her voice was squeaking. Her legs were jelly. She was going to faint right there on the spot.

Carla, get yourself together.

"I'll come by at six and pick you up."

"Six-thirty, if you can." Thankfully at least part of her brain was still functioning. "I need time to close up."

"Six-thirty. See you then." And then he headed to his truck and Carla stumbled back to the counter, leaning on it, staring out into space.

She had a date with Christian.

She had a date with *Christian*.

Suddenly, she was very glad she had the counter to lean against. She had a date with one of the cutest single guys in Sawyer. Things like this just did not happen to Carla Grahame.

She immediately snatched her cell phone up from behind the counter and speed-dialed one of her closest friends, Hannah Morland. "Guess who I have a date with?!"

CHAPTER
SEVEN
CHRISTIAN

Do you always begin conversations this way?
~Westley in *The Princess Bride*

CHRISTIAN TURNED DOWN the rutted dirt road that led to the Miller Family Farm, a huge grin seemingly etched onto his face. He'd asked Carla out. He'd done it! Sure, he had a butt-ugly piece of shit in the backseat with absolutely no idea of what to do with it, but that was *well* worth the price of admission.

At the Party from Hell, when – shocking even him – he'd actually gotten up the nerve to ask her to stay, his mother had then spent the evening riding him like a rented mule. He'd rearranged speakers, chairs, tables, lighting, and every other conceivable item at the party – most of it twice – and by time he'd come up for air, she was gone. He couldn't blame her, and he was damn sure she wouldn't want to hear from him again. Why she hadn't kicked him out of the shop as soon as he'd shown his face was beyond him, but he wasn't about to look a gift horse in the mouth.

Now he just had to figure out what to do on Friday night at 6:30.

His heart skipped a beat in his chest. Suddenly, what hadn't seemed all that important that morning was now paramount. He'd been so nervous about getting up the nerve to ask Carla out, he hadn't bothered worrying about what they were going to do on said date.

But now, that seemed like the most important question in the world. If he didn't get it right...

Well, that didn't bear thinking about.

As he drove past the main house, he spotted Stetson giving Jennifer a long and lusty kiss on their front porch. Shit yes – he could ask Jennifer! The idea had briefly flitted through his mind of asking Yesenia or his mother, but Jennifer was a much better idea. He pulled into the turnaround in front of the house and bounded over.

Stetson pulled away from his wife and gave Christian a dirty look for interrupting them, but he hardly even noticed. Not when he had such an important topic to discuss. Now that he was close enough to the house, he could hear Flint, their toddler son inside, chattering away with Carmelita.

"What should I do on a date with Carla Grahame?" he blurted out.

Jennifer's mouth went into a perfect O and then she broke out into a huge grin.

"You asked Carla on a date?" at the same time that Stetson said, "What, the florist?"

He sounded shocked.

"Yes, the florist," Jennifer said, poking him in the side. "Florists need love too, you know."

"I just...I've never seen her on a date before," Stetson mumbled.

To be sure, Christian counted this as a positive in Carla's favor – he rather liked the idea that she hadn't dated every guy in town before him.

Which Yesenia would scold him but good for thinking that if

he ever said it out loud – it was very machismo of him and he knew it – but he couldn't help it.

Something else that didn't bear thinking about.

"Girls like romantic dates," Jennifer said just as Stetson said, "You could go to a movie."

Jennifer snorted with derision. "That is *not* romantic," she informed her husband dryly, shaking her head at his apparently awful idea. "Everyone does that. Plus, it's the world's worst first date. You go into a dark room and both stare at a screen for two hours. How are you ever going to get to know each other?"

"Not everyone can spend the first few weeks of a relationship investigating their future spouse's financial statements," Stetson said with a laugh.

"I do *not* recommend asking to go over Carla's books as a first date. Or as an ever date." She let out a huge sigh of disappointment at the quality of her husband's input. "No, Carla is a true romantic. I mean, I don't know her all that well because I didn't grow up here, of course, but what I've seen of her around town, she wants big. She wants romantic. She wants to be swept off her feet."

Christian, who'd been thinking that asking Jennifer for help had been a stroke of pure genius, was now seriously regretting his decision. Big? Romantic? Swept off her feet? Dinner and a movie sounded doable. This…this sounded like Christian needed to rent a limo and fly her in a helicopter and…

This was *not* going well.

"You could give her flowers!" Stetson interjected.

Jennifer gave him another dirty look. "She's a florist. Flowers are *not* going to impress her. How is it that you got married again?"

"My charm, and that move in bed…" He whispered something in her ear and she went bright pink, shoving at his shoulder.

"Behave yourself," she scolded him, but the look in her eye

told Christian a different story. "Okay, Christian, what do you like about Carla?"

"Her…smile," he finished lamely. He was about to say her tits but then realized at the last moment who he was talking to – his boss' wife. He was *not* going to discuss Carla's tits with Mrs. Boss.

"She does have a very friendly, warm smile," Jennifer said seriously, but he could see the sides of her mouth twitching and was just sure she was laughing at him.

Yesenia it was. He'd ask her for help. She'd been laughing at him since the day she was born; at least that wouldn't be something new.

Frustrated, he turned to walk away, and Jennifer called out, "No, sorry. I'm sorry. Come back. Let's brainstorm. *Other* than Carla's, uh, smile, what do you like about her? Like, what do you like about her personality? What does she like to *do*?"

Do? Other than arrange flowers in vases? Hell if he knew. In fact, this seemed like a damn good question to ask her on that mythical first date he was never gonna get planned at this rate.

"That funny movie!" Stetson burst out. They both turned to look at him, surprised. "You know, that cult classic. She's always quoting it." More blank stares. "There's a giant in it, the guy almost dies, there's a marriage in it. Mawage," he intoned in what had to be the world's strangest accent. "Mawage is wot bwings us togeder today."

Christian just stared at his boss wide-eyed. He'd lost it. His boss had officially gone 'round the bend.

"*Princess Bride*!" Jennifer burst out, whacking Stetson on the arm in her excitement. He rubbed at the spot ruefully, but Jennifer ignored him. Considering the fact that she only came up to Stetson's shoulder and must've weighed at least a hundred pounds less than her husband, Christian was pretty sure Stetson was going to live through the experience. "I'd forgotten about that, but you're right. She just loves that movie.

Have you ever watched it?" she asked, turning back to Christian.

Her bright green eyes practically pinned him to the spot. She was a petite, gorgeous thing, but she'd always made Christian just a little bit nervous. He couldn't quite put his finger on it, but over the years, the feeling had never subsided, and here it was again.

He was going to fail her test.

He mutely shook his head.

"There you go. You can watch *The Princess Bride* together, then. If you're going to date Carla, you definitely need to watch that movie. Otherwise, half of what she says to you won't make sense."

Date Carla? That sounded…serious. He was going to go on *a* date with Carla, and then decide after that. He hadn't had a steady girlfriend since high school.

His nerves were starting to crawl up his throat, strangling him in place, when Stetson interjected. "So, darlin' wife, you think they should sit in a dark room for two hours and stare at a screen, eh?" he asked dryly. "What a…novel idea."

She turned and glared at him, lips pursed, hands on hips. "This," she informed him haughtily, "is totally different. This isn't just *a* movie. It's Carla's all-time *favorite* movie. By watching it, Christian will understand her better. Now," she said, turning back to Christian, supremely confident that she'd made her point, "do you have a place to watch it with her?"

"The trailer?" Christian ventured. He lived in a single-wide trailer on the Miller Farm; it was part of his pay for being head foreman of the ranch. It wasn't much, but it was his home.

"No, that won't do," Jennifer said distractedly, pulling at her dark brown hair. "I mean, it's fine and all. It's just not first-date material. I've got it!" She snapped her fingers, excitement lighting up her face. The happier she looked, the more worried Christian got. He was just the foreman of a small family farm.

He didn't fly helicopters or rent limos or wear tuxedos or whatever insane idea Jennifer had just come up with.

But she was also the boss' wife, and a body didn't tell the boss' wife no if he wanted to keep his job for any amount of time.

With a strangled inward groan, Christian waited to hear the plan.

CHAPTER
EIGHT
CARLA

Hold it, hold it. What is this? Are you trying to trick me? Is this a kissing book?
~Grandson in *The Princess Bride*

FRIDAY DRAGGED ON like no day she'd ever lived through before. Every time she checked the clock, only mere minutes – sometimes only seconds – had passed since the last time she'd looked.

As insane as it sounded, she was almost getting to the point that she was wishing it was Valentine's Day.

Almost.

At least on V-Day, she would be insanely busy which would make time fly, but of course, today had to be a slow day for business instead.

She'd actually sent Valrea home early, which she never did – she could *always* find something for her high school assistant to do – but Val had kept asking her what was wrong and Carla wasn't sure she could utter, "Nothing, of course!" in a chipper voice one more time.

It was better for her to be antsy without company, she

decided, not to mention that paying someone to keep a barstool from floating away wasn't good business.

Finally! She looked at the clock and saw that it was 6:00 straight up. Okay, maybe 5:58, but who was counting? She put the till into the safe, threw the deadbolt on the front door into place, flipped off the open sign, and headed for the stairs in record time, her feet hardly touching the boards as she flew up them. She ducked automatically as she went through the open doorway at the top, avoiding the steep pitch of the roof. She'd only had to whack her head on that beam one time before becoming a lot more careful about paying attention to where her head was in relation to the roofline.

For the millionth time, she inwardly sighed at the size of her apartment. Yes, it made sense for her to live above her shop in a converted attic to save money, but oh, how lovely it'd be to walk from the bed to the toilet at night without worrying about braining herself on an exposed rafter as she went. A kind-hearted person might call this a studio apartment, but in Carla's opinion, that was too generous by half. It was probably only slightly larger than the shoe boxes used to deliver the custom-made boots to André the Giant, aka Fezzik from *Princess*.

As she tripped over Bella who was busy wrapping herself around Carla's feet, she decided "slightly larger" was her putting on her rose-colored glasses again. Her converted attic *was* the size of a shoe box for a pair of André's boots. After all, the giant wore a size 24. In men's.

"Hi, hi, hi," she said distractedly, picking up Bella and giving her a quick version of the loving that her kitten always got upon her arrival. Bella didn't know what a rush she was in, and wasn't about to take no for an answer. Her rusty purrs filled the cramp space and then she began enthusiastically grooming Carla's face with her sandpaper tongue.

"Thank you," Carla said with a laugh. "Now, go behave yourself. I've got work to do!" She laid Bella down on the bed, hoping she'd take the hint and settle in there but of course, the playful kitten instantly bounded off the bed and wove herself between Carla's feet, not content to sit on the sidelines when her momma was home.

"I'm sorry, baby," she murmured as she washed her face thoroughly and then began meticulously making herself up again. "I promise we'll play tonight when I get home. I sure wish Leo would come up here and you two could be friends, but considering that Leo is four times your size and hates your guts, it's probably a good thing he doesn't come up here regularly and beat you up. The last thing I want is you two yowling at each other as you tear around above the heads of a bunch of customers."

She pulled her favorite dress off the hanger with a happy sigh. There weren't many things that made her much-too-big-around figure look good, but this dress was one of them. Cobalt blue, it made her indecisive hazel eyes appear bright blue, and also emphasized her generous chest, which she figured was one of the few positives about her body. Hopefully Christian was a boobs guy, because she had boobs aplenty – enough for a dozen women.

As she wiggled into the dress and zipped it up the back, she realized a fatal flaw in her plan – she had absolutely no idea where they were going on this date tonight. She was so rarely asked out, she'd forgotten to get even the most basic of information. What if Christian wanted them to go hiking or something? She pulled a face at herself in the mirror as she patted her hair back into place. She'd simply have to tell him that she'd have to change. This dress and these spiky heels were *not* hiking material.

Just then, she heard a muffled knock on the front door of the store and only barely stifled back a scream of panic. She knew he was coming over. She knew he'd knock on the door. But the anticipation had only made the actual event just that much more nerve-wracking.

After one more swipe of bright red lipstick, she made her

way down the stairs much more carefully than she'd gone up them just 30 minutes earlier. She hadn't been wearing heels before, and didn't fancy breaking her neck on the way to her first date in years.

Leo, the commotion of the knocking and Carla's footsteps on the stairs wakening him from his evening nap, came wandering over to watch the proceedings and make sure to be given at least one round of pettings if at all possible. He was *always* up for a round of pettings, if not ten.

Carla glimpsed Christian's face through the window panes in the door and then flipped the deadlock back and swung it open.

Oh.

My.

There was no way this man in front of her had meant to ask *her* out on a date. He'd swapped out his jeans and work shirt for a pair of khakis and a button-up shirt, the top two buttons undone, leaving a triangle of tanned skin that Carla very much wanted to explore with her tongue. His hair was gelled and combed off to the side – more formal than his normal look, but oh-so-handsome. He was tall for a guy who was Mexican, which was good because she didn't aspire to towering over her date in her heels. Her mind flashed back to the party and she realized that as a whole, the Palacios family tended to the tall side. That was nice. Her family did too.

And why on earth am I thinking about this right now?!

"Hi!" she blurted out. He went to pull on the brim of his hat in greeting, realized he didn't have one on, and dropped his hand back down by his side. This tiny crack in his self-possession made her grin.

It's possible he's as nervous as me.

Not likely, but possible.

"Let me lock up and we can head out!" she said brightly, turning the key in the lock and then jiggling the handle to double-check that everything caught as it was supposed to.

"I've never had anyone break into my shop," she said as she followed him over to his pickup and he helped her inside. The feel of his calloused hand in hers had lightning shooting up her arm. As soon as he got in on the other side, she picked up right where she'd left off.

"But just in case, I always lock up and put my money into a safe each night. Teenage boys. They are a magnet for trouble, and I like to help them choose to cause it elsewhere."

Silence. He still hadn't said anything.

If possible, her panic – and thus her mouth – kicked into yet a higher gear. Her mother had always said that she could talk the ear off a dead person, and this was a trait that only got immeasurably worse when she was nervous.

So of course tonight, it was at catastrophic levels.

"I'm not saying that all teenage boys are troublemakers, of course!" *Shut up, Carla, shut uppp!* "I'm sure there are some good ones among them. They just have that reputation, you know. I'd like to hire a teenage boy to work in the store – give him something to do that isn't causing problems, but guys don't seem to want to work with flowers."

She was about to dive headlong into a diatribe about how flowers weren't *just* for women to enjoy when she realized they were pulling into the parking lot of the Old Horvath Mill.

This stunned her so much, she actually managed to lapse into silence. The old mill? They were going to the old mill?

She'd been here a few times on Saturday morning, attending the new Farmer's Market that Penny and Troy Horvath had started up not too long ago, but it was Friday night, which was most definitely *not* Saturday morning.

Clearly, Carla, you have a dizzying intellect.

But not even a line from one of her favorite movies could calm her nerves at a time like this.

He pulled into a parking spot and shut off the engine, hopping out and hurrying around to help her out of the truck. She was still mute, thank the heavens above, and completely confused. If she'd had to guess a hundred places that they'd go on their date tonight, the Old Horvath Mill was nowhere on that list.

He slid back the giant wood door on its track and stood aside to let her through. One foot inside, her jaw dropped in shock.

"What the…" She trailed off, hurrying forward and then spinning in circles, trying to take it all in. There was a huge projector's screen hanging down from the ceiling. Elegant couches, and tables laden with food and drink, and flickering candles, and fairy lights strung everywhere, and…

"You did this?" she whispered. "You did this for *me*?"

"Well, I had a lot of friends' help," he said modestly. "You like it, then?"

"Like it? Oh Christian, I *love* it."

This wasn't a pity date. No one went through this kind of hard work and effort for a pity date. She'd almost convinced herself over the previous few days that this was a bet gone wrong. Or chivalry taken to an extreme. Or an overactive tendency towards pity. Or a penance prescribed by a priest. Or maybe even a wide masochistic streak.

This, though, blew all of those theories out of the water.

Which only left one…that he liked her.

Which *couldn't* be.

She trailed along behind him to the buffet table, resolving to leave the mystery of why they were on this date for another time. Right now, she fully intended on enjoying herself, because God knew, with the averages she was batting at, it'd be a decade before she got to go on another one.

They filled up their plates, Carla carefully taking tiny portions of each proffered dish. She couldn't eat like she normally did in front of him. She'd simply pretend as if she ate like a bird at every meal, and then she'd eat again when she got home. He'd *never* like someone who had a "hearty appetite," as her mother had always put it. And honestly, it wasn't so inconvenient to cook another meal when she got home.

Not if it meant getting another date sooner rather than later.

Moving to the couch where TV trays had been set up, she did her best to settle into place and not spill her food everywhere, but the opening strains of the soundtrack to *The Princess Bride* made all decorum flee her mind.

She gasped. "You love *The Princess Bride* too?!" she squealed, turning to Christian, her mouth agape. "I didn't know you liked this movie! What's your favorite line?"

"I, um, haven't watched it before."

She froze in place, staring at him, trying to comprehend, but failing. "Haven't…watched…" she mumbled. "I…*how*? Okay, look, I'll do my best not to recite every line in the movie as we watch it, but I promise nothing. Half the fun of this movie is saying the lines along with it. Hold on – if you haven't watched this, why did you pick to watch it with me?"

"Some very good advice," was his cryptic answer.

Which just reinforced her theory that this wasn't a pity date. No one decorated an old mill to the nines and catered a meal and asked for advice so they could fulfill their part in a bet gone bad.

"He's gonna pinch my cheek. I hate that," Fred Savage's character said, and Carla giggled like she did every time she heard that line.

Ugh. This was going to be impossible, not laughing and reciting every line in the movie, but Christian didn't know yet what a freak she was, and she didn't dare let him figure it out.

"Buttercup was raised on a small farm in the country Florin," Grandpa told his grandson in the movie.

Carla settled back with a happy sigh. Food, cutest guy around, and best movie ever. If she managed to keep from annoying her date, this would end up the most perfect first date of all time.

She just had to keep her mouth shut.

She could do this.

CHAPTER NINE

CHRISTIAN

> I give you full marks for bravery.
> ~Prince Humperdinck in *The Princess Bride*

CHRISTIAN SWUNG UP into the cab of Stetson's latest acquisition – a Case-International Magnum 400. It was so new, the leather seats were still (mostly) clean. He swiped at the light layer of dust and then settled in, letting out a happy sigh. Field work had become a hell of a lot nicer with this tractor around, now that his boss allowed him to play with the new toy too.

Stetson had practically danced a jig when Jennifer had given him the go-ahead to sign the paperwork for it. Considering that Stetson and Jennifer had met because she'd been part of the bank's team sent out to repossess the Miller Family Farm just a couple of years ago, Christian felt like this meant he could finally draw in a full breath. He knew finances were better with Jennifer in charge of them – Stetson had no head for numbers and was more likely to fly to the moon next week than balance a checkbook – but still, "better" wasn't much of a measuring stick when you were starting out at "verge of bankruptcy."

They had to be doing *much* better if Jennifer said yes to buying a beast like this. Whistling softly, Christian started it up and put it into gear, heading back out to the north 40. It'd been off the pivot long enough that the ground would let him disc between the—

His internal train of thought came to a screeching halt as he saw a figure out in the field, standing there patiently as if waiting for him to show up.

He shielded his eyes from the early morning glare of the sun and squinted. That looked like…

Carla?

As he got closer, he could see her fine figure – curves in *all* the right places – and her thick brown hair blowing in the gentle morning breeze. Either it was Carla, or she had a twin.

He pulled up to a stop next to her and he could see her lips moving as she tried to shout something up to him, but of course over the deep rumble of the diesel, she didn't have a chance. He cut the engine.

"—here!" she shouted, and then turned a bright pink at the sudden quiet.

He opened the door and swung out, quickly taking the built-in steps to the ground.

"Hi," he said. He sounded a little breathless, which he decided he'd attribute to the stairs he'd just come down. His eyes skimmed over her features, drinking them in – her wide red lips that were ever ready to break into a smile; her large hazel eyes that constantly intrigued him. He never knew what to expect – dazzling blue with hints of green? Sparkling green eyes tinged with blue? This morning, in the field of lush green against a sky of brilliant blue, her eyes were a mix of the two, creating a color he swear he'd never seen before, and loved all the more for it.

Also, he came from a family where it was sacrilege to leave the house without putting on makeup, and he could see that Carla was cut from the same cloth.

He liked that.

He liked that very much.

After their spectacular date 10 days ago, he'd been at a complete loss as to what he should do. He'd wanted to ask her out again, of course – watching *The Princess Bride* with her was more fun than he'd had in the last year combined together – but he'd blown his wad. He had *no* idea what to do as Date #2. Turned out, he still didn't own a jet or a tuxedo, and flying her to Paris was still out of the question. After watching *The Princess Bride* with her, he'd realized that Jennifer had been right: Carla wanted big. Carla wanted romantic.

Christian didn't do big or romantic.

So, he did nothing. Well, except worry and stew about it.

But, nothing productive.

"Hi," he said again, stupidly. "What are you doing here?"

She nudged the basket at her feet, which he'd somehow missed until now. He blamed the shirt Carla was wearing, and more specifically, her tits inside of said shirt. Little things like oversized picnic baskets were easy to overlook with Carla around.

"I brought you some breakfast," she said with a brilliant smile. "I thought you might be hungry."

Breakfast? He didn't eat breakfast – he never felt hungry first thing in the morning – so he always made up for it with a big lunch and an even larger dinner.

He felt thick and stupid, staring at the basket on the ground and then up at her. Girls didn't do this. Girls expected guys to sweep them off their feet.

Which he was totally going to do with Carla. As soon as he found the right broom.

Which was why, every time he'd seen Jennifer in the last week, he'd ducked out the back door and made a run for it. She would want to put together elaborate plans for the next date, and there was simply *no way* he could outdo the first one. He was going to wave the white flag of surrender.

He was a failure.

After that mega-star, Zane Risley, had set the bar stupidly high by renting out the most expensive restaurant in Franklin just to take his *nanny* out on a date, the men of Long Valley had been royally screwed. The way Christian figured it, he didn't have a chance.

But now Carla was standing there, a basket of food at her feet, and he still hadn't said a word.

Considering how he spoke two languages, it was amazing how both of them could desert him just when he needed them most.

"One of my friends from high school talked about doing this with her husband," Carla continued on, blessedly filling in the silence. "It's called a tractor date. It's simple, really. I sit up in the jump seat next to you and we plow the field together and then afterwards, we eat the breakfast that I packed." She shrugged, and the pink began to steal back into her cheeks. "It's not nearly as amazing as your date was—"

"It's perfect," he cut her off. "Really…perfect."

No private chartered jets to France. No expensive meals that cost him a week's wage. Just the two of them, riding in a tractor.

If Carla could find romance in that, who was he to question it?

He helped her up into the cab after they stashed the picnic basket in the shade, and after starting up the engine, he slowly let off the brake. They began rolling down the field, and just as easily started rolling into a conversation.

Although they'd both grown up in Sawyer, only a year apart, they'd run in different circles, and he didn't know nearly as much about her as he wanted to. But somehow, he still found himself talking about his life instead of hers.

"I'm the only boy," he confirmed, in answer to her question. "I have six sisters."

"Six sisters?!" she gasped, and then laughed. "I knew you had a lot of sisters, but *six*?!"

"Yup, and every one of them is younger than me," he said with a groan, making a tight turn and then heading back the way they came, a few dozen feet to the east. "I was that tyrannical older brother, so my sisters took turns hating me or loving me. It depended on if I was breaking some noses after a guy broke their heart, or running a guy off after he dared to kiss one of them in front of me. Bastards," he said in disgust, and Carla let out a belly laugh.

"Tyrannical is right," she got out through her laughter. "I bet your sisters have some stories to tell."

Christian rolled his eyes at that – his sisters' judgment was *not* to be trusted, and they should feel thankful he saved them from more than a few slimy bastards.

"Mom stopped having kids after Rosa," he said, ignoring Carla's comment, "and everyone thought she was done, including her, when along comes Yesenia. Six years after Rosa. There she was, the baby of the family...right up until Nieves was born, another five years later. That time, the doctor tied her tubes while he was in giving her a cesarean. Said it was his duty as a doctor to save her life. She'd fought it tooth and nail beforehand – my mom's a good Catholic, and birth control is off the table for her." He shook his head dolefully. "I'm damn glad the doctor did it anyway. Nieves was the hardest pregnancy of all – my mom was flat on her back the whole time. The moment she got up and started moving around, she started bleeding."

"Oh my goodness," Carla said softly, just audible over the rumble of the engine. "Your poor mom."

He nodded, thinking back. It'd been rough when Nieves was born, and he didn't often reminisce about it, happy to just forget about the chaos and struggle.

Somehow, though, telling Carla wasn't the painful experience that he'd expected.

"She was 45 years old, with a newborn baby. The oldest of my sisters had already had kids, so the moment Nieves was born, she was an aunt. Honestly, we're all just glad Nieves doesn't have anything wrong with her. Well, at least not anything that couldn't be fixed with some strict rules." He chuckled without a dash of humor. "I'd always thought my younger sisters were spoiled compared to me, but when Nieves came along, I realized I'd had no clue what the word 'spoiled' meant."

He paused for just a moment but before Carla could ask any more probing questions, he decided that it was time to turn the tables on her.

"What made you decide to be a florist?"

"Oh!" she said, clearly delighted to be asked about a favorite topic of hers. "That's easy. May Day!"

He was in the middle of a turn at the end of the field so he had to finish it before he could look at her. "May Day?" he repeated skeptically. "Like, help, help, I'm in trouble?"

"Oh, you're right! I'd never thought about that before." She chewed her luscious bottom lip, deep in thought, and he tried to keep his mind out of the gutter and focused on whatever she was about to say. "I wonder why they're both called the same thing. No, remember back at Cleveland Elementary, how we made baskets and flowers out of paper to give to our moms on the first day of May?"

"Oh. Uh, yeah, of course."

She shook her head. "You don't remember it at all," she said dryly, and before he could defend his honor and come up with a convincing recollection of this event he did not remember in the slightest, she continued on. "Well, I had so much fun putting these baskets together, when I got home, I decided that it'd be even *more* fun if I use *real* flowers. Of course!"

She let out that delighted laugh of hers that Christian was sure he could never tire of listening to.

"But, my mom wasn't much of a gardener, and I quickly stripped our beds clean of any blooming flowers. It was only the start of May, after all. There were still snowdrifts in the shade."

She breathed in deeply, as if stealing herself for the part that came next, and in spite of himself, Christian held his breath. Whatever Carla was about to confess to, he was sure it couldn't be terrible – she wasn't capable of terrible – but that only made it all the more intriguing.

"Weellll," she drew out slowly, clearly trying to postpone the confession of her sins, "Mrs. Anastos lived next door with her gorgeous flower beds, and I figured she wouldn't mind if I took just a few so I could deliver flower baskets to every home on the street. How could she not be happy with me spreading cheer and love everywhere, right?"

She groaned, and Christian laughed. Just as he'd expected – Carla's terrible "sin" was helping herself to some flowers.

"I don't remember where Mom was at while I was stripping our neighbor of every flower in her garden, but the shit really hit the fan when Mrs. Anastos got home from the weekly shuffleboard game down at the old folks' home, and saw that her flowers were decimated. There I was, ringing the doorbell on every house on the street, and everyone was *so* happy to get these little paper baskets of flowers, thanking me for my kindness, and here comes Mom down the street with *that* look in her eyes. I wasn't sure if I was gonna live to see the sunset that day."

She chuckled ruefully, her boobs bouncing delightfully against his arm in the process. "I spent the whole summer doing yard work for Mrs. Anastos. For free. It was my punishment, but all I could think was how much fun it was to hand people flowers. I was *hooked*. I learned a lot from my neighbor – like how to forgive overeager kids who strip your prized garden of every petal – but also what the names of the flowers were and which season brought which variety. I worked several summers after that for her; luckily, she was kind enough to pay me after that first year! Finally, I was old enough to drive to Franklin and work at the floral shop there, so that became my job during high school."

She shrugged with a self-deprecating laugh. "But yes. You're on a date with a flower thief. I probably should've told you beforehand."

A date. He liked the sound of that, even if it was with a confessed flower thief.

"I will restrain my impulse to call Sheriff Connelly and report you," Christian said dryly.

"Thanks," she said with an impish grin that sent a bolt of lust straight to his dick. Did she know what she did to him, sitting in the cab of a tractor, so innocent and beautiful?

She couldn't know how gorgeous she was. Hell, he hadn't realized it himself until Mother's Day. Somehow, he'd overlooked her all through high school and beyond.

Not anymore.

"So tell me something about your family," Carla said, clearly wanting to change the subject back to a topic not related to thievery. "Something you wouldn't normally tell a girl on a second date."

His mind froze for a moment as he scrambled for something to say, and then snapped his fingers, rotating the steering wheel with his other hand as they made the turn at the bottom of the field. "Yesenia is going to college," he said proudly. "The only one in the family to do it. My parents are a little weird about it – if *I'd* been the one to go, that would've been fine with them. Of course, we were too poor back then, and I had to go to work right away out of high school. But for Yesenia to go as a girl…"

He trailed off, not wanting to air dirty laundry about his family with someone else, even if that "someone else" was his date, and even better, Carla Grahame.

"I'm helping her pay for it," he plunged on, getting to the important part of the story. This was definitely *not* something he would've mentioned on a second date – or a twentieth – under normal circumstances, but Carla was so damn good at asking great questions, the info was spilling out of him without him quite realizing it. "She's working and she has a first-generation college scholarship, but it doesn't cover everything. It's…not always fun," he said delicately – *understatement of the year, right there*, "but she's the smartest kid in our family. It wouldn't be right for her not to go to college – to just get married and pop out seven kids of her own. My other sisters have that covered. Yesenia…she's different."

Carla pulled his left arm against her generous chest, squeezing it tight. "That is so sweet, Christian," she said softly. "Not many brothers would do that."

He shrugged, feeling his bicep slide against her tits, and deciding in that moment that every night that he'd eaten Ramen Noodle or the Yellow Death was worth it.

"Yesenia was born four months before I graduated from Sawyer High School. She was my *fifth* sister. A new baby girl? Nothing special in our family at that point. Except, she was. From the beginning, there was a bond between us. She'd wrap her tiny fist around my finger and pull it to her mouth, sucking on it. When I left the night of graduation to go sit with my classmates in the auditorium, she put up a huge fuss that I'd dared to leave her behind. My mom eventually had to take her out. I was there when she took her first steps – she was holding onto my fingers. She became my shadow around the farm, following me and asking me a million questions. She can fix a tractor almost as well as I can. I can't believe it's been 20 years since yet another squalling, red-faced baby girl was born into the Palacios family. She's…well, she's Yesenia. She's different," he said again, lamely.

"You graduated in 2000, right?" she asked.

"Yup. Best class of the century." He winked at her.

"I do believe that was the class of 2001," she said haughtily, and then ruined the effect by laughing. "I always told my mom that she should've had me a year earlier," she said wistfully. "To be the first graduating class of the century…"

"Not many people can say that," he agreed. They were getting to the end of the field, and he lifted the discs on the hydraulic and then made the slow sweeping turn back towards the barn. "I think I'm ready for some of that breakfast you made us. Are you hungry?"

"I thought you'd never ask."

CHAPTER
TEN
CARLA

Since the invention of the kiss, there have been five kisses that were rated the most passionate. The most pure.
This kiss left them all behind.
~Grandfather in *The Princess Bride*

AFTER ARGUING – and losing – that she should be the one to empty out the picnic basket and spread the goodies out on the ground, Carla leaned back on her hands, legs crossed in front of her, and watched Christian with a happy sigh. She could get used to having someone else take care of her.

"Did you hear the latest about the Roberts' mansion?" she asked lazily, turning her face up to the warmth of the sun.

"No, what's happening with it now?"

He was nearing the bottom, where she had the cheesecake stashed away for dessert. She had no idea what food he liked to eat, so the whole meal had been a giant stab in the dark, with a heavy emphasis on "giant." She'd packed food for an army, figuring that if she offered enough variety, she was bound to bring at least a few items that Christian liked to eat.

"I've heard a woman is interested in it," she said, closing her eyes and soaking in the warmth. Nothing was better than early summer weather. She tilted her head towards Christian and cracked one eye open, eager to see his reaction to the news. "She came all the way from back east somewhere to look at it."

There was a moment's pause, and then they both burst into laughter.

"Some lady flew all the way here to look at the *Roberts'* mansion?" Christian finally got out, and shook his head in dismay. "I hope she brought her hazmat suit with her. I don't mind mucking out horse or cow shit, but mice and rats' poop and piss? *Hell* no."

Carla shrugged and moved to sit cross-legged. "It… wouldn't be my cup of tea," she said tactfully, "but that mansion *is* beautiful. Four stories? Seventeen bathrooms? I can't remember how many bedrooms, but yeah. The place is huge. With enough money, someone could turn it into a hotel or something."

"And every square inch of the place is stuffed to the rafters with shit," Christian said, passing one of the paper plates in its bamboo holder to her, and then began loading up his own. "I don't care how pretty the stained glass windows are. There isn't anything wrong with that place that can't be cured with a match."

"Christian, no! You're one of those who thinks the county should 'accidentally' set fire to the joint, aren't you?" She shook her head in dismay. "Homes of that age and stature aren't replaceable, you know."

He paused with his breakfast burrito partway to his mouth, thinking. "I do like older homes with character," he finally allowed, "but in the case of the Roberts' mansion, there are mountains of trash between you and that character. There wasn't a newspaper or receipt or junk mailer that Mrs. Roberts didn't love. I think if you dug deep enough, you might find the stone tablets from Moses buried in there."

"Exactly!" Carla said, delighted that he finally understood. "Think of what treasures are buried among the junk. Sure, you have to dig through a lot of empty tin cans and newspaper circulars from fifteen years ago, but I bet there's some really cool stuff in there."

He arched an eyebrow at her. "Let me guess," he said dryly, "you're one of those who thinks there are gold bars buried under the trash."

"Maybe," she said primly, not sure if she wanted to admit to the fact that the idea had flitted more than once through her mind. "I don't know. Mrs. Roberts does seem the kind to hoard gold bars." Christian laughed at that, and she sent him a quick grin. "But whether the famed gold exists or not, I'm interested in her years as an interior decorator. Did you know that she used to have clients who'd sit on a waiting list for a year, just for the privilege of paying her to decorate their homes?"

"Oh wow," Christian said, his chocolate-brown eyes going a little wide at the idea. "I didn't know. I knew she was into decorating, but I didn't know she was *that* much in demand."

"I bet she had some gorgeous pieces," Carla said with a wistful sigh as she took a bite into a piece of cantaloupe. "To go from being one of the top interior decorators in three states to… well, how she died…"

She trailed off at that. Mrs. Roberts' end was rather gory and sad, and not at all what Carla wanted to think about, and *definitely* not what she wanted to discuss while eating.

"So, did the buyer from back east leave already?" Christian asked, clearly trying to steer the conversation back into less macabre territory.

"No," Carla said with a light laugh, happy to leave talk of Mrs. Roberts behind. "Last I heard, she's in negotiations with the county. She wants to buy the property for the back taxes owed on it, and not a penny more. The county commissioners aren't happy – they've had it on their books for a year now, and you know they'd originally put that two-million-dollar price tag on it."

They both sighed at the insanity of someone paying two million dollars for the kind of headache that the Roberts' mansion would surely be. No sane person would ever pay that kind of money for a hoarder's mansion.

"Had you heard they'd dropped it to a half million?" At Christian's nod, she continued, "Having someone walk in and say she wasn't going to pay a penny above and beyond the back taxes owed on the place...I wish I'd been a fly on the wall for *that* county commissioner meeting. Everyone knows it's a millstone around the commissioners' necks, and who knows. They just might be desperate enough to say yes."

"More power to her," Christian said, raising his glass of orange juice in mock salute. "Whatever she does, she's gonna have two dozen people telling her that she's doing it wrong. I hope she has skin of leather. There's no better way to guarantee that you get plenty of unwanted advice than to pick a project like the Roberts' mansion."

Carla opened her mouth to agree wholeheartedly – Sawyerites were many things, but short on opinions wasn't one of them – when she noticed that Christian was peeling the paper cup off the last blueberry muffin. That part of the breakfast, she'd gotten from Gage at the bakery, of course – she could make a decent batch of muffins herself, but Gage's were better. No surprise there.

She'd gotten a baker's dozen so she could have some leftover for breakfast for the next week, but littering Christian's paper plate were ten discarded paper cups. She looked at the container with the sausage links in it. Empty. She eyed the Tupperware that had been filled with cantaloupe. Gone. She even picked up the thermos that'd been filled to the brim with orange juice before she set out. Not a drop left.

She'd packed enough for an army, and he'd single-handedly – well, with a tiny bit of help from her – inhaled it all.

"How?" she whispered, looking up at Christian wide-eyed. "How do you stay so skinny?" she blurted out, and then clapped her hands over her mouth.

She'd broken the cardinal rule of a fat person – never talk about weight with a skinny person. It always ended with either them proclaiming that they had *sooooo* much to lose (usually while pinching nonexistent fat to prove their point) or them telling her that she just had to watch what she ate.

Or worst of all, both.

Hold on, are you trying to tell me that I shouldn't eat a plate of donuts for breakfast and a bag of chips for lunch every day? Golly gee whiz. That'd never occurred to me before. I didn't know that I couldn't eat my way through the dessert menu on a daily basis and still stay skinny. Pray tell, enlighten me.

But Christian just looked down at his perfectly flat abs and then over at her, confusion writ large across his face.

"Genes, I guess," he said, and shrugged. "My sisters all hate me for it. I've never understood that. They all want to be super skinny, like a guy should want to bang a woman who looks like she hasn't even hit puberty yet. I've always liked women with meat on their bones. Substantial. I don't find it sexy to be with a woman who looks like a child. It makes me feel like a pervert."

Oh.

Maybe Christian could eat more food than two grown men put together and still stay skinny without even trying, but Carla decided on the spot that she'd forgive him for that flaw.

In fact, in that moment, she thought she could forgive him for just about anything. A man who *liked* meat on a woman's bones? Who didn't want someone who could pose for a fashion magazine in their spare time?

Yup, she could forgive him for just about anything at all.

He leaned forward then, pulling her out of her thoughts, his question stamped on his face.

Could he…?

She leaned forward too, meeting him halfway.

This kiss, in the history of kisses, blew all of the rest of the kisses away. She could hardly breathe; she couldn't think. He turned her inside out, and she enjoyed every moment of it.

They pulled apart and he whispered, "Whoa."

Her thoughts exactly.

CHAPTER
ELEVEN
CHRISTIAN

Have you any money? ~Inigo
I have a little. ~Fezzik the Giant
I just hope it's enough money to buy a miracle. ~Inigo
In *The Princess Bride*

CHRISTIAN YAWNED SO HARD, his jaw cracked as he pulled on his sleep t-shirt. It was only 9:45 at night, but like an old man, he was already heading for bed.

He'd always been an early bird, but even still, it was hard to want to get up at four in the morning to cut hay. Thank God he wasn't allergic to hay like he was cats.

Cats...

He scratched absentmindedly at his forearm, where he'd had that terrible allergic reaction after stupidly petting Carla's cat. She'd mentioned her cats a couple of times since then on their dates, and he knew how much they meant to her.

How could he tell her that he couldn't breathe around them? To break her heart like that...He hadn't meant to keep it a secret from her; he just hadn't found a good time to slip it into the conversation.

Yet. He would soon, though. It was only fair.

As he was pulling back the covers on his bed, ready to sink into his mattress for the night, he heard a muted knock on the front door, and let out a string of Spanish swear words that'd have his grandmother rolling over in her grave if she'd heard him. He was *so close* to sleep.

Could he ignore the knock and pretend he hadn't heard it? He would've given his right nut to do just that, but he couldn't. Whoever it was, it was someone he cared about. Door-to-door salesmen didn't bother with his single-wide trailer. One look at it, and they kept going.

Not to mention that Marshmallow hadn't started barking his fool head off, which meant he recognized the vehicle pulling up.

With a groan, Christian shuffled to the front door and found his younger sister – well, that was all of them – Yesenia, on the doorstep, her features cast in shadows by the dim porch light.

"Hey, *hermanita*," he said, forcing a note of cheerfulness into his voice as he opened the door wider to let her in. Once she was inside and he could see her better, he realized she wasn't there to pay him a social visit. "What's going on?" he asked, trying to keep his voice neutral even as his hands curled into fists at his sides.

Some guy had attacked her, he was sure of it. Christian was well aware how gorgeous his sister was, and what assholes there were in the world. Even now, with her hair disheveled and her eyes red from crying, she was beautiful. He was going to track the guy down and leave him for the buzzards to find.

"Tuition is going up this fall," Yesenia said, dropping to his dilapidated couch and burying her face in her hands. Her shoulders shook with silent sobs as Christian stood there, frozen, only his fingers moving as he slowly uncurled his fists.

No guy. No attack. No rape. He was grateful, but…

"By how much?" he asked, trying to keep calm. It was already a Herculean effort to help her get the tuition bill paid each semester. How could he pay more? He didn't want his sister leaving college saddled with debt – it went against everything the Palacios family believed in.

"Two thousand dollars." Her voice broke as she said the words, just as his heart broke to hear them. Two thousand? He didn't have an extra two thousand dollars sitting around. If he had, he would spend it on Carla, anyway.

Carla.

He wanted to do some weeping of his own. He wanted to spoil her – give her chocolates and take her out to fancy dinners and show her the world on his arm, or at least the inside of a nice restaurant.

Why now?

"It's an extra two thousand in tuition," Yesenia said, her voice dull and broken, and he was sure – absolutely sure – that he didn't want to hear the rest of the sentence, "and I also have lab fees this semester. It's another $1500 on top of it all."

Christian dropped to the couch next to his sister, his legs no longer able to hold him up. An additional $3500? He couldn't. He didn't have—

Yesenia turned into him, burying her face in his chest as she sobbed. He held her, stroking her hair back as he tried to wrap his arms around the enormity of the problem.

If he could just convince his parents to help out…but even as the thought crossed his mind, he shoved it away. Yesenia was a girl. Yesenia was supposed to get married and pop out kids and let her husband take care of everything. She was *not* supposed to go to college and have a career.

It did not matter how smart she was; Yesenia'd had the bad luck of being born a girl.

His parents were willing to splash out stupid amounts of money on things that did not matter –*quinceañeras* that were fit for a princess – but Yesenia hadn't wanted a *quinceañera* fit for a princess.

She'd wanted to go to college.

"I'll just borrow the money," she said, straightening up and wiping the tears from her eyes. "Everyone borrows money. It'll be—"

"You are *not* going to leave college in debt!" Christian snapped, and immediately regretted his tone. She shrank away from him, and he blew out a frustrated breath. "I'm sorry." He closed his eyes and breathed in slowly. "I didn't mean to be so…" He waved his hand in the air, brushing it away. "We'll figure it out. We always have. You're already working during the semester and that slows you down, so it isn't like you can take on another job during the school year."

They had seven semesters of this left. Not, of course, that he was counting or anything. But in his not-so-humble opinion, May of 2024 couldn't come fast enough.

He'd never, ever say that to Yesenia, of course.

She sighed, her long, dark hair a tangled mess, her mascara smeared across her face. She was normally so particular about her appearance. If she looked in the mirror, he was sure she'd let out a shriek of horror.

"I wish I could find a second job this summer," she said miserably. "Danyard's is always so good about taking me back, but I need to find something for the evenings and weekends."

Danyard's, a local office furniture company, was always so good about rehiring Yesenia every summer because she was the hardest worker they had, and they knew it. They paid her minimum wage – a crime in Christian's book – but Yesenia said she liked the fact that it started so early in the morning and gave her from three o'clock on to work somewhere else.

Not, of course, that this gap in her schedule had done her any good this summer.

"Your shift down there already starts at 6:30 in the morning," he reminded her. "You can't work *too* late into the evenings."

She shrugged. "I can sleep when I'm dead," she quipped, trying to smile.

And I'll eat when I'm dead. But he didn't say it out loud.

Yesenia already worried about how often he ate macaroni and cheese – aka, the Yellow Death – for dinner. He refused to make her worry more.

Finally, she slipped out the front door when she realized how late it was. "I know Stetson has you cutting hay right now, which means you'll need to get up in just a couple of hours. I'll let you sleep." And then she was gone into the night.

Christian forced his weary body to bed, staring up at the ceiling as he tried to figure out what to do. What'd he been thinking, dating Carla? Here she was, this successful businesswoman. She had employees. She'd been running Happy Petals for years. She even had her own house, unlike him, who lived in a single-wide trailer for free as part of his pay package from Stetson.

Huh. Actually, come to think of it, he'd only ever seen Carla come down the stairs of the florist shop and greet him there. Where *was* her house? He needed to ask her on their next date.

He beat his fist dully against his forehead.

If they should have a next date. Maybe he should just break things off with her now, before she figured out she was too good for him.

God, life sucked so hard sometimes…

CHAPTER
TWELVE
CARLA

Nonsense. You're only saying that because no one ever has.
~Westley in *The Princess Bride*

JULY, 2020

CARLA TOOK A SIP of her coffee and settled back against the bench seat of the bakery with a happy sigh. When Hannah'd had the temerity to get married, it'd thrown a real wrench in the works for the meetings of the Early Spinster's Club, and she and Michelle had floundered around a bit, unsure of what to do. They couldn't have meetings for a club with *two* people in it.

And then Michelle had struck up a conversation with Autumn one day while at the shop, waiting for Carla to finish helping a customer, and began probing for deets when it came to Autumn's love life. Carla had missed the whole thing, what with being busy and all with her customer, but Michelle told her all about it with relish afterwards.

"I told Autumn her boyfriend, Johnny, is so worthless, she might as well be single—"

"You didn't!" Carla had broken in, and then had started laughing. "Oh, Michelle."

Her friend had just shrugged. "I told her she could be an honorary member of the club, and that since we needed a secretary, she could do that."

"What did she say?!" Carla had asked, torn between horror and laughter. Only Michelle would tell someone that their long-term boyfriend was a pile of worthless shit.

"She asked when the next meeting was. I figured we could go back to our schedule from before, so next Wednesday afternoon. She said she'd be there."

And, she'd shown up. Bouncing brown natural curls and brilliant dark green eyes, Autumn was now officially the newest member of the Early Spinster's Club. She was so damn gorgeous, there was no way she'd last long – she was sure to get married way before lifers like her and Michelle – but still, Carla liked having Autumn there. She loved Michelle with all her heart, but sometimes, her snarkiness was a bit much to take without anyone else there to help buffer the storm.

"I was pissed as hell with him," Michelle said darkly to Autumn, deep into a story about her latest run-in with a negligent animal owner. "Treating animals like that? I told him he had a week to get the property back into shape and good-quality hay for his horses, or I'd be back with Sheriff Connelly in tow. I also told him to take a damn shower. He smelled like the south end of a north-bound mule."

Autumn let out a whoop of laughter at that and Carla shook her head even as she chuckled. There was an eight-year difference between Michelle and Autumn, so they hadn't had much of a chance to hang out before now, and Carla was happy to see them hit it off. Such age differences that'd seemed so huge in high school now seemed trivial.

Thank God we've left high school behind. Life was better as an adult, no question about it.

Michelle, spurred on by the reaction of her new audience, launched into one of her favorite diatribes. "Did you know that male animals that've been castrated are much healthier than their full-strength brethren?"

"Really?" Autumn said, her mouth hanging open at the thought. "I didn't know it made a difference."

"Oh yeah. Guys are *much* better off with their nuts removed," Michelle said baldly, eliciting another round of belly laughs from Autumn.

Carla chuckled even as she made the mental note to never let Christian hear Michelle pontificate upon this particular theory. She was pretty sure he wouldn't appreciate it.

And then, the air changed. She'd never been able to explain it properly to Michelle or Hannah – Michelle had said that Carla was "weirdly sensitive to things that didn't matter" the last time she'd tried to explain the sensation – but it was a sensation Carla couldn't ignore. There was something going on. Sitting up, she looked around the bakery and immediately realized where it was coming from. The harried woman at the front counter, talking to Sugar, was practically spewing anxiety.

"Are there...teenagers," the woman stumbled slightly over the word, "around here who want a job for a couple of weeks?" She had a slight nasal quality to her voice, a flat accent that told Carla that she wasn't from around here.

Northeast? Maybe? Why was a lady from the northeast wanting to hire teenagers?

Scratch that. What was a lady from back east *doing* in Sawyer, Idaho?

Sugar's brows knitted, and Carla could tell the full-time barista was trying to figure out the same thing. "What're you wanting the teenagers to do?" she asked. She was tugging on her braid of straight brown hair, just like she always did when she was confused.

"Clean-up work," the woman said vaguely, waving her coffee cup in the air.

Dimly, Carla could hear Michelle going into the finer details about how castrated males were healthier than full-strength males, but Carla ignored her. That was just Michelle being Michelle.

This lady at the check-out counter, though, stuck out like a whale floundering around in the Amazon rainforest. There was a story here, and interested in human beings like she was, Carla wanted to figure it out.

"What are you cleaning up?" Sugar pressed her. Carla mentally clapped in appreciation of Sugar's persistence.

"I bought the old Roberts' mansion," the woman finally said, and with that, the buzz in the bakery disappeared. Even Michelle stopped pontificating upon the benefits of male castration – only in the animal kingdom, of course – and turned, mouth open, to the woman at the counter.

"Did she just say she bought the Roberts' mansion?!" Michelle gasped under her breath.

Of course! Carla almost slapped her forehead. *The county clerk had told me all about her when she came in to pick up those flowers for her daughter's birthday. What would the chances be that two women from back east were wandering around Sawyer at the same time?*

She was even more petite and more beautiful than the clerk had described, though. Carla had conveniently left that part out when talking to Christian – telling the guy she was on a date with that a drop-dead gorgeous woman had just moved to town hadn't seemed like a stellar plan.

Now that Carla had clapped eyes on the woman, though, she realized words didn't do her justice. Even Autumn would stay single forever with this woman in the availability pool. At least, the county clerk had said she thought Keila – "Pronounced like 'tequila' without the T," as the clerk had explained – was single. She'd never been seen with a guy; wasn't wearing a wedding ring; and the paperwork for the mansion'd had just Keila's name on it.

Carla wasn't sure if the clerk should really be gossiping

about the transactions that took place down at the county courthouse, although it *was* true that it was all public knowledge, and Carla *did* love hearing the gossip. She was careful to never spread any herself, of course, but she loved being in the know.

The ringing silence of the bakery finally broke under a tidal wave of questions.

"Does it still stink?" shouted Mr. Maddow.

Not to be outdone by his friend, Mr. Behrend hollered, "Has the back half fallen in on itself? I heard it collapsed last year. Least, that's what the sheriff said when he came back after he found the dead body."

Questions were swirling in fast and furious now, and Carla couldn't keep track of who was asking what. Someone was shouting about gold bars and someone else was asking about the cockroach infestation, but if Carla thought it was overwhelming, she could plainly see it was affecting the newcomer a hell of a lot more.

The deer-in-the-headlights look on her face said it all.

Carla hesitated, not sure if she should stand up and throw herself in front of this woman to defend her from the rest of the town or leave her be, when Mr. Stultz's voice rose above the rest as he shouted, "How much did you dicker the tax man down to? I heard the county commissioners were downright *pissed* that you got the place for a song and a dance."

Like shutting off a tap, the bakery was silent once more, every eye pinned on the woman at the cash register.

Keila fixed a haughty stare on Mr. Stultz and said icily, "I *really* don't see how this is any of your business."

And with that, Carla was quite sure what she needed to do.

"See y'all later," she said under her breath as she pushed herself up from the booth.

"Where are you going?!" Michelle whisper-yelled after her, but Carla ignored her. Whatever this woman was thinking buying the old Roberts' mansion, she wasn't going to win any favors in Sawyer with that attitude.

Maybe it really wasn't the business of anyone in Sawyer to know how much she paid in back taxes for the falling-down mansion, but that didn't mean that she could actually state such things out loud. Not as an outsider, anyway.

"I'll help you find some teenagers," Carla said loudly, grasping the tiny woman's delicate elbow and steering her towards the front door. "Morning, Mrs. Gehring. Morning, Mr. Willow. Don't forget to pick up your flowers for your granddaughter's birthday, Mrs. Worsop – the bouquet is ready," and then they were out the door and heading down the sidewalk towards Happy Petals. "I'm Carla Grahame, by the way," she said conversationally, walking fast and forcing her companion to keep up. "And you are Keila Wilson?"

"How did you know that?!" the woman gasped, her cherry red lips making a perfect O. Carla almost asked her what brand and shade she used – she was sure Christian would love that color on her – but forced herself to stay focused.

"Small towns," Carla said cheerfully, keeping them moving at a brisk pace. They had to get to shelter before some enterprising Sawyerite decided to run after them. As it was, she'd count her blessings if she didn't "randomly" have a half-dozen people remember that they needed to stop by for some flowers *right now*, once word spread where the new owner was hiding. "Everybody knows everything. You'd have better luck trying to hide a secret from the CIA than from the people of Sawyer. Here's my shop."

She unlocked the front door and hurried inside, deftly hitting the light switch for the open sign while also hanging up her keys.

Moving in slow motion, Keila walked in behind her but then simply stood there, frozen to the spot. Carla hastened to reassure her.

"I own Happy Petals," she said, hoping Keila wouldn't take

offense at her stating the obvious. Why else would she have a key to the front door of the business?

But Keila seemed to be a little slow on the uptake. Maybe she was still in shock from the Muffin Man encounter. Her bright blue eyes – the exact color of her shirt – blinked just as slowly as she looked around, as if trying to figure out where she was at and what was happening.

"The good news is," Carla said, steering the convo back to the disastrous first encounter with the locals, "Sawyer may be filled to the brim with inquisitive, nosy people, but they're also sweet and kind. For the most part. But if you need something, the people here will take the clothes off their backs to make it happen."

That seemed to do the trick. As if waking from a dream, Keila had the wherewithal to send her a clearly dubious look, but instead of arguing, circled back to her original question. "You said you could help me find teenagers to clean up the mansion?"

Right. She'd said that, hadn't she.

She'd been in somewhat of a panic, simply trying to save the woman, but clearly Keila was single-minded about the whole thing.

"Sure, sure," Carla said absentmindedly as she mentally flipped through the possibilities. "I'm assuming you're wanting teenage girls, right?" As they talked, she went back to putting the finishing touches on Iris' monthly bouquet.

Not pregnant.

Again.

Gah. It was stupid awkward. When Carla saw her on the street, she wanted to give the frail red-head a hug, but she also couldn't acknowledge that she knew what was going on. As a florist, she had to help people get through their problems, while also pretending that they didn't have any.

It was an interesting balancing act, for sure.

Keila got a mulish look on her face. "I'd hoped to hire some teenage boys, actually, but that very rude man down at the hardware store told me that every teenage boy worth a bucket of warm spit," she pulled a face, clearly indicating her thoughts on warm spit, "already had a job for the summer, and the good ones have two. Is that true?"

Finished with Iris' bouquet for the month, Carla began cleaning and facing the flowers, pulling a bouquet that looked past its prime to throw away. She hated it when flowers didn't get to go home with someone to make them happy, but she never wanted to sell them when they got to this point, either. High quality was part of what she offered her customers. "Yeah," she said as she worked. "It's true. Where are you from?"

Keila looked startled but answered, "Boston." As soon as she said it, things clicked into place for Carla. *That* was the accent she was hearing. Not just northeast somewhere, but the very distinct Bostonian accent.

She loved the thrill of figuring things out, and matching the accent together with the town was like sliding a puzzle piece into place. She still had no idea *why* a woman from Boston, Massachusetts would be in rural Idaho, but that would be the next mystery to solve.

"Right," Carla said, trying to figure out how to word this next part as delicately as possible. "Well, this probably isn't a thing in Boston, but here in Sawyer, there's a lot of hard physical work that needs to be done. Feeding cows, stacking hay, moving water, castrating and branding calves…it isn't that girls aren't hard workers and aren't willing, but quite often, they lack the muscle necessary to pick up a 90-lb hay bale and toss it into the back of a truck. Teenage boys – the ones worth talking about, anyway – tend to get snapped up real quick. There are some teenage girls who will help out on a farm or ranch, but they mostly stick with babysitting, working at the grocery store…things like that. Mr. Burbank," (who *was* rude, but Carla decided to keep her thoughts to herself on that topic), "is right – it's the middle of summer. These teens have already been working at their summer jobs for a couple of months. I promise you, there isn't an available teenage boy in town who you'd want to hire."

Just then, the front door to the shop opened and Carla turned, automatically sliding her professional smile into place, until she saw it was Autumn coming in, and then it melted into her friendly smile instead. It was so fun to have Autumn as a business partner. Instead of being alone in the shop, alone in the decisions that she had to make, she had someone else to run things past. She hadn't realized how much she'd love that until it happened.

Autumn shot Keila a harried smile and then pulled Carla off to the side. "I've got Mrs. Hoffmeister wanting to talk to me," she whispered, "about the flower arrangements for the retirement party for her husband, but she wants to go through every detail of every flower, and…I tried to tell her that it'd be best to call you, but she keeps claiming she can't find your number." She rolled her eyes dramatically. "Can you call her? She's driving me crazy."

"Yeah, of course." They moved over to the front counter so Carla could scribble a quick note and stick it to the computer screen. Otherwise, she'd never remember to call the client back. Mrs. Hoffmeister was a difficult woman on the best of days, so it'd be all too easy to "accidentally" forget she was supposed to call her.

Finishing up, she looked at the two women. "Keila, this is Autumn. Autumn, this is Keila Wilson. Keila just bought the Roberts' mansion and is looking for help to clean it out. Autumn has a small office here in my shop that she uses to run an event planning business out of." She couldn't help the note of pride in her voice at that. It had been one of her finer ideas, if she did say so herself.

Keila put her hand out to shake Autumn's, and then Carla turned to the newcomer, snapping her fingers, a huge grin spreading across her face. "You know who you should hire?" she asked rhetorically. "Christian's sisters!"

Keila gave her a blank look, and Carla realized belatedly that that wouldn't mean much to her new Bostonian friend.

Autumn chimed in. "Oh, that's a great idea! Rosa was just telling me the other day that her younger sisters were on the hunt for a job."

"Christian," Carla explained to Keila, "is my…boyfriend." She stumbled over the word, not sure if her tongue was going to handle it or not. Such a weird word to use. Boyfriend…boyfriend…*were* they boyfriend and girlfriend? He hadn't asked her to be his girlfriend, but she also wasn't sure what the etiquette on that was. Did he have to ask? Or was it just assumed?

If she'd had more experience with this sort of thing, she would know the answer to those questions. Alas…

"Anyway," she hurried on, feeling a blush stealing into her cheeks, "Christian has six younger sisters. He's the oldest, and there are no other boys in the family."

Keila just stared at her like she'd grown a second head, and Carla laughed.

"I know, right?" she said dryly. "Seven kids in one family. Welcome to Idaho. Anyway, most of them are married and have plenty to keep them busy, but Yesenia is always looking for a way to make more money for college, and Nieves needs to do something this summer that doesn't involve kissing her boyfriend."

Not that Carla had anything against kissing, of course, but it didn't seem healthy for a 15-year-old girl to be *this* obsessed with boys. There was something about Nieves that made Carla think there was more to her than just boy obsession, but so far, she hadn't had that theory borne out by facts. If Nieves wasn't sucking face with her boyfriend, she was texting him. Getting her to do something this summer that didn't involve a phone screen would be an excellent step forward.

"Autumn, you should text Yesenia and Nieves. See if they're free."

Autumn smiled at Keila, her natural friendliness on display. "You'll like Yesenia," she said in a confidential tone as her fingers flew over the screen. "She's a hard worker."

Carla couldn't help but notice that Autumn left Nieves out of the compliment, and mentally applauded her tact. Hiring Yesenia meant she'd keep Nieves focused and working. Nieves by herself…was not a great idea.

As they waited for Yesenia and Nieves to show up, they fell easily into chatting.

Keila leaned forward as if about to share a secret. "I'm going to turn the mansion into a bed and breakfast," she said, her voice low.

Carla clapped her hands with glee. "I was *just* telling Christian the other day that someone should turn it into a hotel." She decided to opt for her own bit of tact and leave out the part where they'd laughed uproariously at someone flying from one side of the continent to the other to buy the place. "It's certainly big enough. Seventeen bathrooms?! I mean, c'mon. No single house needs *that* many bathrooms."

"As soon as I read about it, I knew it's what I wanted to do with it."

Carla opened her mouth to probe more – read about it? Where? How? – but Keila's next words made her forget the questions. "I had you on the list to talk to," the woman said, her giant blue eyes pinning Carla in place, "so I'm glad we ran into each other down at the bakery. Once the B&B is up and going, I'd like to arrange to have you deliver fresh flowers for the foyer every week. A huge, gorgeous bouquet on the table in the entry would strike the right tone for the guests coming in."

"Ooohhhhh…" Carla breathed, and her face split into a huge smile. "I would be *delighted*. Oh, to do a new bouquet every week, and always use whatever's in season right now…I'd cut you a great deal if you'd give me total leeway on which flowers

I use. If you want the bouquet to be roses every week or something, that's a different story. But if I can change up the bouquets depending on the time of year and what's in bloom, we could totally make that work."

"I'm not a huge flower person," Keila confessed, "so I'm happy to let you decide. Whatever you think is best."

Before Carla could press her for more details, the bell over the front door tinkled and Yesenia and Nieves came in, looking dressed to work. Well, Yesenia looked ready to go, with her hair in a braid and work jeans on, but Nieves was buried deep in her phone, not even looking up to say hi, and her jeans looked artfully distressed. Those rips and holes definitely didn't come from cleaning out horse stalls or washing cars.

Carla mentally sighed. Nieves was…

Well, spoiled rotten. She remembered again how Christian was helping to pay for Yesenia's college while Nieves was getting fancy *quinceañera* parties.

Sometimes, life just wasn't fair.

After the round of introductions, Keila said, "I'd like to get started right away. There's a lot that needs to be done."

Carla thought that was probably the understatement of the century, but her naturally inquisitive and friendly nature drove her to find out *just* how true that was. "Would you be willing to let us tour it?" she asked hopefully. "Mrs. Roberts wasn't exactly one for having a lot of visitors, and I've always wanted to see the inside."

Just from what Carla could see from the road, she knew it was gorgeous. And huge. And a real mess. The landscaping alone was in terrible shape.

Keila nibbled on her bottom lip for a moment, looking torn, and then finally said, "Sure. It'd be good. I could see what ideas you have."

Carla only *just* kept herself from squealing with delight.

They headed out, Keila in a rental car and everyone else in

Carla's Happy Petals van; Carla making sure to lock the door and turn the sign back off on the way out.

Once inside the van, Yesenia – who'd claimed the front passenger seat – confided, "I've never seen it in real life either, but I've heard horror stories. It can't *actually* be as bad as they say, though, right?"

Carla sent Yesenia an encouraging smile. "I'm sure it can't be *that* terrible. Someone was living there just last year!"

Autumn, in the backseat, let out a cough that sounded a lot like, "Yeah right!" but when Carla looked at her friend in the rearview mirror, she was gazing innocently out the window.

Carla let out a sigh, her hands tightening on the steering wheel as she remembered that they'd found Mrs. Roberts' body weeks after she'd died, and with the oppressive summer heat last year...

Maybe the mansion wasn't ready to be a summer home right now, but surely it couldn't be *too* far off the mark.

"I've only ever seen it through the trees as I've driven past," she admitted, taking a right at a stop sign and heading farther out into the country, following Keila's car as she led the way. "I think I've seen the whole county at this point because of the flower deliveries, but of course, Mrs. Roberts wasn't one to get flowers delivered on the regular."

As soon as the words escaped her lips, she felt terrible that she'd said it. Emphasizing the fact that Mrs. Roberts was a recluse without any visitors or friends wasn't a kind thing to do, and if nothing else, Carla was *always* kind.

They took a left and began heading down a dirt lane, huge maples arching over the driveway, enclosing them. It was beautiful in a wild sort of way but they were in desperate need of a trimming, and she worried that some of the lower-hanging branches would take a chunk out of the van's paint job. She gripped the steering wheel harder, doing her best to avoid the worst of the ruts in the road but not sure if she was succeeding or not. She gritted her teeth, trying to keep from breaking a tooth when slamming through a particularly large hole.

Damn. If Keila was actually going to make a go of this, the driveway would have to be completely reworked. She hoped the Bostonian had cash. A *lot* of cash.

With one last curve of the road, the view opened up and the mansion was on full display.

"Holy…" Carla whispered under her breath.

"Shit," Autumn finished from the backseat. Carla noticed in the rearview mirror that even Nieves had stopped texting and was staring out the window of the van, her mouth hanging open.

Stunning. That was the word that kept reverberating in Carla's mind.

It was gorgeous but broken; stately but wildly overgrown. Idaho wasn't littered with historic mansions like the states back east were, and to let this kind of a house fall to ruin was a travesty, in Carla's not-so-humble opinion.

"Wowee, wowee," Autumn breathed. "Yesenia, how many friends do you have? If this is just up to you, Nieves, and Keila, y'all are gonna be cleaning this up for the rest of your lives."

"Not enough," Yesenia said quietly, her large brown eyes, so like Christian's, huge with surprise and what Carla thought might be a little bit of well-deserved terror. "This is…" She trailed off.

Carla rolled to a stop behind Keila's rental car, putting her van in park.

"Well, ladies, let's see what it looks like on the inside," Carla said, trying to keep up a cheerful façade. It was rude to ask Keila what the status of her bank account was, of course, but this house was bigger and more rundown and needed more work than she'd even remembered, and her memory hadn't exactly been positive.

Didn't they make a movie about this back in the 1980s? The Money Pit *with Dan Aykroyd? No, it was Tom Hanks. Well, whoever it was, I think it might've been a documentary of the remodel of this place.*

Keeping her thoughts to herself, they all piled out of the van and followed Keila's petite figure up to the front porch where she unlocked the door, and then turned back to them. "Be careful where you step," she said, a comment that didn't make a whole lot of sense until they'd made their way inside.

Because simply walking in was not possible. Other than the clearance needed to swing the front door open far enough to squeeze through, there wasn't a square inch of bare floor as far as the eye could see. The piles rose and fell like the hills of gold and treasure inside of Aladdin's cave, but in this case, it was nothing but mountains of junk.

Carla had heard it was bad. Carla had known it wasn't going to be beautiful. But this was so far beyond "bad," words failed her.

Shoes and receipts and empty pop cans and stacks of books towered over them. A broken wheel from a bike, rusty coffee cans, and towels encrusted with stuff Carla was *quite* sure she did not want named dotted the piles. A rocking chair sat atop one particularly tall heap, like a throne for a king to survey his domain. Carla wondered for a brief moment if the ghost of Mrs. Roberts came back at night and rocked in that chair, overlooking her estate, and shivered despite the oppressive heat.

"I call it The Hoard – capital T, capital H," Keila said into the silence. They were clustered together – partially still in the open doorway and partially perched awkwardly on top of the shorter stacks at the base of the hoard – and no one was saying a word. "I'd make a joke about finding a dead body in here, but of course, Mrs. Roberts…well, it wouldn't be much of a joke, would it?"

"So you know about that?!" Carla gasped in surprise, and then began coughing. The overpowering smell only made worse from the summer heat meant breathing was questionable to begin with; sucking the air in willy-nilly wasn't her best idea.

"Of course," Keila said blithely. "It was in the original article I read."

This was the second time Keila had mentioned she'd read about the mansion somewhere. But where? And why? Surely the Roberts' mansion didn't make it into the local news back in Boston. Before Carla could think of how to phrase her question, Keila continued on.

"There's certainly more to this place than this square foot we're all squished into," Keila said with a laugh. "Let's explore, shall we? Let me know if you find anything interesting."

Nieves scrambled over to the base of the grand staircase that led to the second floor and stared upwards, clearly trying to find a way to make her way up it. "I haven't been able to make it up that way yet," Keila called out. "There's a back staircase over here that I've used to get to the second floor."

"Cool," Nieves said, and followed Keila through a narrow opening in the garbage to parts unknown. Carla decided to take a left and follow a wide hallway that would surely lead to something beautiful.

What if I get lost in here? What if I have to call someone on my cell phone to have them come rescue me?

She tended to have a pretty good sense of direction, but in The Hoard – which was the perfect name for this disaster zone – there were very few landmarks. Piles of trash on top of mountains of trash, packed to the ceiling in most places.

Carla was starting to wonder if Christian wasn't onto something after all. As gorgeous as this place was, a body would need to excavate literally tons of trash to find that beauty.

Turning sideways, she managed to push her way through a partially open door, popping out the other side into a funny-shaped room. With the piles everywhere it was hard to tell, but she thought it had at least six walls. Light struggled to make it through the dirt-incrusted, large-paned windows on the far side, forcing Carla to squint at what she thought were tatters hanging off a curtain rod. Or, it could be wallpaper peeling. She squinted harder. Yup, those'd been red velvet curtains...at least before mice and age had ruined them.

This was probably a gorgeous room at one point. Oh, to have seen it in its heyday!

Right then, she felt something run across her foot and she looked down just quick enough to see the tip of a mouse tail disappear under the trash.

"Ahh!" she yelled, her hand over her chest, her heart pumping a million miles an hour. She was posed to make a run for the door when a sparkle in the dim lighting caught her eye. There was some sort of figurine on the marble mantlepiece she hadn't even noticed until that moment, buried as it was under the trash. Pulling her shirt up over her nose to block out the smell, she forced herself to climb the less-precarious-looking piles between her and the fireplace, hoping against hope she wasn't walking across a warren of mice or, heaven forbid, rats, as she worked her way across the room.

She plucked the figurine from the mantel, trying not to touch it any more than she absolutely had to, and tilted it towards the weak light from the filthy windows, settling her reading glasses into place so she could have a good look at it. It was a mother cat and her kitten, posed with the mom giving her baby a bath. Both animals' eyes glittered. Carla rotated the cool porcelain in her hands, letting the light catch and shine in the depths of the green jewels.

Carla wasn't exactly a jewelry connoisseur, but she was almost positive these were emeralds.

"Whoa," she breathed, and shoved her glasses back on top of her head.

She scrambled back over the mountains of junk, hoping she didn't get stuck with rusty metal on the way and die of tetanus, squeezed back through the doorway, and hurried down the hall, sidling past some crazy tall piles that seemed to be defying gravity. *One of these piles could fall over and squash me to death.*

She tried not to dwell on that, either.

"Keila," she hollered as she fought her way back to the main foyer. "I found something!"

She heard scuffling emanating from one of the wings and mentally crossed her fingers that it was Keila on her way back, and not some wild animal with rabies. When Keila pushed her way through a mostly closed doorway – such a tight fit, one of Carla's thighs wouldn't fit through, let alone her whole body – and popped out the other side, Carla murmured a quick thank you to the heavens that she was not, in fact, a raccoon intent on eating her for breakfast.

"Look!" she said, holding the delicate figurine out for her new friend to see. "I think the cats' eyes are emeralds."

Keila peered at it, but didn't take it from her. "Pretty," she said unenthusiastically. "Are you going to keep it?"

"Keep it?" Carla gaped at her. "But, I think these are real emeralds!"

"They're small," Keila said dismissively. "If you like it, you can keep it. If you don't want it, do what you'd like with it. If you pitched it back into The Hoard, I think it'd swallow it whole and burp out a thank-you."

Carla laughed even as she cradled the figurine in her hands. If Keila could afford to be so cavalier with emeralds – even small ones – she was playing on a completely different financial field than Carla was. Maybe she did have the kind of cash necessary to bring this mansion back to its former glory.

As the group headed back outside into the warm sunshine, leaving the overwhelming stench behind them, Carla breathed in deeply, appreciating clean, sweet air like she never had before. She could hear Yesenia laying out a work schedule with Keila, promising to ask other friends and family members if they'd like to come help even as Nieves was back on her phone, texting again.

Carla searched through the detritus that always managed to accumulate no matter how often she cleaned out her van, and finally found a soft scrap of cloth to wrap around the figurine to protect it. She'd clean it up and take it with her the next time she went to Boise. See if she could find an antique dealer who could tell her more about it. If it ended up being some priceless antique, she'd have to give it back to her friend, no matter what Keila had said.

She secretly hoped it wasn't worth anything at all – she was already falling in love with the sweet look on the momma's face as she licked her baby clean. Carla'd find a place of honor for it in the shop.

"Ready?" she asked when Yesenia seemed to have wrapped up her discussion with Keila.

"Yeah. Nice again to have met you. See you tomorrow?" She stuck her hand out to shake Keila's, and then climbed into the van. Once her younger sister and Autumn were also in, Carla started up her van, waved to her new friend, and carefully made her way back down the driveway, doing a slightly better job of avoiding the potholes this time around.

"Well, you're in for an adventure, aren't you?" Carla asked Yesenia with a small laugh once they got back onto pavement. "I hope you're excited about this. I didn't mean to volunteer you for something quite that nuts."

Yesenia sent her a happy grin. "This is more perfect than you know," she said cheerfully. "I've been trying to find a good job that would work around my schedule at Danyard's, and it doesn't get much better than this. Keila seems happy to have me put together a schedule that works for me, and says she'll pay cash every week. I don't mind cleaning up a few piles of junk."

Carla laughed at that. "If that's what you consider to be a few piles of junk," she said, still chuckling, "I can only imagine what you were like as a teenager with your mom telling you to clean your room."

As the conversation continued to swirl around the van, Carla thought back to her new friend. There were a few pieces missing to the puzzle here. Why was a gorgeous woman from Boston here in little ol' Nowhere, Idaho? Why was she buying a monstrous mansion that possessed more major problems than it had bathrooms? How could she afford to buy it, let alone remodel it?

Keila Wilson was a mystery, and people person that Carla was, nothing intrigued her more.

CHAPTER
THIRTEEN

CHRISTIAN

> Good. Then pour the wine.
> ~Westley in *The Princess Bride*

CHRISTIAN HEARD the rumble of Adam's truck long before he spotted it, and just at the sound, his heart sped up.

"Hey, I need to go talk to the vet for a sec," he said casually to Dave. "Be back in a minute."

He headed out of the barn and into the bright sunshine, squinting as his eyes adjusted. It was a hot one today, and he instinctively hunted out a bit of shade under a lean-to, to wait for the vet. Adam was there to check on a couple of cows with a nasty greenish discharge, but while he was there...

It'd been a couple of weeks since Yesenia had dropped the bad news on his lap – a nuclear bomb that would destroy his life and all that he wanted from it. He'd struggled with it every day since, knowing that he *should* break up with Carla, but not able to make himself do it. He'd prided himself growing up on the self-control that he had – how hard he could work. How dedicated he could be to completing a project.

But when it came to breaking up with Carla, he'd found his

self-control had gone AWOL on him. A better man than him could let her go, but he couldn't do it.

If he wasn't capable of forcing himself to let her find someone more worthy, though, then he could damn well make sure that she wouldn't have to give up her cats for him. It was the *least* he could do.

"Hey, Christian!" Adam called, swinging out of his truck, bag in hand. "How's it goin'?"

"Good, good. It's a cooker today."

The tall, lanky vet joined him in the shade, leaning up against the other side of the post as he took his cowboy hat off to fan his face. "July is always the worst of it," he agreed. "Makes a body want to spend the whole month in a lake. Just get in and don't come back out again until the weather has a mind to be decent again."

Christian chuckled politely at that, and then dove head first into it. "Is there a way to get rid of cat allergies?" he asked bluntly.

"Cat? I didn't know the Millers had cats," Adam said, looking around as if suddenly expecting one to jump out of the shadows at him.

"No, although Stetson keeps saying he wants to get a couple of barn cats. Keep the mice down." Adam nodded approvingly at that. "It's my…girlfriend." His tongue suddenly felt too big for his mouth.

Was Carla his girlfriend? They'd gone on plenty of dates at this point, but he hadn't formally asked her. Was he supposed to ask? He didn't know. There was so much about dating that he didn't know a damn thing about.

"Oh yeah, I heard about that! Kylie told me about some big date the Miller girls helped you put together down at the old mill with Carla. You're making the rest of us look bad, you know. Now Kylie's asking me when I'm gonna rent out the old mill and decorate it to the nines for a big date with her."

"I figure Zane set the bar so high with his date with his

nanny that the rest of us are screwed," Christian admitted baldly.

Adam let out a bark of laughter at that. "The bar keeps gettin' higher, that's for damn sure. All I had to do to win over Kylie was hire her. Next thing I know, guys are going to have to rent helicopters to take a girl out in the valley."

Christian let out his own belly laugh at that. A helicopter ride in a tux was one of the date ideas he'd been sure Carla was going to require if he was ever going to talk her into going on a date with him. Thank God that theory hadn't ended up being true.

"So Carla has a cat, and it's causing you allergies?" Adam mused, bringing the conversation back around. At Christian's nod, Adam said, "I'm an animal doctor, not a human doctor, to be clear. But from what I understand, it's best to start out with allergy pills like Benadryl, and if that doesn't keep it under control, you can look at doing shots."

"Shots?" Christian tried to play it calm, but his heart went into overdrive just hearing the word. He didn't like needles.

"Yup. It ain't guaranteed, but the idea is, they give you a series of shots and over time, your body stops attacking the cat dander and just ignores it instead. It's a sight easier to just not be around cats, though." He shot Christian a sideways glance. "How serious are you about Carla?"

Christian shrugged, not sure he knew the answer, and not willing to tell the vet in any case. Adam nodded sagely and left it at that. Just one of the many things to like about the vet.

"Well, I better get to it," Adam said, pushing away from the pole and settling his hat back on. "The cows are in the solitary corral, right?"

"Yeah, we separated them as soon as we noticed the problem," Christian said, and they walked together towards the pen where Stetson kept the cows that needed extra attention. "Stetson's out in the back forty, so I'll help you out."

After the vet finished his work and headed off to his next

appointment, Christian decided to take a quick stroll up to the main house and get a glass of Carmelita's world-famous lemonade to cool down with, and maybe oh-so-casually ask her for some help while he was there.

"Christian," Carmelita said with her soft, Hispanic accent, beaming at him as he came in through the kitchen door. "It is hot today. Do you want some lemonade? You come sit at the table. I will get you a glass, and some cookies too."

He smiled to himself. With Carmelita around, no one would ever starve to death. She wouldn't allow it.

"Here, here," she said, fussing over him and setting out a spread worthy of a king at the kitchen table. "I will get you more cookies. Stetson works you too hard. You are only skin and bones. You must eat more."

Just then, he heard the crashing of metal against metal, and even before he turned to look, he was sure he knew who it was.

"I'm sorry, *abuelita*," Flint wailed, crawling out of the pantry over clanking pots and pans. Once on the other side, the sturdy three year old climbed to his feet and threw his arms around Carmelita's legs. "I was going to make you a *secret* pie."

"You are my best pie-maker," Carmelita agreed solemnly, winking at Christian over the blond boy's head. "You pick out which bowl you want to use, and then you need to put the rest back on the shelf. I am too old to bend over so much."

Flint seized a huge bowl out of the bottom of the pile, causing the rest to crash and rattle yet again, and held it up triumphantly. "We will make a secret HUGE pie!" he said gleefully.

Christian laughed into his glass of lemonade. Stetson and Jennifer should count their lucky stars every night to have such a wonderful *abuelita* for Flint such as Carmelita.

"After you two are done making your huge pie," Christian said, "could I talk you into doing a favor for me?"

"Of course, of course," Carmelita said, bringing over a large ham sandwich and chips, not even asking if he was hungry. Maybe she knew he was always hungry. "What is going on?"

"I'm dating Carla Grahame." The words were hard to say, but he managed to get them out. Would it ever be easy to refer to someone as his girlfriend? Even someone as amazing as Carla?

"I heard this from Jennifer!" the housekeeper said with a delighted clap of her hands. "Flint and I, we made your dinner that night at the mill. I like Carla *very* much. You have good taste in women. She has meat on her bones," she said with satisfaction.

Flint had finished stacking the pots, pans, and bowls back on the pantry shelf in a haphazard fashion that was sure to topple back over at any moment, and was now busy tugging a chair over to the counter so he could stand on it as he cooked.

"Get the sugar and salt out and put them on the counter," Carmelita told her little helper, and then turned back to Christian. "Now, you said you are dating Carla. What can I help you with?"

"A big picnic basket," he said, figuring he'd better get to the point before Flint pulled her attention away again. "Carla surprised me one morning with a basket out in the field, and I thought it'd be fun to return the favor. Take her up into the mountains and treat her to a picnic. Get away from this heat."

After their tractor date, they'd gone out almost every weekend, and after a meal at a local restaurant, would go on long walks around the lake, talking and laughing and getting to know each other. He had yet to take her back to his place – his single-wide trailer was not good enough for someone like Carla – but he hadn't seen her place yet, either. Every time he offered to drop her off at her house, she would say she had a few more things to wrap up at the shop so he should drop her off there instead.

All of this meant that somehow, after a month of dates, they still hadn't gotten past first base. But a picnic up in the mountains with no one around and a stream trickling by?

Christian had a lot of plans for this date, and only some of it included food.

"¡*Excelente!*" Carmelita exclaimed, and clearly excited about whatever would make his beloved *abuelita* excited, Flint began clapping. Carmelita laughed and leaned over to press a kiss to his forehead. "It is very exciting, no?" she said, pulling the boy in for a quick hug. "Christian here is a smart man." She looked over at Christian. "I will make you a big basket filled with food. Something to make Carla fall in love with you," and winked.

"I love you," Flint said, and began banging on the counter with a wooden spoon.

"Yes, yes, but maybe not so much noise," Carmelita said, rescuing the spoon from the boy's hands.

With a wave goodbye at the pair, Christian slipped out the back door. Seeing Flint today reminded him all over again about his bond with Yesenia almost from the day she was born. Although he was damn proud of how she'd turned out, a part of him missed having his own little shadow, following him everywhere and "helping" him at every turn, whether he wanted the help or not.

He would be forty in another two years. If he was going to have kids of his own, he'd better get a move on.

Did Carla want kids?

It was too soon to ask, but he needed to gather up the courage to broach the topic soon. He'd always wanted kids – the more, the merrier – and watching Stetson's kid grow up over the past three years had made that crystal clear for him, along with the hoards of his own nieces and nephews.

Kids and Carla…

Somehow, that wasn't nearly as scary as it should've been.

CHAPTER
FOURTEEN

CARLA

What he meant was, I love you.
~Grandfather in *The Princess Bride*

HIKING ALONG a beautiful wooded trail, Carla was busy questioning her life choices. When Christian had promised her a "big date," she'd taken her time picking out her sexiest underwear and matching panties. Satin and lace, they made even her look sexy.

Unfortunately, satin thong underwear wasn't the best choice for hiking, and as she tried to discreetly un-wedge the material from her butt crack, she began to think she should've stuck to her granny panties. Not to mention that her bra, although it made her tits look fabulous, wasn't really meant to hold the girls in place during athletic pursuits.

Note to self: Next time, ask more questions about what, exactly, you're going to be doing on your "big date."

After a few more switchbacks, the trail opened up and Carla gasped with surprise. Okay, so maybe it was actually her just gasping for breath after that steep climb, but she *was* surprised, nonetheless.

"Do you like it?" Christian asked, the nerves showing a little more on his face than he probably realized.

He cared if she liked it. A lot.

She reached over and took his hand, pulling his work-hardened knuckles to her mouth and kissing them. "A lot," she whispered.

And she did. How someone could not was beyond her. The meadow was picture-perfect, like the scene from a postcard.

Except she was lucky enough to breathe it in, not just look at a still photograph and imagine.

The Payette Beardtongue – a brilliant blue flower that was often compared to snapdragons – was in full bloom. It was one of her favorite wildflowers, and watching them sway lazily in the light breeze made her inordinately happy. A ring of grand fir trees encircled the meadow and she could hear the mountain stream they'd crossed over several times on the hike bubbling past. Over it all was the buzz of industrious bumblebees as they flew from flower to flower, and birds serenading them with a mountain love song.

If someone combed the world for a year for a more gorgeous place than this, she was sure they'd come up empty-handed.

"I found it while out hunting in high school." His voice was quiet as they took in the scene. "Here, I'll show you my tree." He tugged her towards an older pine tree, listing to its left, the bark rough and seeping sap. He pointed to a spot that Carla first mistook for simple damage to the tree's trunk until she looked closer.

CP + LS

"Do you remember Laura Smith? My girlfriend in high school?"

She hadn't, until that moment. Laura, who was a year ahead of Christian, was thus two years ahead of Carla, and so they hadn't had much reason to hang out together. A pretty smile? Carla couldn't remember much else.

She nodded anyway.

"After I found this place while hunting, I brought her back here and carved our initials in the tree. I really thought..." He laughed a bit – not bitterly, but the kind one lets out when thinking back to a naïve, younger version of themselves. "She was the one for me." He winked at Carla. "Ah, the stupidity of youth. After she graduated, she wasn't about to wait around for me to finish high school, and was married before Christmas break of my senior year. She broke my heart, but I still consider this to be my tree." He reached out and ran his fingers lightly over the rough bark.

"Have you dated anyone since then?"

"No." He looked up from the tree trunk and smiled at her. "Not until I decided one day to pick up flowers for my mother for Mother's Day."

He pulled his oversized backpack off and set it on the ground, pulling a blanket out first and spreading it out. After he helped her settle in, he began pulling dishes out of the apparently bottomless pit of a backpack.

"You never did tell me that story," Carla murmured as he continued to pull items out. How on earth had he stuffed so much into one pack? "I don't remember seeing you that day. I'm sure I would've remembered if I had." It'd been busy that day at the shop, but not *that* busy.

"I don't think you did," Christian admitted with a sexy grin that made her want to kiss him. Everything made her want to kiss him, but that grin in particular... "I came in, took one look at you helping some old man pick out a bouquet, and fell head over heels in love."

"You did not," Carla protested with a laugh. Men did *not* fall in love with her at a single glance. That was something that happened in fairy tales, not in real life. And especially not in Carla's life.

"I did too," he countered. "I was so smitten with you, I accidentally bought a Congratulations on the New Baby! bouquet that day. Didn't even notice until I got back out to the truck. I only had eyes for you. You were swamped and you never even noticed I was there. Your high schooler helped me instead. Blond gal. Big brown eyes."

"Oh yeah. Valrea. She helps me when I know it'll be a busy day." Carla plucked the stem of a wild blue flax and brought it to her nose to smell it – no scent – and then twirled it in her fingertips. "A new baby arrangement?" she asked, not sure if she bought this story. After weeks of dates every weekend and sometimes during the week, she'd finally convinced herself that Christian really did like her – something that was mind-blowing, to put it mildly – but a guy coming into her store and falling in love with her on the spot…

If he were telling this story about falling in love with someone else at a single glance, she would've eaten it up with a spoon and sighed over the romance of it all. But after many years of singledom – 37 years, in case anyone was counting – she just couldn't believe it was true.

"Yup. For a baby girl, by the way." He handed her a plate and began filling up one of his own. "I pulled the 'Congrats!' balloon out and the little pink baby rattle off before handing it to my mother. Can you imagine what she would've thought if I'd given *that* to her for Mother's Day?"

Carla burst out laughing. "I think she would've had some questions," she said dryly.

"Her and me both," Christian grumbled, and then shot Carla a wink.

Maybe…

Maybe it really did happen that way.

She'd never caught Christian in a lie before now. She didn't have any reason to think he was lying today. Only that the idea was so bizarre; so strange for someone like her. She was the one who watched everyone else fall in love.

What was that saying – always the bridesmaid, never the bride?

Not, of course, that Christian was proposing marriage to her. But still...

"This food is amazing," she mumbled around a mouth full, making the conscious decision to decide on the truthfulness of his story later. For now, she was going to dig in and enjoy the food. She'd long ago given up eating like a bird while on a date, pretending that she wasn't hungry and then eating again when she got home. It wasn't like she was fooling anyone anyway. She was fat, but somehow Christian liked that about her, and she was ready to just own it already. She swallowed some potato salad. "Don't tell me you made all of this."

She'd thought her tractor date and the picnic spread she'd brought that day was pretty good, but looking at this one...

She'd been beat but good.

"Oh hell no," Christian said with a laugh. "I can cook okay – I haven't starved to death yet, anyway – but this is all the work of Carmelita. Do you know her? Stetson's housekeeper?"

"Of course!" Carla said, slathering a homemade roll with thick huckleberry jam. "A real sweet lady. Loves Stetson like her own son, from what I can tell."

"And now, Stetson's son, Flint. I watched them together the other day – Carla, you should've seen it. I don't know if Flint has Carmelita wrapped around his little pinky, or if Carmelita has Flint wrapped around her little pinky. Maybe they're just wrapped up together." He laughed. "Carmelita keeps dropping not-so-subtle hints to Jennifer that they should have another kid. A girl, if she wouldn't mind. Jennifer keeps telling her that that part's up to Stetson." He laughed again, harder this time. "There's little Carmelita, barely coming up to Stetson's shoulder, giving him his marching orders. She told him the other day that she is getting too old to take care of babies, so he better get to it. God bless anyone who dares to stand between Carmelita and what she wants."

They laughed together at that – the diminutive housekeeper ruled the Miller home, and everyone knew it.

And better yet, no one seemed to mind. Jennifer was happy to have the help with the household, considering how busy she was with the accounting firm, and Stetson wouldn't know how to cook anything beyond toast if his life depended upon it.

But if Jennifer does get pregnant...oh, what that would do to Iris' heart.

Iris was married to Stetson's older brother, Declan, of course, and for her sister-in-law to have not one but two kids when Iris couldn't even manage to get pregnant the first time...

Iris would be happy and pretend everything was fine, but it'd kill her to do it.

"—Carla!" Christian snapped his fingers in front of her nose, and she blinked, startled. "There you are," he said with a chuckle. "You disappeared on me."

"I...I did?" She hadn't meant to.

"Yeah. What were you thinking about?"

"I...I can't tell you." He looked at her, surprised, one eyebrow cocked. "It's nothing to do with you," she hurried to assure him. "It's a client-florist confidentiality issue."

"A client-florist confident—" He cut himself off and began to laugh. "You mean like what lawyers have, but with florists?"

Her back stiffened and she glared at Christian. Maybe he thought this was funny, but she did not.

"*Exactly* like that."

He stopped laughing.

"I'm sorry. I didn't mean to offend you," he started out weakly. She could tell he didn't really mean it, though. He genuinely thought the idea was a joke.

It was *not* a joke.

"As a florist, I know everyone's business in town. Who's sleeping with who; who got promoted; who's retiring; who's sick; who's pregnant; who's in huge trouble and sleeping on the couch." She gave him a pointed look at that. If he kept this bullshit up, that'd be the *only* place he'd sleep at her house. "If I walked around and told everyone everything that I knew, how long do you think I'd still be the town's florist? No one would trust me to keep their secrets."

She folded her arms across her chest and scowled at him.

"Oh." He paused for a moment. "I never thought of that. I'm sorry I laughed."

And this time, the contrition was real.

She nodded, accepting the apology, and let her body relax. No one took her seriously when she first mentioned the client-florist confidentiality agreement. She shouldn't have been surprised that Christian hadn't either.

Turned out, she wasn't *quite* ready to let it go, though. "The reason you never thought of it," she said quietly, "is because I don't share secrets. No one in town even thinks to question how much I know, because I never let anything past my lips. If I started spreading gossip around, it'd be damn quick that people would start to think about how much I know."

She sucked in a deep breath and then let it out slowly, determined to let the topic go.

Perhaps if she told Christian about the Declan and Iris in super general terms, it wouldn't be bending the rules *too* much. Sometimes, it was hard not to have anyone to share the burden with.

"Just now," she said, starting out slowly, trying to decide just how much she could say, "I was thinking about a client. Well, a husband and wife. They're trying for kids, and every month, he's sending her flowers when her period starts. It's been going on for months now. You talking about Jennifer and Stetson having another kid…it just made me think about this other couple. They would do almost anything for a baby. It makes my heart hurt."

She felt her eyes tear up just a bit and wiped frantically at them, hoping Christian hadn't noticed. What a boob she was, to tear up over something like this.

"I want to help, but all I can do is send the most beautiful flowers I can get my hands on." She spread her fingers out in the dappled sunlight beneath Christian's tree, stained and calloused from years of thorns and more flower bouquets than she could ever hope to count. "When I was a kid," she mused, "I liked to do my fingernails – I'd even do manicures on my friends. If I didn't become a florist, I definitely would've become a beautician. If 10-year-old me could see how beat up my hands and fingernails are now, she'd scream in fright. It's a small price to pay to deliver love as a job, I suppose."

It was Christian's turn to kiss her knuckles. He looked up at her through thick eyelashes that would make any model jealous, and smiled. "I love every damn part of you, but most especially your hands," he whispered. "They show how hard you work, and how much you care. You give with your whole body. These fingers," he held up her hand in the air, her skin clearly stained a muted brown and green from the countless flowers they'd handled over the years, "are just one of the things that make you beautiful."

He popped the tip of her finger into his mouth and began to suckle on it.

"Oh!" The explosive bit of breath puffed past her lips, and she felt her heart begin to hammer in her chest. The warmth and moisture of his mouth combined with the feel of his tongue against her skin sent lightning bolts down her arm and straight to her heart.

They were alone.

Well, of course they were alone, but…

Ever since their tractor date, Carla had wanted to go back to his place and see about making it to at least second base, but he'd demurred every time, instead wanting to go to her house.

Her house. Ugh. If she had a house, she'd gladly show it to him. But the little tiny attic space above the shop probably wouldn't even properly fit the two of them in it. It wasn't a place she showed anyone – not even Michelle, or Autumn, or Hannah.

It was a little crazy how over the years, she'd always

managed to casually meet people at the shop, or go to their house for a party, or meet up at a restaurant. No one seemed to question where it was that Carla the Florist actually lived.

This had put a damper on her and Christian's relationship, but finally, right now, they were alone. In the mountains.

And she very much wanted to get to second base.

CHAPTER
FIFTEEN
CHRISTIAN

There's a shortage of perfect breasts in this world. It would be a pity to damage yours.
~Westley in *The Princess Bride*

As Christian worked his way up Carla's plump arm, nibbling and sucking on her sweet skin, he mentally pinched himself. Was someone as gorgeous as Carla really wanting this?

He gazed up at her face even as he gently turned her arm to bare the inside of her elbow to his tongue and lips, and saw that her eyes had drifted closed and her lips were in a perfect O as she leaned back on her other arm, her tits unconsciously thrust forward.

The thrill shot through him and straight to his dick as he kissed the rapid heartbeat in the crook of her elbow. She *did* want this.

Not one to question extraordinary luck, he focused on not giving her a chance or a reason to change her mind. It'd been a long dry spell – longer than any red-blooded male should have to endure – but that was about to come to an end, and with one of the most beautiful women he'd ever met.

If he wasn't busy trying to undo the buttons on Carla's shirt, he would've dropped to his knees and thanked God on the spot.

"Oh..." Carla breathed as he was finally able to pull her shirt away, bearing her chest to the gentle breeze, and to his gaze. He stroked his fingertips over the tops of her breasts and listened with satisfaction to the quick intake of breath.

With a bit more fumbling than he liked to admit – it'd been a while since he'd undone the clasp of a bra – he slid her shirt and her bra down her arms and into a pile on the blanket. He'd been a tit guy from the first day he'd had a rush of teenage hormones hit, and Carla's were magnificent. He cupped one in each hand and motorboated between them, sure that he'd died and gone to heaven. Carla laughed at his antics, and he looked up at her with a naughty grin.

"You have *no* idea how long I've wanted to do that. I could die happy with my face buried in your chest."

"You're a boob guy?" Carla asked, and he couldn't help his laugh at the question. Somehow, he hadn't thought she'd know about that kind of thing.

"I mean, I like all of your curves—" he nipped playfully at her breast, "—but your tits are definitely at the top of the list."

"That's good," she said breathlessly, "because it's not like I'm running low on them."

"No, no you are not," he breathed, deciding that it was time to show her just how much he loved her tits. If she was talking in complete sentences, he wasn't doing his job.

Cupping her breast in one hand, he bent over and began suckling on the rosy pink tip. "Oh!" she gasped, her voice a full octave higher than normal. "Ohh...oh, Christian." She'd wrapped her fingers in his hair and was tugging him closer, her breath rapid. "Yes. Oh. I..."

She wasn't making a bit of sense.

Good.

He switched to her other breast, the tip just begging for his tongue as she squirmed and panted beneath him. It pebbled in his mouth as the pitch of her cries increased.

"Chri…ohhh…yeesss…"

Forget full sentences – she wasn't even saying his full name.

He laid her the rest of the way down and then made his way to her slacks. A little fancier than people normally wore on a hike up in the mountains – no doubt his fault for not specifying what they were going to do on this date – but right now, all that mattered was that they contained heaven. Working the button and zipper with trembling hands, he pulled them down and mostly off, getting stuck on her flats but at least he could now see her in all her glory.

And oh, what glory it was. His eyes skimmed her body, her lush curves like those in old paintings, before society decided that broomsticks were in fashion. He hesitated, hardly knowing where to start. His mouth over her mound? Peel her underwear off and bare her fully to his gaze? Suck on her pink toes one by one? Kiss his way up her thighs? Or he could—

"It's okay," she said, jackknifing into a sitting position, scrambling for her clothes, her hair falling forward into her face, hiding it from view. "You don't— I didn't— it's okay. We can just—" She was shoving her arms into her shirt but her bra was tangled up in the mess and she wasn't making any progress.

Which was good, because it took Christian a stunned moment – or ten – to register what was going on.

"Hold on! What's—what are we doing here?" he sputtered, curling his fingers around her arms, arresting her movements. His dick, near to bursting just seconds before, began wilting.

"You don't want me, and that's okay," she said, looking past him, over his shoulder, refusing to meet his eye. "I knew it was too good…I just…did you have to wait until I was naked to figure out I'm fat?!" She was trembling all over but she shifted her gaze to look straight at him. Her blue-green eyes had gone steel gray; all of the color drained out of them by the hurt that was clearly overwhelming her. "I've been fat all this time. It isn't like I gained 50 pounds in the last five minutes. You know what?" She stabbed him in the chest with her index finger. "Next time, when you want to just stare at a lumpy chick, try some porn!" She was shouting now, and the agony in her voice tore through him, slicing him to pieces.

"Whoa, whoa, whoa," he said as calmly as he could, holding up his hands in surrender, but his heart was thumping along in his chest, an out-of-control animal faced with the unacceptable: Losing Carla. "Let's...let's back up the train for just a moment."

She ignored him, struggling to put on her shirt again, but it was twisted somewhere and one sleeve was inside out.

"Carla!" he shouted.

She jerked and then stopped, panting, staring at the ground, back to refusing to meet his gaze. He tried desperately hard not to get sidetracked by her heaving chest and instead chose to stare at the crown of her head.

"Carla, *mi querida*, I don't know what just happened," he said quietly. "I need you to talk to me. I was just looking at you—"

"You were staring at my fat rolls," she said dully. "I get it, okay? I know I'm heavier than most. I just thought you knew that, and I thought..." Her voice grew shaky and he was sure she was on the verge of crying. "I thought you liked me. The way I am. So stupid. Stupid Carla." She swiped at her face, still hiding behind the curtain of her hair, but now he was *sure* she was crying.

Not how he'd wanted this to go.

Worse, he had no idea why things had gone off the rails.

Tentatively, delicately, he tried to figure out what had happened. He was sure that someone trying to defuse a live bomb was less cautious than he was at that moment.

"I think you're gorgeous," he whispered, reaching out and tucking a strand of hair behind her ear. "I wasn't looking at you and thinking you were fat. I was thinking you were perfect. Those old paintings – you know those ones where the women are mostly naked and laying on their sides and you can see all of their curves? Painted a *long* time ago."

"You mean a Rubens' painting? From the 1500s or whatever?"

"Yes! Him!" Christian said, delighted she'd put the pieces together from *old paintings* and *mostly naked women*. "You look like one of those paintings. I had paused because you'd taken my breath away, not because I was turned off by you. Nothing could be further from the truth."

"Are you…really?" she breathed, pushing back her hair as she lifted her face to look at him. Tears had left their trail on her cheeks and he was sure she'd die if she knew how messed up her makeup was, but none of that mattered. He used his thumbs to wipe the worst of it away.

"Yes, really." He chuckled a little and shook his head. "You really don't know, do you. *Mi querida*, every time I look at you, you take my breath away. You are the most gorgeous woman I have ever met. When I was in high school, I was obsessed by Laura and somehow, I guess we just didn't cross paths since. At least not while I was paying attention. But I promise you, I'm paying attention now."

Slowly, giving her time to change her mind and praying that she wouldn't, he leaned forward to kiss her again, and this time, she melted into him. The tangled mess of a shirt went somewhere, and she was tugging at his clothes, murmuring, begging him to let her touch him.

Let her? He wanted to laugh at such a crazy statement. He'd give his right arm to have her touch him.

This time, when he finally got her on her back again, he used his fingers *and* his eyes to feast on her curves.

"*Hermosa*," he breathed as he ran his lips and tongue over her skin. "*Mi hermosa…*"

He couldn't hold himself back any longer. The years dotted with one-night stands and the rare casual relationships hadn't been enough and he was now straining with a need so deep, he couldn't breathe. Settling himself between her thighs, he plunged inside of her, long strokes giving way to shorter ones as his self control slipped, and then disappeared.

"Carla," he cried as his back arched and his body froze, his desire spurting out of him in waves, the world white and featureless around him. He didn't know...he couldn't breathe...

Finally, his body unclenched and he propped himself up on his elbows, looking at Carla through bleary eyes. "Are you okay?" he made himself ask. *Please let her say yes.* He'd lost control there at the end, and he knew it. He wasn't proud of it, but with Carla, he couldn't help it.

"Okay?" she breathed, her own eyes fluttering open. "I could fly."

He laughed at that – now that he'd watched *The Princess Bride*, he knew that was a line from the movie – and then rolled over onto his side, tugging her up against his front, spooning her, and kissed the nape of her neck.

"I could fly, too," he whispered, and together, they drifted off to sleep.

Chapter
Sixteen
CARLA

Buttercup's emptiness consumed her.
~Grandfather in *The Princess Bride*

AUGUST, 2020

Ahhhh…the Huckleberry Festival. Carla grinned with happiness as they wandered through the booths, the sweet smell of huckleberries drifting on the warm summer breeze. This was the perfect date – free, fun, and lots of great samples. There were huckleberry jams and huckleberry pastries, of course, but here at the festival, she could also taste-test huckleberry coffee and huckleberry wine and huckleberry pancakes and her favorite, huckleberry ice cream. Especially right now, in the heat of the summer.

"I keep expecting to see a huckleberry beer for sale," Christian murmured in her ear, and she laughed.

"If we find that, I promise to buy you a six-pack," she said with a saucy wink.

"Yeeaaahhhh…let me try it first," Christian said skeptically. "The huckleberry wine was good, but I'm not so sure about huckleberry beer."

Just then, Carla saw a flame of red that caught her attention and she turned to look…

Iris and Declan were there, wandering around the booths also.

Carla froze.

Shit, shit, shit.

Normally, seeing her friend would be cause for celebration. She'd hurry over and give her a hug and they'd hang out and look at huckleberry paintings and…

But today was not a normal day.

Austin Bishop had called the shop right at closing time the night before – Saturday night – and had asked for a bouquet to be delivered on Tuesday that would put all other bouquets in the history of bouquets to shame.

His wife, Ivy, was pregnant.

Iris' younger sister had beaten her to the punch.

Worse yet, as far as Carla knew, they hadn't even been trying. Ivy and Austin had gotten married in a quiet ceremony last summer, with only a few people in attendance. Carla'd only found out because Ivy had come in and asked her to create a bridal bouquet for the wedding. It was the only flowers she'd had at the affair.

If they'd been trying for kids since then, Austin wasn't following in his brother-in-law's footsteps and sending his wife bouquets each month.

"You okay?" Christian asked, stiffening up and looking around, clearly trying to spot the danger. "What's happening?"

"Oh, uh, nothing," she said, trying to conjure up a believable smile. They should change directions. Hide. "What if we—"

"Hi Carla! Hi Christian!"

And…double shit.

She turned back to her red-haired friend with a huge smile pinned on her face. "Hey Iris! Declan! How are you guys?" She and Christian waited for the other couple to join them since they were under the shade of a huge elm, and didn't want to give up their spot. It was too hot to stand out in the full brunt of the sunshine.

"Damn, this heat," Declan said, once he reached them, and pulled off his hat to wipe at his brow. "I swear I can almost *hear* the kernels of wheat ripening. A couple more weeks of this, and harvest will be here in record time."

"I keep telling Stetson we need to put a camera on the fields," Christian said with a chuckle. "I think we can watch the hay grow in real time. When we get to harvest, you and I are gonna need to arm wrestle for who gets to use the new Case-International Magnum 400. I've been pumping iron every day so I can win." He curled his arm, showing off his biceps like a body builder, and even as Carla laughed at his antics, she felt a little bead of sweat form across her upper lip.

Time had gotten away from them since their hike up to Christian's tree, and they hadn't made love since then. Carla was getting hornier by the day, and just watching the muscles of Christian's arm was enough to get her motor revving.

Declan and Christian fell to chatting about tractor scheduling and when which Miller farm would harvest what – a topic guaranteed to put Carla to sleep in 30 seconds or less – so she turned to her friend instead.

"How are things going for you?" she asked brightly. *Can't talk about bouquets or infertility or Ivy's pregnancy.*

Which meant, of course, that was *all* her brain wanted to discuss.

Helpful, that.

"Good," Iris said just as brightly. "I love the flowers from Happy Petals. Declan is sending me a bouquet every month, of course, and they're just gorgeous. You do *such* a good job. I swear you work magic with flowers, and they always last forever, too!"

"Oh, uh, thanks," Carla said, trying to brush off the compliment. *Talk about something else. Something else. Think of something else.*

She had nothing.

"It really is lovely," Iris said, breaking into the silence. "Getting flowers, I mean. I really—" Her voice broke and before Carla even looked, she knew Iris was crying.

Dammit.

"They...they make a difference," Iris continued valiantly, her voice warbling. The tears were running ever faster down her face.

"Hey, we're gonna go look at that display over there," Carla said to the guys even as she looped her arm around Iris' thin shoulders and led her away.

"Thanks," Iris said, her voice muffled by the fabric of Carla's shirt. She'd practically buried her face into Carla's chest, trying to hide her tears from the rest of the world, but Carla didn't mind. God gave her an extra generous helping of padding for just this reason.

She steered Iris behind a tall row of lilacs, the spring blossoms gone for the year but their greenery forming a perfect barrier, and then pulled her friend into a full embrace. Iris sobbed, her shoulders shaking as she let out the anguish.

"Shhh...it's gonna be okay," Carla whispered as she gently stroked her hand down the cascade of red. She'd always wanted red hair, and seeing the sunlight play with the color reminded her of just how much she'd love to have hair like this, instead of the average dark brown hair. Carla's hair was nothing special – not like Iris'.

We all want what we don't have.

"I'm sorry," Iris said, her voice still shaking as she pulled away, rubbing at her eyes with the backs of her hands. She wasn't using her cane today, and Carla thought about asking if this meant she was getting stronger, when Iris said, "Declan and I have been trying for months to get pregnant. Months and months...actually, over a year now."

Carla nodded, not pointing out that it was her handwriting on the card included in the flowers each month. Declan always dictated the message over the phone, but it was her hand that wrote it.

Next month, honey
It'll happen – keep the faith
I love you more than anything else in the world, even kids

"We started going to a doctor in Boise, actually. Did you know that infertility is one of the last big mysteries of the medical world? That 33% of the time it's the girl's fault; 33% of the time it's the guy's fault; and 33% of the time, they have no idea. They've run every test on the planet on the two of us, and lucky us, we fall into the third category. No one knows why I'm not getting pregnant. There's not a damn thing wrong with either one of us. I mean, other than my car wreck back in 2017. Three years this month for *that* lovely anniversary."

Even if Iris was walking today without her cane, Carla worried that her strength was going to give out, and decided to steer them towards a bench tucked off to the side, thanking the heavens above that it was actually empty. As many people as there were at the festival that day, she was sure this bench was only empty because it was so out of the way from the normal traffic pattern.

They settled down in the shade, Carla listening as her friend unburdened.

"They say the car wreck didn't affect my, you know, ovaries and such, and shouldn't be a factor in me getting pregnant, but I don't know. I think it's my fault. Why we can't have kids, I mean," she said miserably. "I feel terrible. Declan could have a happy life with someone else, and I'm just—"

"Now you hold on a minute here," Carla interrupted. It was rude to interrupt, of course, but she couldn't let her friend continue to spout such craziness. "You and Declan were a year ahead of me in school, sure, but I still watched you two. I've never seen a guy more head-over-heels in love than Declan was with you. When you two broke up and he ended up at the U of I without you, everyone was in shock. You two were the perfect couple. I'm a florist – I have a sense about these things, you know. You two were *meant* to be together. Declan doesn't want to marry someone else, kids or no kids."

Silence. Iris was working up the courage to get to the *real* problem, and Carla gave her the space to mentally steel herself to say it.

And then...

"Ivy is pregnant."

Even as Carla's heart broke from the pain in Iris' voice, she was grateful she'd said the news out loud. Now Carla could stop pretending she was in the dark about the whole thing.

"She finally took a pregnancy test this weekend," Iris whispered. "She missed her period, but she waited weeks to test anyway. She's happy – so happy – but Carla...if that were me...I wouldn't have waited one extra moment to take the pregnancy test. The fact that she could even wait..."

Iris' voice broke as tears began trailing down her cheeks again.

"I'm on a bunch of hormones," she added dully. "The doctor told us that they'll increase my chances of getting pregnant, but that they'll also screw with my emotions. I haven't gotten pregnant yet, but I can tell ya, they got the emotions part right." She laughed mirthlessly. "Declan hates seeing me cry. He doesn't know what to do when I'm over in the corner, bawling. I try to hide it from him. Ugh! Guys are so damn lucky," she announced, straightening her back and glaring at Carla, as if she'd dared to contradict her on this topic.

Carla wanted to laugh at the rapid mood swing her friend was going through, but decided that wouldn't be advisable under the circumstances, and nodded instead.

"Declan gets handed a girly magazine and a cup, and sent to the bathroom to go—" she lowered her voice and leaned towards Carla confidentially, "—jerk off. So they can do a semen analysis on him. Do you know what I have to do?" She straightened up again, her face alight with righteous indignation. "Get undressed and have some guy stick a cold metal spatula up me so he can poke around. It *hurts*. And then all of the shots…No one hands *me* a magazine and tells me to go have some fun."

Carla wanted to both laugh and cry. "It really isn't fair," she agreed, pulling her friend up against her into a one-armed hug.

"I just want to be happy for my little sister," Iris whispered, her shoulders slumping. "Austin is the best thing that's ever happened to her, and she deserves this. I just want it too. Is that so much to ask?"

"No," Carla whispered. "It's not. I…" She hesitated for a moment and then plunged in, feeling like this was a story her friend needed to hear. "I went through the same thing myself."

Iris pulled back, looking at her quizzically. "You wanted to get pregnant?" she asked.

"No," Carla said, laughing for a moment. "Heavens no. Not right now. But, I did watch Hannah meet and fall in love with Elijah. You know that for a couple of years, Hannah and Michelle and I have met together down at the bakery for the Early Spinster's Club?"

Iris chuckled herself. "I'd heard that. We're not *that* old yet, are we?"

"Late 30s?" Carla said skeptically, one eyebrow arched. "Not exactly young spring chickens. But anyway, Hannah had always been the one in the group who didn't want to date anyone. I wasn't even sure if she *liked* guys, honestly. Michelle and I would drool over Gage or some other hot guy coming into the bakery, and Hannah was over there in the corner, not saying a word. Whenever she was forced to be around a guy, she shut up completely and would do her best to hide behind me."

"I'm laughing because it's true," Iris said with a chuckle. "Hannah was *not* boy crazy."

"No, she wasn't. And then, she found the love of her life and was *so happy*, and she wasn't even trying. She hadn't wanted it for decades like I had. I had to put on my happy face, and I *was* happy for her. I just wanted it myself, too. It wasn't fair how easily it came for her."

It was Iris' turn to pull Carla into a one-armed hug. "But you've found your own guy now," she said. "And he seems to adore you."

"I have found my own Westley," Carla said with a secret smile. "But all these years...I didn't know how it'd work out. You never know until it happens, and then looking back, it seems destined to have worked out that way." She patted her friend on the hand. "Speaking of, we should probably go back and find our men before they send out a search party for us."

"How does my makeup look?" Iris asked anxiously, looking straight at Carla to give her a clear view. "Declan just hates it when I cry..."

Carla wiped a bit of stray black away and then tucked a piece of her thick red hair behind her ear. "You look beautiful," she reassured her friend. "I've always wanted red hair, you know."

"Really?" Iris asked in surprise as Carla helped her to her feet and they began walking slowly back towards where they'd last seen the guys. Carla took her friend's elbow, not sure if her gait was steady enough on the uneven ground. "I've always loved your hair and complexion. Your skin is dark and doesn't show every blush like mine does. It'd be lovely to have dark brown hair and skin that actually tans, not just turns a darker shade of pink."

"We always want what we can't have," Carla agreed with a light laugh. "I was just thinking that earlier today, ironically enough. There they are. Hey Christian! Declan!"

The men turned as one and began hurrying towards them. "We couldn't figure out where you went," Declan said as they got closer. "I was thinking we were going to have to call out a search party for you two. Is everything okay?"

"Oh yeah," Carla answered breezily, lest her friend not be able to lie convincingly. "We found a nice bench in the shade and sat for a bit. Figured we'd let you two talk out every bit of the harvest and get it out of your systems so we didn't have to listen to it."

Christian chuckled. "Very sweet of you," he said dryly.

"I know!" Carla shot him a saucy grin.

They all paused for a moment, that awkward moment when no one was quite sure if they were going to stay together or split apart, and then Declan broke the silence.

"We were just about to go check out more food vendors. I heard there's frozen huckleberry yogurt this year, and elephant ears with huckleberry syrup. Do you guys want to join us?"

Christian looked at Carla, who grinned happily. "I can *always* be persuaded to eat an elephant ear." She slipped her arm into Christian's and together, the four of them began heading towards the elephant ear booth, run by the local Boy Scout troop.

Carla squeezed Christian's arm against her side and sighed happily. Iris was right.

She had found her Westley, and she was never going to let him go.

CHAPTER
SEVENTEEN
CARLA

You keep using that word. I do not think it means what you think it means.
~Inigo in *The Princess Bride*

With an economy of movement, Carla pulled the two bouquets out of the display case, quickly rearranging the other flowers to help fill in the gap, and then carried the wilting flowers to the back. For the millionth time, she wished she could figure out what to do with old flowers. Simply throwing them away seemed so wasteful. This was the part of the job she'd hated since high school when she'd worked at the flower shop in Franklin, and then at Boise State University when she'd worked at the Toadstool.

Unfortunately, it was one part of the florist industry she had yet to solve.

She heard the front doorbell tinkle, and hurried back out front, wiping her hands dry on a towel slung over her shoulder.

"Oh, hello Mrs. VanLueven! Mrs. Zimmerman. How are you?" She sent them a genuine smile. Two middle-aged women who did a lot for the community, she'd worked with them on a few projects, and was always happy to help with more. Like every small town in America, Sawyer was a better place to live because of their community volunteers.

"Well," Mrs. Zimmerman said officiously, "I don't know if you've heard about all of the issues that returning military men and women are having after serving in war zones, but Carol and I read an article a month ago about soldiers with PTSD, and we've decided that this is what we're going to focus on now. We've put together a plan on how to tackle this, and are reaching out to businesses around the valley to make it happen." Carla pasted a smile on her face as the flood of words washed over her, hoping she didn't look as overwhelmed as she felt. "You know how we were sending care packages to our Long Valley service members? But then we realized *everyone* does that, and the real hard part is when they come home. *That's* when they need our support."

"Nancy, what do you think about these?" Mrs. VanLueven called out, pointing to a mammoth arrangement of flowers that'd normally be at home at a statesman's funeral. But before her friend could respond, she turned to Carla, who mentally braced herself for whatever was coming. "We need your help decorating for these meetings."

"They're going well!" Mrs. Zimmerman put in brightly.

"No, they're going terribly," Mrs. VanLueven said bluntly. Carla covered her mouth with her hand, doing her best to hide the laughter bubbling up inside. Carol VanLueven had a reputation for saying it the way it was, but still, seeing it up close and personal was a bit overwhelming.

She wondered for just a moment if Michelle and Mrs. VanLueven liked each other, or hated each other. Two people with such strong personalities...

It would be the *Clash of the Titans*, but in real life.

"Well, the gift boxes we sent the soldiers went well," her friend pushed back feebly.

"Yes, of course. Those were easy, though," Mrs. VanLueven

said dismissively. "Paperbacks, beef jerky, lip balm, playing cards...it's not hard to gin up a nice box for a bunch of soldiers. But we've found that it's a lot harder to get them to come to meetings and talk. You know, about their feelings and things."

"So we need your help!" Mrs. Zimmerman said, turning back with a pleading look to Carla. "We need flowers that will help the men and women relax. Talk. Open up about what happened to them."

All laughter drained away at that, bubbling panic quickly replacing it. Sure, Carla was someone who believed wholeheartedly in the healing power of love, and of course, flowers helped someone know they were loved, but they weren't magic.

Even flowers had limits.

"Ummm..." she stalled, trying to think of how to tactfully say any of that, especially to a powerhouse like Carol VanLueven.

Everyone in town knew two things:

1) Carol got things done; and

2) Standing in her way was a *really* bad idea.

She was Kylie Whitaker's mother, of course, and although the vet's wife had some of her mother in her, she wasn't nearly as...opinionated.

Which was good. A small town like Sawyer couldn't handle *two* Carol VanLuevens.

"Ummmm..." she said again, flailing around blindly. "Did you two have any particular flowers in mind?"

"Happy," Mrs. VanLueven said.

"Welcoming," Mrs. Zimmerman put in.

"Let the men—"

"And women!" Mrs. Zimmerman cut in.

"—know that they are loved," Mrs. VanLueven finished.

"Well," Carla said, thinking fast, "what about sunflowers? White daisies? Nothing says welcome and happy more than those flowers."

"Oh, I like it!" Mrs. Zimmerman said with a delighted clap of her hands. They turned to look at Mrs. VanLueven, the *real* decision maker.

"Good," the middle-aged woman said thoughtfully. "Yeah, that might work. Maybe now we can get more than Gunner Nash to show up."

"And Carol practically had to twist his arm off to make that one happen," Mrs. Zimmerman said confidentially to Carla. "Do you know Luke's younger brother? He's been in the Navy with my boy for years now, but his time is up and he's come back home. We think if we can get him to come to the meetings, he'll convince some others to attend too."

"Yes, sunflowers and daisies should help," Mrs. VanLueven said decisively. "Okay!" She clapped her hands together, clearly done and ready to tackle the next item on the list. "Carla, you deliver three vases next Wednesday to the event room down at the senior center and send me the bill. Nancy, we need to go to the bakery next. I think donuts will help."

"Oh yes!" Mrs. Zimmerman said, her eyes lighting up as the two women headed for the door. "My boy loves donuts, especially with sprinkles on them. We should get—"

The door closed behind them, cutting off the rest of her sentence. Carla sagged against the counter, staring sightlessly out the glass front door. She felt a bit like she'd just lived through a human tornado.

Sunflowers, daisies, and donuts with sprinkles are supposed to help soldiers relax and talk about trauma, while two women with coffee pots hover around the edge of the room, occasionally barking things like, "Share more!" "Talk!" "Open up!"

Wow.

She knew Carol's reputation, of course – she was a woman who got things done – but she was beginning to get the vaguest inkling that the formidable woman didn't *quite* understand how group therapy worked.

Just then, her cell phone began to play the opening bars to *Mama's Song* by Carrie Underwood.

Mama, you taught me to do the right things
So now you have to let your baby fly…

"Hey, Mom!" Carla said cheerfully, tucking her cell phone between her cheek and shoulder as she perched her reader glasses on the end of her nose to see as she scribbled herself a note about the flowers. Heaven forbid she forget.

"Hi, dear. How are things down at the shop?" They chatted for a moment, and then her mom got right to the point. "At Knit Wits the other night, Mrs. Crofts asked me what I thought about your new boyfriend, and I had to admit to her that I hadn't met him yet – no one has. I've invited your sisters and brother over for Sunday dinner, and I want you to bring Christopher—"

"His name is Christian," Carla cut in. Her mother knew that, of course, but was apparently happy to take the guilt-trip route during this conversation.

"—Christian with you and introduce him to everyone," she continued smoothly. "I'll make my specialty – pot roast and potatoes. See you at three?"

"Uh, sure," Carla said, biting down hard to keep from pointing out that they lived in Idaho – *everyone's* specialty was pot roast and potatoes.

"Good, good. Love you!" And with that, she hung up.

What is it about women of a certain age feeling like they are the boss of the rest of us?

Switching over to iMessage, she quickly sent Christian a text. She could only hope he wasn't actually busy on Sunday at three.

CHAPTER
EIGHTEEN
CHRISTIAN

Anybody want a peanut?
~Fezzik in *The Princess Bride*

COULD SOMEONE DIE OF NERVES?

Christian was about to find out.

The cauldron of snakes he'd apparently swallowed when he wasn't looking were writhing around in his stomach, and he was a little afraid that if he didn't die first, he was going to puke up his guts instead.

What on earth made him think that he could meet Carla's family? When she'd asked him, he'd said yes because of course he'd said yes – telling Carla 'no' wasn't an option. But still, it was one thing to say yes to meeting her family; it was another thing to actually do it.

He gripped the neck of the wine bottle that Jennifer had told him to bring like a man clinging to a life preserver. He'd panicked when she'd asked him what gift he was going to bring to the party, and sensing that his answer was going to be, "Uh, a gift?" Jennifer had steered him toward the wine aisle, even telling him which kind to get.

He hadn't always been a fan of Jennifer – he felt like she

could see deep into his soul with those piercing green eyes of hers, and that he was failing the test she was silently administering.

But the more dates he went on with Carla, the more he began to appreciate Jennifer. She was *much* too skinny for his taste, but after she'd helped him plan and decorate for his first date with Carla, Christian had decided that Stetson had won the Wife Lottery. All of the help she'd given him since just reinforced that belief.

Leo wrapped his way around Christian's feet, loudly meowing his demands to be petted, but Christian just shook his head at the cat. "I fell for that once," he told the feline. "Never again." The last thing he wanted was to break out in hives while trying to chat up Carla's family.

Just then, Carla appeared at the top of the stairs to the attic, wearing a flowy colorful dress that made her look like a million bucks. "Sorry!" she called as she hurried down the creaking stairs. "I didn't mean to take so long."

"Did you get dressed up there?" Christian asked, peering past her and up the stairs. He'd never actually been up there, and was curious if she only stored a change of clothes, or had a full closet, or—

"I just freshened up," she said and leaned over to give him a kiss hello.

What was probably meant to be a peck on the lips quickly turned into a whole lot more. He *missed* Carla in every way possible. Ever since their trip up to the mountains, Christian had been busy scheming, trying to figure out how to get Carla to another horizontal surface – or hell, even a vertical one would do at this point – as long as it gave them privacy.

Well, any horizontal or vertical surface *not* within the walls of his single-wide. He wasn't *that* desperate. If only she'd take him back to her place, but it never seemed like the right time for her in her busy schedule.

Many more kisses like this, though, and he was going to

throw caution to the wind and make love to her on the counters of Happy Petals.

"Whoa," she said finally, pulling back and staring up at him with lust-glazed eyes. "Hello to you, too."

He sent her a cocky smile, and leaned forward to kiss her again when the allergies hit.

Like a spigot turned on full blast, his eyes began watering, his nose itchy, and he began sneezing again and again, hardly able to draw in a breath between.

"Are you okay?" Carla asked, patting his shoulder. "Do you need to go home? Are you getting sick—"

He opened up the front door of the shop and charged outside, gasping in deep breaths of clean air, free of cat dander while Carla locked up the shop.

Finally, he turned to her, pasting on what he hoped was another cocky grin and not the drowned-rat look he was afraid he had going on.

"Sorry about that," he said breezily. "I guess I just got something in my eye. You ready to go?"

She cocked a skeptical eyebrow at him, but slipped her hand through his elbow and let him escort her to his truck. Once inside, he pulled the Benadryl chewables out and quickly tossed one into his mouth, hoping the antihistamine would kick in fast. He didn't want to show up at the Grahame household with red-rimmed eyes. He could only guess what they'd think about that.

He should just tell Carla already, but he'd gone this long without telling her, and now, he just didn't know how to broach the topic. He couldn't ask her to give up her babies. He'd seen her coo and love on her cats – they meant the world to her.

He'd gone to the doctor last week, who had referred him to an immunologist. This seemed like code for "stupidly expensive," but he didn't have a choice. He had to figure this out.

Sitting next to him in the passenger seat and giving him directions as they went, Carla made it hard to keep his eyes on the road. Would she notice if he drove up into the mountains and made love to her there instead?

Somehow, he thought she might.

"Turn left here – the one with the white van in front of it," she said, pointing. He pulled in behind the van and turned the engine off.

The sudden silence was stifling.

"Do I look okay?" he blurted out. *This is not a good idea. They are going to know I'm not good enough for their daughter. Run. Run now—*

"You do!" Carla said with a reassuring smile. "You look handsome in that button-up shirt. Don't worry – my family will love you!"

His chest tightening, Christian reluctantly got out and went around to the passenger side, helping Carla out and down to the ground. With her hair pulled up into an elegant bun and long earrings swaying hypnotically, she was any guy's dream girl, and the desire to help her right back up into the truck and drive away before he could screw this whole thing up was overwhelming. Right now, no one knew if the Grahame family would like him or not.

Better not to know than to open your mouth and remove all doubt, right?

Wasn't that some saying by Abraham Lincoln? Or Benjamin Franklin? Maybe it was Mark Tw—

"Carla! Christian!"

They turned to find a woman who looked *exactly* like Carla but 25 years older standing on the front step of the house, waving energetically at them. "Come, come!" she called out.

"C'mon," Carla said, tugging at his arm. "We can't stand out here all day."

Shoes filled with concrete, Christian moved as slowly as he dared towards the middle-class home, a brick structure with large windows overlooking the street. It was a nicer home in a nicer part of town, and suddenly, Christian was very, *very* sure he was in over his head. He was the son of migrant workers. He was just a farmhand himself. He couldn't afford something like this. He needed to run—

"It's so good to meet you," Mrs. Grahame said, enfolding him in an embrace that said without words that she meant it. "I've been excited to clap eyes on you for a while. You're just as handsome as Carla said you were."

"Moooommm," Carla said, and Christian was sure she was embarrassed to the tips of her toes, but he couldn't help the grin that spread over his face. Carla had been telling her mom that she thought he was handsome, eh?

He walked into the house with a bit more spring in his step.

"Hi, I'm Samuel Grahame," an older man said, sticking his hand out to shake. "You can call me Samuel." Carla may've been the spitting image of her mother, but Christian could tell at a glance that it was her father from whom she'd inherited her arresting blue eyes with hints of green. Mr. Grahame's eyes had faded a bit with time, but they were Carla's, all right.

"Hi, Samuel," Christian said, returning the firm handshake, the name feeling strange on his tongue. *Mr. Grahame* seemed *much* more appropriate. "I'm Christian Palacios. Nice to meet you."

"Come in, come in. We shouldn't all crowd in the entryway. Let me introduce you to my son, Sammy, and my other daughters, Vanessa, Kate, and Jackie. Just warning you now: There are a lot of us. It's probably going to be quite overwhelming."

Christian shrugged. "I'm the only boy in my family, too, but I have six sisters. At four, my mother was only getting warmed up." He winked at Samuel, who let out a roar of laughter.

"I like this one, Carla!" he called over Christian's shoulder. "Come. Let's meet the rest of the clan."

After that, it was an overwhelming mass of adults and small children who seemingly belonged to no one at all and ran willy-nilly, screaming and yelling and beating each other with foam swords.

In other words, he felt *right* at home. After a scrumptious meal of pot roast and potatoes – Christian'd had to run back to the truck to grab the bottle of wine he'd been so nervous, he'd left it behind – they got out Uno and began playing. It became quickly apparent that card games at the Grahame household was all about building alliances, and trash-talking your opponent.

"A red reverse," Carla crowed, laying the card down atop the precarious pile. "Whatcha gonna do about it, huh?"

He pretended to study his hand for a moment, and then laid down a blue reverse. "Nothin' much," he said nonchalantly as the family broke into cheers. Defeated, Carla began pulling cards from the stack one at a time, muttering more than a few choice words under her breath with every draw.

After the game – which Christian had won, and had thoroughly enjoyed rubbing it in Carla's face, as any good boyfriend would – they packed up and headed out into the warm evening air to calls of goodbye and invitations to come back again soon. He was in a daze.

Did that really go as well as he thought it did?

He sneaked a peek at Carla and she beamed up at him.

"They love you!" she half whispered, half laughed.

"They do!" he said in disbelief, still a little stunned by that stroke of pure luck.

More than that, though, he was even more stunned by an even better stroke of pure luck – somehow, this beautiful woman liked him. After an evening of watching Carla eat and laugh and talk, he couldn't stand it anymore.

As soon as they got into his truck, he pulled her towards him, kissing her hard. He *wanted* her.

"Let's go back to your place," they both said, and then stopped.

CHAPTER
NINETEEN
CARLA

I'm not saying I'd like to build a summer home here, but the
trees are actually quite lovely.
~Westley in *The Princess Bride*

CARLA LOOKED AT CHRISTIAN in surprise. Her place? They didn't want to go to her place. She had yet to see Christian's house and she really wanted to, plus her "house" was a converted attic.

No, it was much better if they went and saw his place.

"But, I haven't seen your house yet," she finally said.

"I haven't seen yours," he countered.

She stopped, biting her lip and staring at him. "My house isn't very interesting."

"Neither is mine."

This really, really wasn't going well.

She was still biting her lower lip, staring at him, when he groaned and turned away. "Please, don't do that thing."

"What thing?"

"Stare at me like that. With your lip and stuff."

Automatically, she looked down to see what was wrong with her lips, but of course, she couldn't see them. She flipped the visor down and looked in the small mirror. "What's wrong with my lips?"

Hmmm...

Actually, she should probably apply another coat of lipstick. She rummaged around in her purse, searching for it.

"Nothing. It's just..."

She touched up her lipstick, and he grew silent again. She finished, studied herself in the mirror, decided this was as good as it was going to get, put her lipstick back into her purse, and looked at him expectantly.

"It's just what?" she prompted him when he didn't say anything. He looked like he was in pain. "What's wrong?"

"Carla, you could kill a grown man off," he growled.

"I...what?!" She would never hurt a man in her life! Why would he say something like that?

He closed his eyes and let his head drop back onto the headrest, beating against it softly. Carla was wondering if he was having a seizure or something when her mom popped her head out the front door. "Everything okay?" she called.

Oh yeah. They were still parked on the street in front of her parents' house.

They should probably go somewhere. Anywhere.

She gave her mom a thumbs up and a jaunty smile, and then turned to Christian. "We gotta go, even if it's just to the park. My mom'll be over in a minute if we keep sitting here, and I really don't want to tell her that we're debating about where to go have sex."

He nodded, still looking like he was in pain, and pulled out into the street. They headed to the park and he pulled into a nice sunny spot, letting the warmth of the sun heat the cab.

She realized that soon, it'd be winter. There was something she didn't want to think too much about. She hated winter – everything dead and frozen, no flowers in bloom except poinsettias and honestly, those shouldn't even be counted as flowers.

She decided to focus on her boyfriend's reticence to showing her his place instead.

"Why don't you want me to see your place?" she asked softly, putting her hand on his arm and stroking it.

"I could ask you the same thing!" he countered.

Ugh.

"I'll show you mine if you show me yours," she finally blurted out when the tension in the cab reached epic proportions and she couldn't stand it anymore. He turned and cocked an eyebrow at her, and she laughed. "Oh Lordy, I sound like I'm in sixth grade," she said with a groan, waving her hand in the air as if to wipe the words away. "I do not think those words mean what you think they mean," she said in a terrible thick Spanish accent, quoting one of her all-time favorite lines from *The Princess Bride*.

"Okay, but really," she said finally. "I'll show you my place if you show me yours."

He drummed his fingers on the steering wheel, staring at her, his face a blank mask of nothingness, and then after an eternity – or two – nodded.

"You first," he said. She glared at him. He shrugged unrepentantly. "You know the rule – women first." He put the truck into reverse and then stopped in the middle of the street. "Where *is* your house?"

"Let's just go to the flower shop."

He cocked an eyebrow at her again.

"Just go. I promise, I'll show you everything."

Maybe if she stripped when they got up to the attic, he'd be too sidetracked to realize that she lived in quarters better suited for a 20-year-old bachelor. A *poor* 20-year-old bachelor.

The drive over was dead silent, the tension thick enough to cut with a knife. She didn't know why he was so worried – it wasn't like he lived in the kind of square footage only a mouse would find luxurious. She trailed him miserably from the truck to the front door and then, left with no other choice, she unlocked it, her hands visibly shaking.

Without looking back, she started up the stairs.

Only her parents knew where she lived. Her siblings had never asked, and everyone else was fine with her simply saying, "Meet you at the shop!" when they wanted to get together for something.

No one seemed to question the fact that the florist in town was always at work. Maybe Sawyerites thought she was a workaholic who never left her business to go home.

She'd heard of people sleeping on couches at work so they could get up and get more done before actually going home for the night. That's probably what everyone thought she did.

There was a theory she could get behind. She wasn't much for lying, but in this case, she wasn't so sure she'd set a person straight if that's what they believed. It was a sight better to be thought of as a workaholic instead of what she really was: Stuffed into living quarters too tiny to hardly turn around in.

Even as she ducked through the open doorway to her attic room, her breath was getting choppy. Why did she care so much about where she lived? Why did it embarrass her so much?

Were there even answers to these questions?

All she knew was, in that moment, she would've chosen to strip down naked and run down the streets of Sawyer rather than show Christian her place.

Naked and jogging down Main Street would've made her feel less exposed.

"Welcome to my abode," she said sarcastically, sweeping her arm to indicate the tight quarters, and rapped her knuckles against a figurine, knocking it to the floor.

Of course.

It was the momma cat with her baby from the Roberts' mansion, and her breath hitched just that much tighter with panic at the thought of breaking it. She still hadn't gotten it into an antique shop to have it evaluated, and a chip off the momma's ear would—

She bent over to snatch it off the ground just as Christian did, and they smacked heads together. Groaning, Carla rubbed her head, grabbed at the figurine again, studied it for damage – none that she could see – and plopped it down onto an overstuffed shelf she kept promising herself she'd clean off one day.

"Well, are you happy?" she snapped, and then groaned again. Christian's back went ramrod straight at her tone, and he looked pissed. "I'm sorry. I just…I'm not proud of this place, is all."

"Why?" Bella had made it out of her hiding place and was wrapping her way around their legs, meowing and begging for attention. They both ignored her.

"Why?!" she snapped back. "Are you…look at it! It's tiny. No shower. No washer and dryer. I still have to do my laundry at my parents' house, and take a shower there too. It's *embarrassing*."

"You're embarrassed?" His face was unreadable.

"Well, yeah…? I guess. I just…what kind of a 37 year old am I, anyway? I'm a successful businesswoman. I should at least own my own shower, dammit."

She felt tears welling up in her eyes and was astonished. Why was she being so emotional about this? She wasn't even sure.

All she knew was, she hated being this exposed. She was a very outgoing, loving person, but there were parts to her life that she didn't share.

This was *definitely* one of those parts.

"If you're a successful businesswoman," he said slowly, "but you hate this place, then why live here?"

"Well, because I hate debt even more. Like, with a living, fiery passion, I hate it."

They were standing too close – with only a few free square feet available, it shouldn't be surprising, but still.

She couldn't breathe.

She took one step over and then plopped down on the edge of her bed. There. If they were really dedicated to the cause, they might be able to fit a yardstick between their bodies. This would have to do. Bella jumped up onto the bed beside her, continuing to wrap herself around Carla, meowing incessantly.

"I'm almost done paying off my student loans for my bachelor's degree," she said dully, picking up Bella and settling her on her lap, "and then I want to start saving for a down payment for a house. It's not sexy. It's not the cool-kid thing, I know."

She was staring at the floor, unable to meet his eyes.

"My parents taught us kids from a young age to never go into debt for anything, and then I did anyway, to go to college. I hate the debt. It's just hanging over me, like an ax that can drop at any moment. Threatening me. Oh, how I wish I hadn't taken it on. So *stupid*.

"I thought I *had* to get a business degree if I was going to run a business. Turns out, lots of people simply take online courses and learn what they need to as they go along. I waayyy overthought the situation, and ended up with this debt. This is one of the reasons that I love what you're doing with your sister. Yesenia deserves to start her career without student debt strangling her every moment of the day."

She was drained, all of the fight gone out of her. She wanted to curl up on the bed and go to sleep; let the world and all of its problems fade away. Bella had settled into a ball on her lap, purring her contentment with the world.

At least someone was happy. Carla sure wasn't. She was damn exhausted.

Slowly, Christian nodded, his face still inscrutable, and then held out his hand for hers. She cocked an eyebrow at him, but complied, setting a grumpy Bella down on the floor, clasped his hand, and let him pull her to her feet.

Without a word, he headed back towards the open doorway.

Still holding her hand by awkwardly hitching it up behind his back, he headed down the stairs, her right on his heels, until suddenly, he seemed to be hit by a sneezing attack. He leaned against the wall of the stairwell as sneeze after sneeze overtook his body. Finally, he straightened up, and, never letting his grip on her hand slacken, started back down the steep stairs again as if nothing had happened.

"Christian!" she said, a little annoyed now. "Are you okay? That was a hell of a lot of sneezing you just did. Are you getting sick? Maybe we need to go buy you some orange juice or something."

He didn't answer.

Equal parts curious and annoyed, she managed to lock the front door to Happy Petals one-handed. He only let go of her hand after he helped her into the truck, but hurried over to his side and retook possession as soon as he slid inside.

She was his lifeline, and she didn't have a damn clue of why.

Her imagination, usually so eager to fill in the blanks, was giving her a shrug of the shoulders this time. No crazy theory that she'd disavow later on had ever popped into her mind.

She had nothing.

She wasn't sure she liked that state of affairs.

They were driving out into the countryside now, and Carla figured that she could at least guess where they were going – the Miller farm. Stetson, the youngest Miller brother, owned it now with his darlin' wife and son.

He also was, of course, Christian's boss.

Christian took another right and with that, Carla knew for sure that they were heading to the Miller farm. There was nowhere else to go after this point *except* the farm.

And this was a big deal because…?

She turned and studied Christian's inscrutable face. If she lived to be 100, she'd never understand men.

CHAPTER
TWENTY
CHRISTIAN

True, but that's hardly common knowledge, now is it?
~Westley in The Princess Bride

HE WAS GOING TO SHOW Carla his piece-of-shit single-wide, and *then* they could talk about crappy housing. Hers was crowded and small, sure, but it was also cute. Everything Carla touched was cute.

His single-wide was *not* cute. It was many things, but "cute" was not on that list.

He couldn't look at Carla, even as he clung desperately to her hand. What if he looked at her, and he broke, and he turned around and headed back to town? He'd promised her that he'd show her his, if she'd show him hers. He couldn't break his promise.

But showing his piece-of-shit single-wide to her was…

Terrifying.

Yeah. That.

Because there was *no way* she'd want to date him after this. Of course, there was no way she'd want to date him if he broke his word, either.

He felt a sheen of cold sweat cover his body.

The truck bumped its way into its usual parking spot in front of the single-wide, through the ruts and holes, and came to a stop. They both sat and looked at the trailer for a moment, its dull, worn metal siding glinting in the rays of the evening sun.

Somehow, it looked even worse than normal – more dilapidated. More rundown. More shitty.

Or maybe it was because he was seeing it through her eyes: The cobwebs everywhere. The torn screen on the front window that he'd "repaired" with duct tape. A dirt yard.

Oh Lordy, the dirt yard. When he'd moved in, there hadn't been a yard, and he sure as hell hadn't had the time to put one in himself.

He hated it – on windy days, it meant there was a fine layer of dirt covering everything – but he didn't have the time to do anything about it. Being Stetson's foreman was *more* than a full-time job. Between that and spending time with his family, there wasn't much leftover for niceties like a green lawn. He'd kept meaning to, but…

The screen door – which had never latched properly – creaked in the wind, slowly banging open and closed as the shifting winds pushed it around.

Carla still hadn't said a word.

Christian was pretty sure he was going to puke.

Yanking his hand out of hers, he threw open the driver's door, slamming it shut behind him. He'd stayed calm on the way over by holding Carla's hand, but now that he was here and she wasn't saying anything, just passing a quiet judgment on him, he couldn't bear to sit next to her anymore.

Why had he agreed to her stupid idea anyway? At least if Carla had broken up with him because he'd gone back on his word, he would've kept his pride. She never would've known this was where he lived.

Now she was going to break up with him *and* he had no pride left.

He cursed a blue streak, really letting rip, and was just getting to his all-time favorite Spanish cuss words when Marshmallow, his Great Pyrenees, came trotting over. His tail was wagging gently as he sat in the dirt next to him, waiting for his pettings. He was a regal dog that liked to pretend that he didn't need pettings, but that was bullshit. As soon as Christian would stop petting him, Marshmallow would instantly nudge his hand, reminding him that he wasn't done being petted yet.

Marshmallow's viewpoint on "enough" was a little sketch.

Christian let out a long sigh as he stroked his hand through Marshmallow's thick fur. Carla was still hiding in the truck – he hadn't looked back at her because he was afraid he'd lose his shit if he laid eyes on her traitorous face – but the truck behind him had been as silent as a graveyard at midnight. No squeak of the door opening. No slam of the door shutting.

Traitorous was right. Damn her soul to perdition and back. She'd forced him to open up like this, and then did just what he thought she'd do all along – finally figure out that she was too damn good for him. Why couldn't she just have believed him when he told her that? Why did she insist on seeing proof before stomping his heart into the ground?

His temper snapping, he whirled around to storm over to the truck and tell her *exactly* what he thought of her…and only barely kept from bowling her over. Somehow, she'd snuck out of the truck and over to stand behind him without making a damn noise.

"Shit, Carla!" he bellowed, springing backwards in shock, coming down on Marshmallow's paw, who let out a loud yip of pain. "God!" he yelled, stumbling forward again and trying to get his bearings. If he stepped on or ran into or hit one more thing, he thought his head would explode.

He forced himself to close his eyes, and breathe in slowly, then back out slowly.

"Sorry, I'm sorry," he whispered, turning around and stroking Marshmallow's head, feeling like an awful human being. "I didn't mean—"

"Oh!" came a squeak of terror behind him. "Oh my!"

He jerked his head around, trying to spot the threat so he could take it out, but found nothing. He looked back at Carla, who was looking straight at Marshmallow, her eyes wide and her breath shallow.

"He's, uhh..." she squeaked, her voice a full octave higher than normal, "he's big."

"Marshmallow?" He looked back down at his dog as if seeing him for the first time. "Yeah. I mean, he's a big boy all right, but he's a real lover. He'd never hurt you."

"Marshmallow?" Carla repeated faintly, and then laughed. "Your dog's name is *Marshmallow*?"

He scowled at her. He was still pissed, even if she'd finally managed to get her ass out of the truck. "Yes, it is," he said tightly. "Nieves named him for me years ago, and honestly, it fits. It was either that, or Snow Drift. During the winter, with his all-white coat? He disappears."

But still, she just stood there, her hands clasped behind her back as she stared at the sweetest dog on the planet as if she expected him to rip out her throat at any moment.

"Dammit, Carla, he's a sweetheart," he growled. "Stop looking at him like that. Great Pyrenees are bred to guard sheep in the Pyrenees mountains between Spain and France, and are some of the smartest dogs you'll ever meet, and loyal to boot. Unless you're a coyote or wolf, or you attack something that he considers to be his property, he'll love you forever."

"How much does he weigh?" she asked as she clasped her hands in front of her instead. He figured that was some sort of progress. Maybe.

"Just under 125 pounds. So before you ask, yes, he eats a lot of dog food, but he also pulls his weight around here, guarding and watching over the farm."

Her fingers were fidgety and twirling around each other now; her teeth were chewing on her bottom lip. He was on the verge of barking at her to just pet Marshmallow already, but then, she beat him to it.

"Hi, Marshmallow," she said, her voice quaking as she held out her hand for him to sniff. Perfunctorily, he did, and then moved over to sit down next to her so she could do her job and pet him.

Uncertainly, she patted him on his head and then yanked her hand away like she'd just touched hot coals.

Marshmallow rolled his head and looked up at Christian with what he'd would swear was disgust in the dog's big brown eyes. If Marshmallow could speak, he would surely be saying, "Can you believe this woman? She doesn't even know how to *pet* properly."

Somehow, this trip to hell – aka, his place – had turned into a "How to not be afraid of a large dog" session instead, and Christian jumped on it with both hands. Anything that meant not taking Carla inside was a-okay with him. Maybe they could just learn how to pet a dog, then climb back inside his truck, and drive back to town as if this was nothing more than an excursion to meet Marshmallow. Forget the rest had happened.

"Look," he said, "I know he's big—"

"His head is bigger than Leo!" she broke in. Her hands were back to fiddling, her anxiety not lessened in the slightest by touching the dog.

"—But he wouldn't hurt you if his life depended upon it," Christian continued, ignoring her comment. Actually, he was pretty sure Marshmallow's head was bigger than Leo and Bella put together, but he wasn't about to say that. "He protects his herd, and in his world, that's me, and to a lesser extent, the other guys who work here and the Miller family. He doesn't pick a fight unless he has to; he prefers howling and marking his territory, but I've come outside some mornings to find his muzzle and paws stained red from blood. He's nocturnal by nature, so he stays up all night and guards the farm while us humans sleep, and then sleeps in snatches throughout the day to repeat it again the next night. I swear he sleeps with one eye open. I promise you, *he won't hurt you*. Now, put your damn hand out and scratch him behind the ears like you would your cat."

Carla sent him a doubtful look but reached out tentatively and scratched the Great Pyrenees behind the ears. With a happy sigh, Marshmallow leaned against her legs, tilting his head to the side to give her easier access to just the right spot.

She laughed a little. "You *are* a big love, aren't you?" she murmured in wonderment, switching to his other ear. Marshmallow just leaned in harder, and Christian wasn't sure who was going to land on the ground first – Carla from being pushed over by his dog, or his dog falling over to give Carla full access to his belly.

"Good," Christian grunted. He was tempted – oh so tempted – to say, "I told you so!" but swallowed the phrase instead. Nothing good ever came from telling a woman, "I told you so."

Just as he was starting to think that they could make their way back to the truck and pretend like none of this had ever happened, Carla straightened up. "All right, let's do this thing."

Christian stifled a groan – he should've known it'd be too much to ask for Carla to just forget why they'd come out here – and with leaden feet, turned to the house. What he wouldn't give in that moment to be anywhere else but there.

"Does Marshmallow live inside with you?" Carla asked as she followed along behind him.

"No," he said, dragging his feet, hoping to somehow put off the inevitable. "He's definitely an outdoor dog." Maybe, an earthquake would hit. "Marshmallow's never even tried to come inside. I think he'd hate it in there." Maybe, Yellowstone would blow its top. "Out here, the world is his oyster. He can run and chase and bark and jump in the canal and do whatever he wants."

Nothing. Not a single well-timed explosion.

"Inside, he'd be cooped up, just staring at four walls. I think he'd go crazy." His shoes were filled with cement, dragging with every step. "Not to mention that he runs through every mud puddle in the county. You don't want him tracking all of that inside."

And yet, no matter how slowly he walked, they still somehow made it up onto the shitty front porch, the gray, weathered boards creaking underfoot, a couple of them loose and promising a broken ankle to an unsuspecting soul. He knew better than to step on those boards, but Carla didn't. That was all this excursion to his house needed – a trip to the hospital afterwards.

He hesitated, his hand on the doorknob. He couldn't remember – had he even made his bed that morning? That was a rather hit-or-miss affair.

Maybe he should beg for five minutes to straighten up.

No. Clean or dirty, it was still a hunk of junk. No amount of cleaning would fix that.

With an inward groan, he opened the front door. "After you," he muttered, stepping aside and gesturing her in.

Well, it was fun while it lasted. Sure, she was a nice piece of tail, but that didn't mean he couldn't be fine by himself again. He was almost 40. He'd been alone this long. He could be alone another 40 years.

He was fine.

Just fine.

"Where's your bedroom?" Carla asked quietly. He pointed to the right down the short hallway.

"Mine is on the left; there's a guest bedroom on the right," he said dully. "*Not* that I have guests. Stetson used to make all of the single guys share this place but when I was promoted to foreman, I said I wanted a place of my own. No more roommates. It was about 2016 or so when I got the place to myself."

Four and a half years. All that time to make it his home, and he never had. Even when he'd stopped having to have roommates, it still wasn't his happy place. It wasn't *his*. It was just where he slept, and when he had to, where he cooked.

It sure as hell couldn't be where he made love to Carla. That wasn't ever going to happen in this hellhole.

He realized with a start that Carla was most of the way down the hallway, opening up the door to his bedroom before he could stop her. "Hey!" he hollered, hurrying after her. What was she thinking, going into his bedroom like that?! He didn't say she could see—

His brain fizzled to a stop. Carla already had her shirt off, and was unhooking her bra, her back to him. "Wuh…" he stuttered, his brain frozen. She leaned forward, letting her bra straps slide off her arms and onto the floor, and then turned to look at him, completely topless. There were her delicious tits, just begging for him to play with them, and he wasn't entirely sure he knew words anymore.

Any words.

He saw her lips move and a part of him knew she was talking, but the rushing in his ears made it impossible for him to hear her. Maybe in 20 years, he might be immune to the sight of her body, but he sure as hell wasn't today.

Definitely not today.

In a dream, he saw her moving towards him, in his bedroom, in this house he swore he'd never show her, and she was undoing his belt, tugging it out, pulling his zipper down, cupping him through his boxer briefs. He wasn't sure he wanted this, but he also knew he could never tell her no. He was embarrassed by his home, sure, but not *that* embarrassed.

Not embarrassed enough to turn down the opportunity to make love to Carla Grahame.

CHAPTER
TWENTY-ONE
CARLA

They're kissing again. Do we have to hear the kissing part?
~Grandson in *The Princess Bride*

WAS IT BAD that she was forcing this to happen?

Well, maybe 'force' was the wrong word. She wasn't raping him, after all. She was just taking the lead. There was a difference. She was a woman who knew what she wanted and how she wanted it. That was allowed.

Okay, so that wasn't it at all. The truth of the matter was, she was starting to understand Christian. It didn't take Sherlock to figure out that he was embarrassed about where he lived, something she could more than relate to, and making love in it? It was the ultimate show of acceptance. She could tell him all day long that his place outranked hers – he at least had a damn shower and a kitchen sink – but he'd never believe her.

This was her speaking the truth without words – something more effective than words – that in her world, *he* was what mattered. Not where he lived or what he made.

Only him.

She stepped back out of the circle of his arms and pulled the side zipper down on her swishy skirt, as she liked to call it, letting the whisper of fabric pool around her feet.

Christian's dark chocolate eyes went black with lust and, sucking in a breath, took a step towards her.

"No," she breathed, and his hand stopped mid-air. "Not yet."

Despite her I-am-a-woman, hear-me-roar thoughts of just moments before, the truth of the matter was, she'd never taken the lead in the bedroom. Based on her *very* extensive survey of romance novels, rom-coms, and the occasional R-rated movie, she'd always known her handful of experiences in college had fallen short of how mind-blowing sex should be.

Way short.

Six weeks ago, Christian had showed her that she hadn't been wrong her whole life. Love really was magical, and today, she wanted to be in charge of that magic.

His eyes held the question he didn't ask as Carla stepped out of the pooled skirt, feeling the cool of the AC air flow over her skin, pebbling her nipples.

Or maybe it was the lust growing inside of her. She could be in charge, and she could *like* it.

With trembling hands, she tugged on the waistband of Christian's smart, new dark blue jeans until they slid over his slim hips and pooled around his ankles. Too late, she realized her mistake – he still had his cowboy boots on. He wouldn't be able to step out of his jeans like she'd stepped out of her skirt.

With a disgruntled sigh, she let him take control again for just a moment, toeing off his boots and dropping his jeans in a pile. When he straightened, she grinned naughtily at the jutting front of his boxer-briefs.

"Is that a pistol in there, or are you happy to see me?" she murmured in her best Mae West voice as she moved forward to cup him through the fabric. He reached for her again but she leaned up and tapped her finger lightly against his lips. "Not yet," she whispered again.

He groaned.

She grinned.

Slowly, she began unbuttoning his dress shirt, each slide of a button through the cotton revealing another inch of tempting tanned skin. Just for a moment, she pondered the idea of buying him a pearl-snap button-up shirt – or ten – to make access to his chest an easier affair, but then decided against it. She liked unwrapping him slowly, like a birthday present just for her.

The last button released, she slid her hands up his sculptured chest, feeling the muscles jump beneath her fingers, and then, her hands at his rounded shoulders, she pushed the shirt down, letting it slide down his arms to join the jeans on the ground.

That was better. Now they were even – her in her panties, him in his boxer-briefs. Starting at his earlobe, she began trailing kisses down his neck, nibbling and sucking, feeling the excited heartbeat against her lips at the base of his throat.

"Carla," he moaned, the sound vibrating through her lips. "Please…"

Ignoring his pleas, she continued further down to one of his brown nipples, flicking at it, tonguing it, and his pants grew harsher.

"Carla!" he groaned loudly. "I can't…I need…" He buried his hands in her hair, trying to pull her closer, trying to direct her lips.

She pulled back with a breathy laugh. "I don't remember saying you can put your hands in my hair," she scolded him. He dropped his hands to his sides, his eyes glowing lava hot with need.

"You can't expect me…"

He couldn't seem to finish.

She didn't mind. If he was talking, he obviously had too much blood north of the waistline.

Speaking of…

She dropped to her knees in front of him and tugged at the waistband of his boxer-briefs, finally slipping the fabric down far enough that his dick sprung free, bouncing a bit with the force of the release. She laughed, feeling like a daredevil as she wrapped her fingers around him. When she'd had sex in college, it'd been drunken affairs in the back of a car or in a twin bed, hurried along by the scare of being walked in on by roommates. She wasn't entirely sure she'd ever wrapped her fingers around a dick before, but she was sure that she hadn't on as magnificent a specimen as Christian. Somehow, it was soft yet hard; velvet yet steel.

Sucking in a breath for courage, she leaned forward and wrapped her lips around him.

"Oooohhhhh…" Christian groaned, his hips jerking. "I…you…"

Gloating at what she'd managed to turn Christian into – a conglomeration of cells screaming with delight – she slowly moved her mouth down his shaft, trying to bury it completely in her throat. She choked and instinctively pulled back before she did something awful, like have her gag reflex engaged, causing her to throw up all over her boyfriend.

That would be a story for the grandkids.

"Why, the first time I went down on your grandpa, he was so big, I choked on him and puked all over the plac—"

Christian buried his hands in her hair and pulled her off him, breath choppy as he stood there, clearly trying to regain his composure.

"I…need…a…minute," he rasped. His eyes were closed; his face showing a desperate kind of pain. "There's only so…so much a man…can take."

She sat back on her haunches and grinned up at him, thoroughly enjoying the fact that she'd made this beautiful specimen of a man almost cry with the pain of holding back.

But, she couldn't tease him forever. Twisting around, she

found her skirt on the floor and patted to find the tiny pocket that was worthless for almost anything – why was it that women were never given normal-sized pockets in their clothing, as if they could never have anything they needed to carry on them? – except holding one tiny, incredibly important thing: A condom.

She ripped it open and placed it on the end of Christian's straining dick, slowly rolling it in place. Just like the banana she'd been handed in the 8th grade to practice on. *Thank you, sex ed.* They'd forgotten to use a condom while up in the mountains, but this time, she was smart enough to plan ahead.

With a hiss of breath, Christian hauled her to her feet, spun her in a circle, and dropped her down on the bed. He was done letting her be in charge, which was probably good anyway. She'd just about run out of ideas on what should happen next.

With one smooth thrust of his hips, Christian was inside of her and breathing hard, trying to hold back, but she didn't want him to. She wanted him to take her like a dying man in the desert sucked down water.

She wanted to be desirable.

She wrapped her legs around his hips and lifted herself to him, pushing him deeper inside of her. Oh, that felt *good*. She strained, pulling him as deep as he would go.

"Christian…Christian…Chris…" she panted and begged, and he broke. Plunging forward, he began his rhythmic strokes.

"Yes…please…I…" The world was building to a crescendo around her and she couldn't stop it or control it and she didn't want to, and then—

Her back arched and she let out a guttural scream of delight as the world vanished and all she felt was pure joy and lust and desire roll through her, wave after wave, and her hair grew damp and a part of her realized that she'd been crying.

Was it normal to cry tears when orgasming, she wondered idly as her body softened and she sank back down into the mattress, Christian's body above, hot and hard and oh so sexy.

His eyes fluttered open and he gave her a crooked grin. "Welcome to *mi casa*," he said, and she laughed.

"Thanks," she whispered as he crawled up onto the bed beside her, pulling her against him, and together, they drifted on the wings of sleep and love.

CHAPTER
TWENTY-TWO
CARLA

If you haven't got your health, you haven't got anything.
~Count Rugen in *The Princess Bride*

OCTOBER, 2020

IT WAS FUNNY HOW LIFE WORKED, she thought with a happy sigh as she stirred her tea.

Michelle was pontificating on something – it sounded like she was explaining her male castration theory to their newest member of the Early Spinster's Club, Keila – but Carla couldn't keep her mind focused on what her friend was saying.

She took a sip of her tea instead, pondering her own personal housing crisis. Ever since the night of I'll-show-you-mine-if-you-show-me-yours six weeks ago, Carla and Christian had spent every free waking hour together. No more stupidity and misplaced pride keeping them apart.

Thank heavens.

Over that time, talk about "I need to find a new place to live in that is larger than a shoebox" and "I need to find a place to live in that isn't a single-wide trailer in the middle of a dustbowl" had morphed into "We need to find a place to live."

She couldn't put her finger on the exact moment that'd happened – it just sorta did. Being around Christian was like slipping into a pair of faded, comfy jeans. They fit together and already, Carla could only vaguely remember BC time – Before Christian. How had she lived without him? How had she *wanted* to live without him?

She took a sip of her tea, and like dropping a stone into a deep well, it seemed to take forever before the tea actually hit her stomach. Her hollow, empty, cramping-from-hunger stomach.

How had she gone this long without eating?

Even that time she'd gotten really stupid in college and had gone on an ultra-low calorie diet in an attempt to shed some weight, she hadn't been *this* hungry.

She had a bear claw in front of her – always a fav – but in the midst of this personal famine she was suffering through, it looked simply putrid. Disgusting. What had she ever thought she liked about bear claws? They were all dark brown and ugly and smelled terrible.

Autumn's orange-glaze muffin – not even touched yet – was just across the table and Carla's gaze lit on it like a drowning man spotting a life preserver. Orange glaze? Her mouth watered. Clean and bright and citrusy, it was *exactly* what she wanted just then.

"Do you mind?" she croaked, already reaching for the muffin. There was a tiny, distant part of her brain that knew what she was doing was rude, but she could hardly hear it over the roar of the hungry lion that'd taken up residence in her stomach. "I'm sorry," she said around mouthfuls. It tasted even better than she'd imagined it would. "I haven't been able to keep anything down lately. This is…"

She looked down at the empty muffin paper. How had that happened?

"Gone?" she said stupidly.

"You haven't been able to keep anything down?" Michelle asked archly.

"Yeah," Carla mumbled, looking back towards the display case. Were there more? Surely there were more of these bits of heaven.

"I'll go see if they have another one," Autumn said, a lilt in her voice that Carla couldn't quite place, and slid out of the booth. Carla made a mental note to give her a bouquet of flowers to take home with her. This kind of friendship was above and beyond.

"How long have you been having a hard time keeping shit down?" Keila asked, and even in the depths of her hunger, Carla smiled at the tough Boston accent of her friend. It was so different from the Idaho drawl Carla had been hearing from birth, and she liked it.

"Ummmm…" Carla's gaze had followed the path of her friend's trek to the front counter. Autumn was pointing at the display case and Gage was reaching in to grab something. *Good*. They did have more.

Michelle snapped her fingers in front of Carla's face. "Carla!" she barked. She jerked around to look at her friend.

"Yes?" she said tightly, trying not to let her annoyance show. Couldn't they give her a minute? Give her some space to breathe?

"How long have you been strugglin' with keepin' shit down?" Michelle asked, enunciating every word like she was talking to a slow, rather stupid child.

"I don't know. A while," she said defensively. Michelle cocked an eyebrow at her. Carla paused for a minute, thinking. "The Morton wedding!" she said with satisfaction, proud of herself for remembering. "I almost threw up on the boutonnieres. Barely made it to the trashcan. I just kept thinking how angry the mother of the bride would be if I delivered corsages with puke on them."

Autumn was at her elbow, pushing an orange-glaze muffin

beneath her nose, and Carla dug into it, reveling in it. Finally, here was some food that wasn't going to leave her puking over the trashcan. It was exactly what she needed, and her stomach roared its approval.

"When did the Mortons get married, anyone remember?" Michelle asked the table as Autumn slid back into place across from Carla.

"A little over three weeks ago," Carla said around the heaven in her mouth. "The 19th of September." It was her job to remember the big days in her customers' lives. What kind of florist would she be if she forgot something like that?

"You've been sick for three weeks?!" Michelle looked apoplectic.

"I guess." Carla shrugged, and then looked with bewilderment down at the muffin in front of her. Or rather, the empty paper muffin cup. Only a few scattered crumbs attested to the fact it'd once held a muffin.

Was Gage cheaping out on his customers and making his muffins smaller than normal? How was a girl supposed to fill up if the muffins were bite-sized?

There was a long silence and Carla looked up to catch the significant glances Michelle, Autumn, and Keila were sharing. They seemed to be having a silent conversation that she wasn't invited to.

"What?" she said defensively. "What's wrong? Why are you guys looking like that?"

"Autumn, get her another muffin," Michelle barked, a drill sergeant come to life. "I'll run across the street to the pharmacy. Keila, keep her from pitching over from starvation. Ready, set, break!"

"The pharmacy?" Carla asked in bewilderment to Michelle's retreating back. She swung her gaze towards Keila, her friend's chameleon eyes a light gray today. "Why is she going to the pharmacy?"

Keila, a little green around the gills, looked like she'd rather be anywhere on planet Earth than in that booth at that moment. Carla narrowed her eyes at her new friend. Something was going on here, and she'd be damned if everyone would continue to leave her out of...*whatever* it was.

Autumn was back faster that time, shoving the muffin into view.

"Oh, thank you, Lord!" Carla said ecstatically, digging into it. Why had she ever bothered with bear claws? What'd she been thinking? With the existence of orange-glaze muffins in the world, eating anything else was just a travesty.

She closed her eyes, savoring the taste on her tongue. Now that she'd partially filled the giant, gnawing hole in her stomach, she could at least chew before swallowing.

Keila and Autumn chatted lightly, ignoring Carla for the moment, which suited her just fine. If no one was asking her questions, she didn't have to worry about being rude and answering with her mouth full.

Hardly any time at all passed, and then Michelle was sliding back into the booth, sending significant glances at Autumn and Keila. "Has she figured it out yet?" she asked. They shook their heads.

Carla sent her friend a glowering look. "*She* is right here. What haven't I figured out yet?"

"When was the last time you had your period?" Michelle whispered, ignoring Carla's question. Carla paused, confused. What on earth did that have to do with the price of tea in China?

"I don't know." She shrugged. "It's always pretty light – I don't get cramps or heavy bleeding or any of those terrible symptoms people complain about. I just throw a pad on for a couple of days and call it good. I've never paid much attention to..."

She trailed off, her mouth forming a perfect O.

"I'll go get you a muffin this time," Keila said tactfully, sliding out of the booth.

"I think she's finally put the pieces together," Autumn said dryly.

Carla simply stared at Autumn and Michelle, her jaw practically scraping the table top, feelings and thoughts and emotions all running together, no hope of separating them out.

"Yeah, I think so," Michelle said with a chuckle. "Carla, I do believe you're gonna become a momma."

"You keep using that word. I do not think it means what you think it means," Carla whispered.

Autumn looked at Michelle, startled.

"*Princess Bride*," Michelle said, waving the unspoken question away. "And I *do* think it means what I think it means," she said dryly to Carla. "Just how careful have you and Christian been?"

Carla's mind instantly flashed to all of the times that Christian had wrapped up carefully…but then that one time he hadn't. Their first time, up in the mountains in that meadow. It had only been once. Surely she couldn't be pregnant after only one slip-up.

"It only takes once," Michelle said quietly, as if reading Carla's mind, scooting over so Keila could sit down again.

Carla's hands shook as she unwrapped the muffin, mindlessly stuffing bites into her mouth. Pregnant. She could be pregnant. With Christian's baby.

Then the muffin was gone – where did it go?? – and Autumn was gently tugging on her hand, pulling her out of the booth. "Let's head back to the store," she said, putting a steadying arm around Carla's waist.

"Is she okay?" Gage called from the front counter.

"Oh yeah, she's fine. Just didn't eat enough this morning, I think. I'll get her back to the shop," Autumn called back breezily. Carla loved her eternally in that moment for not blurting out the truth.

"You're a good friend," she mumbled under her breath, her arms and legs shaking spastically. She was going to collapse at any moment. Suddenly, her shop seemed miles away, even though it was only a few blocks down the street. It might as well have been Jupiter. Her body refused to cooperate with something as advanced as walking.

Pregnant? I can't be pregnant. I mean, I want to be pregnant. But later. Christian and I are still learning about each other. I don't even know if he likes cheddar or provolone cheese more! I can't bring another human being into the mix. I don't know anything about this human being. What if it likes cheddar but Christian likes provolone?

In a distant part of her mind, she realized that Michelle and Autumn were on either side of her, holding her up, with Keila trailing behind. The words they were saying swam lazily into focus, and she finally figured out they were discussing the merits of different kinds of cheese.

"What...what about Swiss cheese?" Carla mumbled to Michelle as Autumn slid her own key into the lock and opened up the store. Which was very, very good, because unlocking a door seemed like a herculean feat in that moment.

"You were talking about cheese – what the baby would like versus Christian. So we were just discussing our favorites."

"I was?" Carla whispered, surprised. She hadn't meant to say any of it out loud.

Michelle helped her slide into her work chair and Carla gratefully sagged into it, her brain already running a million miles per hour, cheese completely forgotten. Where would they live? Surely not in the little attic space above the shop, and not at Christian's place either. It was fine for a bachelor, but not her and a baby. Suddenly, their search for a home of their own took on a new level of urgency.

Autumn put a cool washcloth on Carla's forehead and slipped a glass of water into her hand. "Drink something. I think it'll help."

Carla really wanted more than water in that moment – maybe a stiff drink, or seven – but if she really was pregnant...

"Hold on – you bought a *pregnancy* test!" she gasped, her mind clearing for the first time.

Michelle pulled a small brown bag out of her purse with a sly grin. "I got a few probing questions from Mrs. Morland but I refused to say a word. If everyone in town thinks I'm preggers by morning, I'm totally blaming you."

Carla let out a bark of laughter and then clapped her hand over her mouth. "Oh, I'm sorry!" she whispered.

"It's fine." Michelle didn't seem bothered in the least. Of course, nothing much ever bothered Michelle. "Now, let's get you peeing on a stick, shall we?"

CHAPTER
TWENTY-THREE
CHRISTIAN

I trust you with this secret.
~Prince Humperdinck in *The Princess Bride*

CARLA WAS ACTING…weird.

Which sure, they'd only been together since June, so maybe this wasn't weird at all for her. Maybe this was what she was always like, and the last few months were the exception.

But he really didn't think so. He didn't remember her being particularly "off" during high school, and there'd never been a whisper around town that Carla was soft in the head.

But there was no denying that "weird" was exactly what she was being right now.

She'd called him up, demanded that he come over *right now* to talk, but after dropping everything and speeding off to town, leaving a rather pissy Stetson behind, Carla was now refusing to say a word. She'd shut off the lights in the shop, flipped off the open sign, and locked the door. She was pacing around the shop like a caged animal, muttering under her breath, and he swore he'd heard her say "provolone" at one point, but every time he'd asked her what was going on, she'd snapped at him, so he'd sat down on a stool and was now patiently waiting for that moment when she'd clue him in on what was going on.

Screw that.

He was fast losing his patience and had half a mind to walk out the front door. She could call him when she was actually ready to say or do something beyond talk to herself. Did he really need to be here as she had the world's longest one-sided conversation?

Stetson is gonna kill me. I left him with those damn cows, about ready to check for —

"Christian, I need to talk to you!" Carla announced suddenly, coming to a complete stop, hands on her hips, glaring at him.

As if he was the reason she hadn't said anything yet.

He was tempted – *oh* so tempted – to reply with a scathingly sarcastic comment, but he wanted to know what in the hell was going on more. Maybe only a tiny bit more, but it did, in the end, win out.

"Okaayyy…tell me what's going on." He used his best level-headed, kind boyfriend voice, and was pretty damn proud of himself for pulling it off successfully, if he did say so himself.

"I…well…I…do you love me?" she demanded.

"Uhhh…" he sputtered. Out of all of the directions that he'd imagined for this conversation, this was *not* one of the possibilities that had occurred to him. "Is, uh, is there a reason that you want to talk about this right now?"

He did love Carla. He loved her more than he loved any other person in his life. But he'd wanted to tell her in a more romantic way than her demanding answers in a quickly darkening flower shop.

"Because I need to know right now!" she yelled, rounding on him. "I can't tell you…I just need to know, okay? Do you love me?"

He felt the hackles rise a bit on the back of his neck. This wasn't how he'd intended this particular conversation to go.

This demanding, pushy woman wasn't Carla. She wanted flowers and chocolates and romance. Surely she didn't want to be told that he loved her for the first time at emotional gunpoint?

He stood up from the bar stool at the work table, and stalked over to her. He wasn't sure if he wanted to hug her or tell her to get lost. As he got closer, though, and could see – in the rapidly darkening store – the way she was standing with her shoulders tense, eyes wild…

Something was going on.

Something she wasn't sharing with him.

At the last moment, *hug* won out, and he pulled her into his arms. She was stiff as a cardboard cutout at first and then she began to loosen, sagging against him, shoulders shaking, and he realized that she was crying as his shirt dampened from the moisture.

"Shhhh…" he whispered, stroking her back. "It's all going to be okay. I promise. Whatever's happening, it's all going to be okay. I can help you." With what, he didn't know, but he made the promise anyway. Whatever was causing this, he'd make it all better, or die trying.

She let out a strangled bark of laughter at that, pulling back in his arms and looking at him. She looked fragile in that moment.

Carla was many things. Boisterous. A true lady. Kind. Giving. Thoughtful.

But fragile?

Never fragile.

"I'm pregnant."

CHAPTER
TWENTY-FOUR
CARLA

And remember, this is for posterity, so be honest. How do you feel?
~Count Rugen in *The Princess Bride*

SHE'D GONE and done it. She'd told him. She couldn't take the words back. She couldn't flee the country and raise the baby on her own. She couldn't pretend that it wasn't real any longer.

She'd told him the truth.

His arms, so warm and welcoming around her just a moment before, went stiff. His whole body went stiff. He wasn't breathing. He wasn't moving.

She was being held by a statue.

"I'm…I'm pregnant," she said again, because it'd been horrible enough to say the first time, so why not repeat it? "I'm about three-and-a-half months along, from what I can tell. I'll be going in to see a doctor to get my first check-up, but…"

"Pregnant," he breathed.

Good. He was still alive. That was good.

"Yes. With a baby. Christian, we're going to have a baby…?"

She hadn't meant for it to come out as a question, but it did anyway.

"Oh my God, we're gonna have a baby." He sat back down with a thunk on the barstool. "We're gonna have a baby? Oh my God, we're gonna have a *baby*!"

He was back up off the barstool and hugging her, twirling her around, knocking the barstool over and Leo went screeching into the other room but none of it mattered. He was raining kisses on her face, hugging and kissing and whooping with joy.

She finally leaned up against the work counter and said dryly, "So. I take it that you're happy about this?"

He laughed weakly, leaning against the counter too. Were her knees as wobbly as his?

"I'm pushing 40. I've never been married. I'd given up on having kids." He shrugged. "If you're the oldest of seven children, either you want kids of your own, or you'd rather have your dick cut off with a rusty blade."

Carla let out a raucous bark of laughter. Christian sent her a wry smile.

"Sorry. If Carmelita had heard that…no dessert for me. Anyway, I'd always wanted kids. My sisters have 'em in spades, and that's cool, but nieces and nephews just aren't the same. I want to teach *my* kids how to change a tire and how to work hard and how they should prioritize college like their aunt Yesenia so they don't end up like a farm hand like their old dad. My parents are pretty good parents for the most part, but I'd like to think I could do some things better. Like encourage our girls to work for their own careers.

"*Our* girls…" he repeated in a breathy whisper and then stared at her, his shadowed brown eyes studying her like she held the key to eternal life.

"Do *you* want this baby?" he asked. The room, the air, eternity was suspended in that moment.

She nodded, a little wobbly still from the whiplash of

emotions. "I...I do. You know that my brother has his kids and I love 'em dearly but you're right – nieces and nephews just aren't the same. I...I didn't think I'd get married, and I didn't let myself dream that I'd get to have kids of my own. Kids were for people who'd found their own Westley, and I never had..."

She drew in a deep breath.

"Until you."

He was raining down kisses then, all over her face and neck and chest, and then he pulled back sharply. He felt around until he found the little lamp she kept to provide ambient lighting when she needed it, and flipped it on. She could mostly see his face again, and found that it was criss-crossed with worry and fear.

It was clear the gravity of the situation was beginning to sink in for him. He was starting to worry about where they were going to live, and how they were going to afford this—

"I'm allergic to cats," he announced.

She began to sink down onto her barstool, almost fell over sideways because of course, the barstool wasn't there anymore – they'd knocked it over during their celebration – righted it, and *then* sank down onto it. "You...what?"

"I'm allergic. I didn't want to tell you because you love cats, and I didn't want you to feel like you had to choose, so I'm taking allergy pills and the immunologist is starting me on shots, and I don't want you to give up Leo or Bella, but I can't breathe when I'm in here. Not very well, anyway," he added.

She started to laugh then. Laugh and laugh and laugh. Out of all the many – *many* – things she thought Christian would be worried about, her cats were nowhere on the list.

It wasn't until she'd wiped the tears off her cheeks and straightened up on the barstool that she saw how perfectly rigid Christian was. "I...I'm sorry!" she said, gulping in air, smothering the desire to let loose with another round of gut-busting laughter. "I'm not laughing at you. I just didn't expect...

out of all the things to bring up in this moment, 'cats' was not on my list. Cheese, maybe, but not cats."

"Cheese?"

"Never mind," she said, waving her hand in the air dismissively. "For the record, if you were deathly allergic to cats, I'd give Bella and Leo away to close friends who I know would take care of them. I love them, but I'm not Michelle. I'm going to pick you over a cat any day of the week. Second of all, it's very sweet of you to do shots so you can be around them. I hate needles," she shivered at the mere thought of them, "so I think that's very brave of you. More than cats and cheese, though, we need to talk about housing. Where are we going to live?"

The little shop grew silent again as Christian stared at her, worrying his bottom lip.

CHAPTER
TWENTY-FIVE
CHRISTIAN

I swear it will be done!
~Prince Humperdinck in *The Princess Bride*

He was starting to wonder about Carla's obsession with cheese – was this a pregnancy thing? Did he need to buy her seventeen different kinds of cheese? – but she was right. They had bigger fish to fry.

"Obviously, upstairs isn't going to work," he said slowly.

"The lack of any kind of bathing equipment is a definite downer," she put in dryly. "Not to mention that when you have a baby, you're doing nothing but laundry. Lugging it all to my mom's house and back is a no-go. Plus...where would we even keep the baby?"

It was obvious she'd spent more than a little bit of time thinking about this. He felt blindsided – he hadn't had days or weeks to wrap his mind around her pregnancy like she had – but he'd do his damndest to catch up.

"The dresser," he said simply. "Before cribs, parents used to keep their babies in a dresser drawer. That's...that's where my mom kept me." He felt the tips of his ears go red. Carla was a white woman. She wasn't poor as a church mouse growing up. She wouldn't understan—

"That's really sweet," she said softly, putting her hand on his arm. "But considering we can hardly walk around when we're both up there, I think it's not the most practical long-term solution. Someday, the kid is gonna want out of the dresser drawer."

Christian let out a soft laugh at that, feeling the tension begin to ebb away. Carla was the least judgmental person on the planet. She wasn't going to break up with him simply because his parents used a dresser drawer instead of a crib for the first eight months of his life.

"My place…" He shook his head, not able to even finish the sentence. The tension was rising in him again, reappearing as quickly as it'd disappeared. "It isn't fit for a baby and you. I can only just tolerate it for myself. You can't live there. But I can't afford to move somewhere else – free rent is a big part of the benefit package of working for Stetson. He can't exactly set up a 401k retirement plan for me or give me top-notch health insurance, but free rent is a hell of a perk, which is why I haven't moved before." He gulped and then continued on. He had to tell her everything – lay it all out on the table, and let the chips fall where they may. They were in this together now.

"You have to know: Yesenia isn't going to graduate from college until 2024. That's, like, four years away. I can't abandon her now."

"And I still have years of student loan payments left to make," Carla said morosely. Christian moved in front of her, pulling her against him as he stroked her back. He felt her relaxing into him.

She trusted him.

Oh God. Lord, please help me. I don't know how I'm going to do this…

But he had no choice. Carla and their baby needed him. He had to make this work.

"Let me look at rental ads tomorrow," he said quietly. "See what I can find. The baby won't show up next week – we've got, what, five-and-a-half months before this baby will make its appearance? We'll figure something out, I promise."

She nodded against him, her trust in him complete.

Now he just had to make sure that it was earned.

CHAPTER
TWENTY-SIX
CHRISTIAN

> You think it'll work? ~Valerie
> It'd take a miracle. ~Miracle Max
> In *The Princess Bride*

THE COWS MOO'D to each other as they ambled into the next field, thick and lush with clovers and grass. Just a few days here in the triangle pasture, and then they'd make the move to the field closest to the barn. After years of rotating in a giant circle from pasture to pasture, ending up back where they started and beginning the cycle again, the mama cows knew just where to go next, and made sure their calves made the move safely. After only a few moves, even the calves caught on and were happy when a farmhand showed up to lead them to fresh, green pastures.

The Goldfork Mountains were already covered with a dusting of snow, and Christian knew it wouldn't be long before the green fields would be covered in a blanket of white. This meant selling off most of the herd except the yearlings and the mamas, and hauling hay bales out to the remaining cows. There'd also be a lot of checking to make sure that waterers hadn't frozen over, and…

It was hard to remember during the winter just why it was he lived in Idaho.

"Lookin' good," Stetson said, pushing his hat back on his head and wiping at the sweat on his forehead. He leaned against a post with a sigh. "I can't believe the trailers are coming next week. The herd's about to get a whole lot smaller."

"And we'll be on the hook for hay and water, all winter long." Christian's voice made it clear just how enthusiastic he was about that idea.

"Winter does always suck," Stetson said with a what-are-you-gonna-do-about-it chuckle. "Well, we better get headin' back to—"

"Before we go," Christian interrupted his boss, "I wanted to tell ya something."

Stetson looked a little unnerved at that, but nodded. "Spill."

"I...well...Carla's pregnant." He was sure there was a better way to broach the topic, but damned if he knew how. Laying all his cards on the table seemed like the only choice he had.

"Oh, well now!" Stetson said, his face breaking out into a huge grin. "Congratulations!" He slugged Christian on the shoulder. "Flint was an oopsie too," he said in a conspiratorial voice, "but I wouldn't trade him for the world. When's she due?"

"April 9th." Christian tried not to show the panic on his face. It'd been nine days since Carla had told him the big news. Nine days of scouring the want ads and Craigslist and asking around. Nine days of not a centimeter of progress.

He'd always known that the rental market in the area was out of whack, what with Franklin being so close by and all. Tourist towns were hell on earth, in his opinion, bringing both loads of strangers through town and also jacking up the prices on everything from milk down at the store to rentals. Anyone with four walls and a roof wanted to rent it out on Airbnb, to a rich tourist. A farmhand? Well, they were plain outta luck.

"Hold on, today is, what, October..." Stetson fished around

in his pocket and pulled out his cell phone. "October 23rd. That's less than six months from now. Did Carla just find out?"

"Yeah. She...didn't notice." He wasn't about to talk about his girlfriend's periods with his boss. Stetson swallowed uncomfortably, clearly not happy that he'd even asked.

"Well, y'all have a lot to figure out. Hey, where does Carla live? I just realized I don't think I know."

"It's a state secret," Christian said with a wry grin, "so you can't tell anyone, but above the flower shop. To save on rent, she's living there."

"Happy Petals..." He scratched his nose, thinking hard. "That's gotta be tiny. Hardly enough room to turn around, unless there's a backside to the building that I've never noticed."

"Nope, it's just as small as you're thinking. Maybe smaller. And then there's my trailer..."

Stetson nodded so slowly then, Christian almost couldn't tell if he was nodding or just sorta bobbing his head around.

"You can't raise a baby in there," Stetson finally said quietly. "I feel bad enough having single men living in a place like that. It's no place for a family."

"The rental market, though. It's...not pretty."

"No, not with Franklin nearby," Stetson mused softly, pulling his hat off and twirling it in circles in his hands. "I keep expecting someone to put a cardboard box up as a rental, and I imagine if they did, they could keep it rented out full time. It's one of the reasons why I offer the trailers for help to live in."

It was quiet then, as Stetson thought things over, and Christian let him. The cows were moo'ing less, now that they were settled into the new field, and were busy munching away. It was a damn pretty sight – dark brown cows scattered out in a field of green grass.

Not as pretty as Carla, of course, but still, it made a heart feel good to look at it.

"Let me talk to Jennifer," Stets said after a while. "After she took over the books, I stopped even stepping into the office, just in case I screwed them up by looking at 'em wrong. You know I didn't have a head for books and numbers. I'll see what Jennifer says."

Christian straightened up a bit, taking the first full breath of air into his lungs that he'd had in a long time. He knew Stetson was a good man. If he could help, he would.

Could it be just that easy?

Lord, he hoped so.

CHAPTER
TWENTY-SEVEN
CARLA

Fencing, fighting, monster, true love, miracles.
~Grandfather in *The Princess Bride*

THANKSGIVING WEEKEND, 2020

Carla was quite sure she hadn't displayed *nearly* enough sympathy and understanding to Christian when he'd worried about meeting her family for the first time. After all, her family was kind and friendly and *of course* they'd like him.

Nothing to worry about.

Not that his family wasn't also kind and friendly, and she was pretty sure they'd like her. And, this wasn't her first time meeting them. She'd helped with Nieves' *quinceañera*, after all. She knew the Palacios family just like she knew everyone else in town.

But it was a very, very different thing altogether to meet them as Christian's girlfriend.

Christian's girlfriend who was also pregnant with his baby, in case anyone cared. *Not* something his family knew – yet – but that was going to change tonight.

She felt her heart rate rev and her palms grow sweaty. There were roughly a thousand different ways this could go wrong, and—

Without warning, Christian sneezed three times in rapid succession.

Carla patted his arm consolingly, happy to focus on something other than her ever-escalating terror. "Sorry," she said for probably the thousandth time. "How are the shots going?"

"Eh," he grunted. "Did you know I could be taking them for the next five years?"

She squeezed his hand in sympathy. She did know that, actually – he may or may not have mentioned this particular fact a couple of times.

A day.

She loved Christian, of course, but she was beginning to discover that he did not suffer in silence. She'd thought more than once that he'd die if he had to be pregnant for nine months, and she was *sure* he wouldn't make it through childbirth.

Not that she was exactly looking forward to it. The horror stories she'd heard all her life sent shivers down her spine at the mere thought. She was already wondering how many drugs the doctor could legally give her. She hoped the answer was, "A Lot."

"Are you cold?" Christian asked, as always, attuned to the smallest change in her. He reached for the climate controls before she could even answer. "Here, we can turn up the heat. It's only the end of November, and the snow's already started. It's gonna be a looonnnggg winter."

She didn't want to tell Christian she'd been shivering at the thought of giving birth, so she just squeezed his hand again and sent him a grateful smile. Maybe he wasn't dealing with the shots all that well, but who could blame him? She didn't want to be stuck with a needle every week or two for five years either. At least she could give birth and then be done with it.

They pulled up in front of Jorge and María's house, pulling Carla out of her thoughts. She looked out the window, automatically cataloging all of the changes that she could see.

Growing up, this had always been Abby Connelly's house, and remembering that the Palacios' owned it now wasn't something Carla was sure she'd ever quite adjust to. She and Abby had graduated together from Sawyer High School, and Carla had spent many-a Friday night here on sleepovers.

When Abby's father lost it to a bank foreclosure years ago, Carla had been away at college but of course heard every gory detail from her mom and sisters. Wyatt Miller buying it and rubbing it in the sheriff's face that he'd "done it all wrong" and lost the farm because of incompetence…

Painful. Maybe that was true, but still, you didn't tell a person that.

Somehow, Wyatt and Abby (and the sheriff) had worked things out, though, and every time Carla saw her old friend around town, she could see how happy she was – like someone had turned on a 1000-watt light bulb in her eyes and heart.

When Wyatt and Abby had decided to build a bigger house and sell the old Connelly homestead plus five acres to their foreman, Carla had heard the news in town like everyone else. At the time, she never would've guessed she'd be back here as the guest of honor at a party the Palacios' were throwing, let alone carrying the baby of the oldest Palacios.

What a small world we live in…

"Are you okay?"

Christian's voice finally penetrated through the haze of memories, pulling Carla back to the present. "Oh! Yes. Sorry. We're good. I was just remembering how Abby lived here all through school, and all of the sleepovers I've had here."

"It is a small world," Christian agreed, and Carla grinned at how his words mirrored her thoughts exactly.

"What?" he asked, cocking his head to the side quizzically.

"Nothing. Let's go. Time to meet the family."

She opened the truck door and felt the wall of mariachi music slam into her. Instinctively, she pulled the door back shut and turned to Christian, eyes wide. He gave her a grimacing smile.

"My family likes it loud," he said by way of explanation. She thought that was rather understating the situation, but she nodded anyway and opened her door again. This time, she was ready for it, and only gasped a little at the sheer volume pouring out of the speakers everywhere.

Christian hurried around to her side of the truck and helped her down, already treating her like glass that could easily be broken. It made her feel loved, and just a little bit smothered. Four and a half more months of this? Being able to breathe was going to have to come up at some point.

With her arm tucked inside his, they began wandering through the throngs, hugging everyone, Christian shouting, "*¡Les presento a mi novia, Carla!*" again and again.

Everyone seemed so friendly, hugging her, welcoming her into the family, and even switching over to English when they realized her Spanish was painfully limited. In turn, Carla quickly figured out some of the elderly in the group didn't speak English any better than she spoke Spanish, so they ended up nodding and smiling at each other a lot. She made a mental note to become more serious about her Duolingo time.

Christian didn't have an accent when speaking English, which made it easy to forget that it wasn't his native tongue. But his family? They were a different story. She needed to up her game and meet them halfway. At least be able to ask them something more than "What is your name?" in Spanish again and again.

As Christian got deep into a discussion with a cousin? Uncle? She wasn't quite sure – about the future's market for beef, Carla spotted Nieves slouched in a chair pulled up to a propane heater, tapping away on her phone, looking bored as always. Without anything else to do, Carla decided to head over to say hi.

"How's the cleaning of the mansion going?" she asked.

Nieves shrugged, not even looking up from her phone as her thumbs bobbed and weaved in a blur over the screen. "Keila's got someone else helping her 'cause school's started."

"Someone else?" Carla repeated, surprised. How had she missed this tidbit of information? She thought back to the Early Spinster's meetings, trying to remember if Keila had discussed cleaning out the mansion at one of them and Carla had just forgotten in the meanwhile, when Yesenia came hurrying over with a huge smile on her face. "Hi, Carla!" she said enthusiastically, giving Carla a big hug. "I'm so glad you could come tonight. How are things going?"

"Good, good," Carla said automatically. "How is school?"

Yesenia rolled her eyes. "If I could just find one person to explain to me how organic chemistry will help me teach new immigrants how to speak English, I'd be a lot more enthused about the class. As it is, it's kicking my ass. Either I graduate, or I go nuts."

"How much longer do you have?" Carla asked, knowing the answer but politely acting as if she didn't have the date burned into her brain.

"May of 2024," Yesenia said glumly. "Not that I'm counting or anything, but that's three years and six months from now. I could give you down to the day, if you really wanted to know."

Carla chuckled even as she gave her young friend a one-armed hug. "It's hard, I know. It'll all be worth it, though. Just think about all of the people you're going to be able to help once you're a teacher." She didn't breathe a word about how much easier life would be if Yesenia wasn't attending college and Christian wasn't her primary support for tuition. Her friend would never know how difficult this made Carla and

Christian's lives; she would never accept the help if she knew just what a burden it was.

Yesenia's face lit up at the mention of her goal. "Helping others is what I'm passionate about. That's the *only* thing that keeps me going."

Just then, the mariachi music died off and everyone turned to the front porch of the old farmhouse automatically, where Christian's father was standing. Just then, Christian appeared at her side, handing her a hot chocolate. She smiled her thanks at him and snuggled into his side, happy just to be there.

As his father spoke in rapid-fire Spanish, Christian kept up a running translation in Carla's ear. "He says welcome to everyone. Thank you for coming. Tonight is a special night, where we meet our son's girlfriend." A cheer rose up from the crowd and everyone turned to Carla and Christian, laughing and waving and calling out greetings. Carla felt her cheeks go red as she waved back. She was a total people person and loved being around others, but being the sole focus of fifty pairs of eyeballs was a totally different kettle of fish.

"This beautiful woman," Christian said in her ear as his father started up again, "has made my son very happy. Soon, maybe he will pull his head out of his ass and marry her, eh?" The crowd broke out into gales of laughter and more than a few people slapped Christian on the back.

"Now, we eat!" he said in English, and pointed to a long banquet table with what looked like enough food to feed an army or two.

The crowd surged forward and Carla felt herself being swept along with them. She rubbed her belly absentmindedly. Her nausea had calmed down some since she'd first gotten pregnant, but she still wasn't always sure her stomach would cooperate. Throwing up on the bushes would probably not impress anyone. Maybe she'd just stick to the bland rice and beans and skip anything with heat in it.

With Christian's help, Carla picked out some dishes she was

sure she could keep down and then they made their way to one of the folding tables with chairs, settling down to eat. Nieves was already there, looking bored, her boyfriend whispering in her ear, but she just shrugged and kept tapping away on her phone. Carla could only be grateful that she was no longer a teenager. There was nothing about that stage in her life that was appealing to her. Nothing at all.

The Spanish rice was flavorful – much better than anything she'd ever gotten in a Mexican restaurant – and she was just starting to dig into it with gusto when she heard a loud commotion break out. Heads were all turning back to the front, and Carla automatically followed the path of their gaze. It was Christian's father, grabbing at a man who looked just like him. "¡Mi tío!" Christian muttered under his breath.

Carla had at least spent enough time on her Duolingo app to know that *mi tío* meant *my uncle*, but instead of this being a phrase of respect, Christian sounded like he very much wanted to shove his uncle's teeth down his throat.

"Christian?" Carla said uncertainly, putting her hand on Christian's arm. "What's—"

Crash!

His uncle, who'd been waving around drunkenly, did a swan dive off the front porch of the farmhouse, crash landing in a banquet table, food and alcohol flying everywhere.

Christian was out of his chair in a flash, sprinting across the crowded, frozen lawn. Yesenia, who'd just come walking up with a loaded plate of food, sent Carla an apologetic smile and shrug, trying to act as if nothing was wrong. "My uncle…he can sometimes drink too much. He got started pretty early this morning. I was worried—"

The shouting at the front tore Carla's gaze away from Yesenia, just in time to see Christian punch his uncle in the face.

Yeah, this wasn't going so well.

"*No se puede confiar en las gringas. Hermosas pero traicioneras,*" the uncle slurred, and Christian punched him again.

CHAPTER
TWENTY-EIGHT
CHRISTIAN

Life *is* pain. Anyone who says any different is selling something.
~Westley in *The Princess Bride*

"No se puede confiar en las gringas. Hermosas pero traicioneras," Tío Nicolás slurred.

You can't trust white girls. Pretty but treacherous.

Even as Christian drove his fist into his uncle's nose again, feeling the crunch of it satisfying beneath his knuckles, he could only hope that Carla hadn't been spending too much time on her Duolingo app. It was bad enough that his uncle was a drunk. It was bad enough that his uncle fell off the front porch of the house and into a table of food and drink. It was bad enough that Christian was punching his uncle during a family dinner.

The love of his life didn't need to hear his uncle's asshole view of her too.

Papá grabbed the front of *Tío* Nicolás' dress shirt, the decorative sequins popping off and sailing across the yard as he hauled him to his feet. Telling his brother just what an ass he thought he was in rather detailed Spanish that Christian very much hoped his mother couldn't hear, *Papá* hauled his brother up and into the house, most likely to dunk his head under some ice cold water. *Tío* Nicolás kept shouting slurs even as he was being pulled away, and Christian contemplated "helping" his father sober his uncle up. He would be all too happy to push his uncle's head under a stream of cold water. Repeatedly, if he could get away with it.

He had more important things to do, though. Searching through the crowd, he felt terror flow through his veins. What would Carla think of his family? He'd met her family. They'd been nice. Normal. Not a single fist fight in sight. What would she think of him?

Duh. The only thing she *could* think of him at this point: He was definitely *not* the man she'd want to marry, and she was probably already deeply regretting getting pregnant with his baby.

The shock was starting to set in. He'd acted instinctively when he saw what was happening. His uncle was always an ass who drank too much, but his father had *promised* Christian that he'd keep his youngest brother under control today.

He didn't know why he'd believed his father. He'd never been able to keep his youngest brother under control before. Why would today be any different?

But the racial slurs against Carla? That was a step too far, even for *Tío* Nicolás.

He had to find Carla. Where was she? He ignored the calls and questions from people as he pushed through them, his eyes hungry only for her.

What was I thinking, agreeing to this? But even if I hadn't, I couldn't have hidden Carla from mi tío *for the rest of her life. He's always at* Mamá *and* Papá's *house, either getting drunk or sleeping off a drinking binge. Sure, like* Mamá *always says, it's better that he's sleeping it off on the couch than driving home, but this—*

Suddenly, he felt someone touching the small of his back and he jumped, letting out a rather heated Spanish cuss word even as he spun in a circle, not sure if he was about to punch someone or hug 'em.

"Oh. Carla," he said, weak with relief, and then pulled her into his arms. "I can't believe...I'm so sorry. So sorry." He rubbed his nose across the top of her head, breathing in her scent. *She's here. She's still with me. It's going to be okay.* "I didn't expect – I didn't think my uncle would get so damn drunk, he'd fall onto a *table*. And what he said about yo—" With a rush of dread, he cut himself off, but it was too late.

"Oh," she said quietly, pulling back just a smidge to look up at him, her big blue eyes swimming with unshed tears. "I wasn't...wasn't actually sure what he said. So he *was* talking about—"

"Don't worry about it," Christian cut her off sharply, pulling her against his chest, stroking his hands down her back. He had to prove to his racing heart that she really was fine. That she was still choosing to be in his arms, despite what had just happened. "My uncle is a bastard. He's the baby of the family and somehow, after all these years, he *still* hasn't grown up."

Carla was melting into his arms then, her curves molding into his chest, tears wetting his shirt.

Dammit.

Carla was crying.

His urge to strangle his uncle was only getting stronger by the moment.

"Is everything okay?" his *mamá* asked, hurrying up to them. "Your *papá*, he push Nicolás' head under the water." Christian sent her a grateful smile for her attempts to speak English for Carla's benefit. It wasn't a language she'd ever really mastered, but she was doing her best.

Mamá didn't notice his smile, though, her attention on the obviously distraught Carla. "Is okay," she crooned, patting Carla on the arm. "My husband's brother...he not a good guy. Do not think about him no more."

"I'm...I'm sorry," Carla said, pulling away from Christian

and wiping her eyes. "*Lo siento*," she added for his *mamá's* benefit.

Look at that. All of those months of working with Duolingo is starting to pay off.

"I just seem to be more...emotional than usual." She shot a pleading look at Christian, and he knew what her problem was. Tonight's dinner was supposed to be their big announcement, when they told everyone the happy news.

Fist fights do tend to put a damper on parties...

Christian hesitated, torn on what to do. He knew his mother would be delighted to hear the good news, but also knew she couldn't keep a secret to save her life. If he told her, half the people at the party would know within five minutes, but that was only because the other half would've found out within two.

Before he could decide if they should move forward with their announcement or not – save this party somehow – *Tío* Nicolás came stumbling back out of the house.

Oh no. No, no, no, no.

Nicolás' hair was wet and in his hand was a cup of coffee instead of a beer can, but he otherwise looked exactly the same.

Not a bit more sober.

"*Hermanito*," his dad said consolingly, coming up from behind, wrapping his arm around his youngest brother's shoulders. "*Volvamos adentro.*"

Carla looked up at him, clearly not understanding that last part. "Let's go back inside," Christian translated in a whisper in her ear. "Honestly, when my uncle's this far gone, he usually passes out. If my dad can just get him into the house and into a bed…"

But *Tío* Nicolás shrugged his brother's arm off his shoulders. "*Niño estúpido*," he spat at Christian. His eyes flicked back and forth between Carla and Christian, and in that moment, Christian was sure that his *tío* would've attacked Carla if they'd been alone together. His blood rain ice-cold in his veins at the realization. "*Enamorarse de una mujer blanca. Tú no eres mi sobrino.*"

Stupid kid. Falling for a white woman. You are no nephew of mine.

Christian shook his head like a boxer after too many rounds in the boxing ring. This couldn't be right. This couldn't be real.

His uncle had always been an asshole of the first degree, sure, and he'd always talked about *that* woman who'd killed his family, who'd taken everything away from him, but somehow, Christian had missed the fact that his uncle hated *all* white women.

Was this new? Or had he just ignored all of the signs?

A strangled yip fell from Carla's lips and Christian realized in a vague sort of way that he was the cause of it. He'd wrapped his fingers around her upper arm and then had squeezed, anger blocking everything else out. "I'm sorry, I'm sorry," he whispered. "I didn't mean to…" He stroked his fingers over the bruised area, promising to himself that he'd kiss every one of those bruises better. Later.

Right now, he just had to face down his uncle. He looked at the wavering, stumbling man on his parent's front porch and said calmly, "*No eres tío mío.*"

You are no uncle of mine.

The whole crowd gasped, and Christian felt the back of his neck grow hot. For a moment, he'd forgotten they had an audience. He wanted to punch his *tío* again just for this.

The gossip about tonight would go on for years to come. No one spoke to their elders this way.

No one disowned their own family.

But if Christian had to choose between Carla or *Tío* Nicolás? He'd choose Carla every time.

Christian's denunciation took a moment to register and work their way through Nicolás' alcohol-pickled brain, but finally, he realized that Christian'd thrown his words right back in his face.

He slurred out a few nasty Spanish swear words – language

that would normally have his mother up in arms and yelling but in that moment, she seemed just as frozen as everyone else – and then with what he probably thought was grace and dignity, he pivoted on his boot, almost slamming into the side of the house, and barely made it through the front door, *Papá* swinging the door out of the way at just the last moment.

A silence fell over the crowd then. Even the barking dogs that normally kept up a constant stream of barks and growls during a family dinner had shut the hell up. Every person was staring at him.

Everyone, even Carla.

Oh, God. *Carla.* What had she understood? What had she picked up? What was she thinking?

Thank God she hadn't asked for a running translation of everything that had just been said. The emotion in the air told her all that she needed to know, he was sure of it.

His arm around Carla's shoulders, he steered her through the eerily quiet crowd, everyone still staring.

Christian just wanted out, he wanted out of there, and he wanted it *right now*. He felt his breath growing rapid, his heart racing. He wanted to go. He needed to be free of the eyes, free of the stares.

Carla stumbled a few times but kept up with him, her arm tight around his waist, using him to hold herself up. She was still there. She hadn't left him. Not yet, anyway.

God only knew that she should.

CHAPTER
TWENTY-NINE

CARLA

My name is Inigo Montoya. You killed my father. Prepare to die.
~Inigo in *The Princess Bride*

CARLA WAS SHAKING and the occasional tear still trickled down her cheek. This was stupid. This was infuriating.

She wasn't normally one to weep like a heroine in a bad novel. Sure, she cried at sad movies – and happy ones, for that matter – and she hated conflict with all her might, so today was officially the first time she'd ever witnessed a fist fight, but still…

It had to be the hormones. She'd heard that when a woman was pregnant, she was more emotional, but it was one thing to hear that and quite another thing to be living through it.

Christian drove them to his single-wide, leading her through to the bedroom, undressing her with delicate movements, so obviously worried that she was going to shatter into a million pieces at any moment. She wanted to tell him that she was fine – she might've even murmured that at one point – but she surely didn't feel fine.

He pulled back the covers, helping her to lay down, and

then spooned her from behind, stroking his hand down her arm, whispering, telling her how much he loved her. How much he loved the baby.

Oh God. The baby.

Could she bring a baby into this dysfunctional family? Christian's uncle seemed to hate her simply because of her skin color. Would he hate their baby too?

"Why does your uncle hate white women?" Carla asked quietly into the semi-darkness of the room. It was night now, but neither of them had bothered to turn on a lamp. She wanted the darkness anyway. She wanted to hide from the world in the circle of Christian's arms, and never come out again.

Christian let out a heavy sigh, ruffling Carla's hair with his warm breath.

"I didn't know he did until tonight, actually," he admitted. "I was worried about him getting drunk off his ass. After all, that's just a typical Saturday night for him. Or Tuesday night, for that matter. My dad was supposed to be slowing him down – giving him water and lemonade to drink between beers – but Yesenia said that he started as soon as he woke up this morning. My dad's best efforts didn't do a damn thing. I do have to say that falling off the front porch and into a table of food is a new low for him." He chuckled humorlessly. "He won't even remember this tomorrow. He won't even remember the party, I'm sure of it. He'll call us liars when we tell him he fell off the front porch. He's…"

Christian let out another heavy sigh, like the weight of the world was on his shoulders. "He's not only an alcoholic, he's what alcoholics aspire to be when they grow up. He has his favorite beer – Corona, in case you're curious – but he'll drink *anything*. My parents tried to help him quit one time, until they found him drinking the cough syrup."

"What?" she interrupted, startled. "Why cough syrup?"

"Brands like Nyquil? Some of their products are 25% alcohol," Christian said with a dry chuckle.

"Wuuuhhh..." Carla had no words. No intelligible words, anyway. "That's craziness."

"Well, after the cough syrup incident, my parents decided they'd allow him to drink all he wanted at their house. As long as he's not on the road, maybe risking his life or someone else's behind the wheel, they're happy. And he's happy, because my mom takes care of him. Laundry, meals...you name it, she does it for him. He still has his own place, but he's rarely there. Life at my parent's house is the easy street for him. Not for the rest of us, though, because now we have to live with him. Thank God for my job here on the Miller farm, so I have my own place. I'm not in the thick of it all the time like Nieves and Yesenia are."

"Sooo..." Carla said hesitantly, not sure how to point out the obvious without being too blunt, "what does this have to do with him hating me because of my skin color?"

"Right. Like I said, I didn't know that he hated *all* white women. I just thought he hated *her*. The woman who killed his family."

Carla froze. She couldn't breathe. *Killed...?*

"Not with an ax or something," Christian said quickly. "She was driving. Not paying attention. She drifted into oncoming traffic and hit my aunt's van head on. *Tía* Gabriela died instantly. My cousins lasted a few days but they hadn't been buckled in. You know how it was in the 1980's. Buckling up every time you got into a vehicle...it just wasn't strict back then like it is now. They were thrown from the van. Even if they'd lived, they would've been vegetables. I was just a toddler when it happened. I don't remember his wife, or his kids. Two boys. I'm sure we played together, but..."

He trailed off then, and Carla let him hold her and simply be for a moment. Even if he didn't remember this, to lose two cousins and an aunt...

"I think that alone would've done my uncle in. But then, the county prosecutor decided not to go after the white woman. She was the wife of the bank president in town. My aunt and cousins were the relations of a poor Mexican family. The woman was sorry, and wasn't that enough? It caused her a lot of trauma. Why, she had to go to therapy and everything!"

Carla snorted with horrified laughter. It wasn't funny. Not funny in the slightest.

But the way he said it…

"My uncle has always ranted and raved about *that* woman. *She* destroyed his family. *She* ruined his life. I really thought he hated only her. I didn't know…If there were signs that it spread beyond that to all white women in general, I missed it. When I was a kid, I called him The Snake – *el Serpiente* – in my mind. Quick to strike, and mean as a rattlesnake. I learned to stay out of his way early on. I'd always wondered if he was this mean his whole life, or if he'd changed because of the wreck and losing his family overnight. My father…" He sighed. "He always makes excuses for him. It doesn't matter what he does or who he hurts, my *papá* will say that it isn't Nicolás' fault. Nicolás is the youngest of the family, and somehow, despite pushing 60, he still hasn't grown up. He's still the baby."

Carla listened, worry growing inside of her as Christian spoke. No matter how sad his uncle's story was – and it was heartbreaking – Carla couldn't let him hurt her child. She would *never* allow that man around her children, no matter who he was related to.

"He can't be around our kids," Carla said softly, liking the sound of *kids*. As in, more than one. Would they have more children? God, she hoped so. She wanted a whole passel. "Our kids are going to be half-white. He's going to hate them, isn't he." It was a statement, not a question, but still, Christian paused and then nodded, his nose rubbing against the back of her head with the movement.

"I wouldn't have said yes before tonight. But now that I've seen him…I never thought he'd disown me. I'm the only son of his favorite brother. The few times in my life that he was nice to me, he told me that I looked like his younger son before the wreck. He says we have the same smile. It's the only kind thing he's ever said to me, but I still didn't expect...Damn, I was stupid to agree to this party. *Tonto*. I don't know why I believed my father when he promised that he'd make my uncle behave."

"It was a nice party," Carla said loyally. "Before..." She waved her hand in the air, encompassing the whole fight. "That," she finished lamely. "Why are you talking about the Lone Ranger, though?"

"The what?" The bewilderment was clear in his voice.

"You said Tonto. That was the Lone Ranger's companion in those movies."

He started shaking in his belly and then a roar of laughter came pouring from his lips. "I'm sorry," he gasped. "It never occurred to me...*Tonto* means fool in Spanish. I was calling myself a fool."

"Oooohhhh..." she said. "That makes a lot more sense." She turned in his arms to face him. She was done dealing with the hurt. The anger. The difficulties of life and family. She wanted to do something else. Or, to be more specific, someone else. "Well, quit being a *tonto* and kiss me. You've got a naked woman in your arms. You haven't forgotten what to do with one of them already, have you?"

"I was trying to be a gentleman," he protested, even as she leaned forward and slipped the buttons loose on his shirt, bearing his tanned skin to her gaze. She kissed the newly revealed spot, running her tongue over his skin, and he let out a groan. "I...I think I can be persuaded to not be *quite* so gentlemanly, though. If you insist."

"Oh, I insist," she said with a small laugh, undoing another button. Suckling another piece of revealed skin. She wanted to forget about dead children and mean uncles and just *be*.

"You know one of the benefits of me being pregnant is?" Carla whispered as she tugged on his belt, freeing it from its loops.

"No, what?" Christian asked in a breathy whisper, his hands running all over her body.

"No need for a condom! I can't get pregnant twice." She grinned at him for a moment and then went back to undoing the top button of his jeans.

"Right," he groaned, as she unzipped his pants. "Turns out, that's a very, very good benefit."

CHAPTER
THIRTY

CHRISTIAN

This is true love. You think this happens every day?
~Westley in *The Princess Bride*

DECEMBER, 2020

CHRISTIAN DRUMMED his fingers on the counter of the bakery, trying to wait patiently for the customer in front of him to make a decision, but it was a struggle. She was a painfully thin, older woman in town – Mrs. Gehring? Maybe? He was never good with names – whose husband used to be a big farmer. He'd died many years ago and she'd sold the farm and moved to town.

Nice, elderly lady. Sweet. Kind.

And if she didn't pick out a donut in the next 13 seconds, he was going to strangle her.

Finally content with her choice, she worked her way to the front door, cane firmly in hand, waving it at people as she went. Christian worried a bit about her aim – was she going to whack anyone with her cane on the way? – but not *that* worried. He had much more important things to do.

Like buy glazed orange muffins. Ever since Carla got

pregnant, these muffins were the one thing she craved day and night.

"You know," Sugar said conversationally as she bagged up a half dozen of the muffins without even asking him what he wanted, "Carla's the cause of more sales of these muffins than the rest of Long Valley combined together. I had Gage asking me why we were going through them like crazy, and when I told him I thought it was pregnancy cravings, he just laughed and laughed."

She handed the bag over with an expectant smile, clearly hoping he'd dish, but Christian just thanked her and headed for the door. He liked Sugar enough, but there was a reason she worked at a bakery. She was a gossip queen, and he wasn't ready to spill.

This was not something he wanted spreading around town. Not yet.

He shouldn't be surprised that the rumors were already flying, though – Carla did have that special pregnancy glow that he'd always heard people talk about but had never seen in person. His sisters and mother had looked miserable sick when they were pregnant, but Carla…she just looked even more gorgeous than normal.

Which was really saying something.

He drove the few blocks down the street and parked behind the flower shop; he would've just walked the muffins down but parking was limited in front of the bakery, especially now that Cady had opened up the Smoothie Queen next door. He didn't want to hog a spot.

He pushed open the glass front door to Happy Petals, listening to the pleasant tinkle of the bell that said *home* to him, and breathed in the heavily perfumed air. Carla said that she'd long ago become "nose blind" and couldn't smell flowers any longer – apparently something common among florists – but Christian could only hope that'd never happen to him. This smell meant Carla, and Carla meant love.

Looking up, Carla saw who it was and sent him a brilliant smile, heading around the counter and pushing her turquoise-rimmed reading glasses into the pile of hair on top of her head.

"Hi, *bebé*," she said with an excited grin, laying one on him that made him wish that they were in a less public place than her flower shop, and then pulled back, looking concerned. "I didn't realize you'd be coming over early. I don't close for another 30 minutes."

He shrugged. "I wanted to bring these to you now," he held out the bag from the Muffin Man and she let out a squeal of delight, "and figured I could hang around until you close if you're too busy to close up early. I have some exciting news I want to share." He wiggled his eyebrows in what he could only hope was a mysterious way, and she laughed.

"Sadly, Mrs. Panuska is coming over with her daughter to approve the final design for the flowers for the wedding this weekend, so I can't close up early. You could always tell me while we wait for them to show up." She looked up at him hopefully as she peeled the paper off a muffin.

He shook his head, trying to look stern and failing in the face of such naked begging. "Nope. This is an 'after the store closes' kind of conversation."

She looked at him, her mouth screwed up as she tried to decide what on earth the big news could be, when the doorbell jingled and in walked an overbearing woman practically towing a younger woman along behind her. This must be Mrs. Panuska and her daughter. Listening to the woman asking all of the questions, the bride-to-be mute as her mother decided on changes in style and colors, Christian decided the daughter was getting married simply and solely to get out from underneath her mother's thumb.

Tyrannical didn't begin to describe Mrs. Panuska.

Bored, Christian wandered into the back and into Autumn's office. At least, it was what he assumed was her office. It had been the last ten times he'd been to the store. Today, however, it just looked like it was ground zero of some kind of fancy fabric explosion.

"Autumn?" he said hesitantly, not sure if she was even in the room. She pushed her way from behind some boxes, swearing as she went.

"Hey, Christian," she said, pushing her curls out of her face. "Come to help me?"

"Uhhh…sure." He had six sisters and a mom. He was used to being voluntold for all sorts of projects.

"Good. Mrs. Panuska will be here at least another 30 minutes, making sure that Carla has *plenty* of time to question her life choices. In the meanwhile, I need you to help me cut this tulle into 3-foot lengths."

Tool, eh? It doesn't look a damn thing like any tools I've ever used, but sure. Why not.

As they laid out and cut the tulle into 3-foot lengths, Autumn pattered on about her worthless boyfriend, Johnny, and how miserable he was lately, and how that was making her miserable, and life was too short to be miserable, and she sure wished he'd learn how not to be miserable, and Christian was *just* on the verge of asking Autumn why on earth she was still with this guy when Carla popped her head around the corner.

"I wondered if Autumn had put you to work," she said with a grin. "Mrs. Panuska is gone and the front door is locked. You wanna go out for a drive? Or up to my place? Or out to yours…?"

"Let's just head upstairs," Christian said, not wanting to wait another moment to tell Carla the big news. Carla looked surprised for just a moment – she knew how bad his allergies could get if he spent too much time in her apartment, even after all of the allergy shots he'd endured so far – but then shrugged and smiled.

"Okay, but Autumn," she turned to her friend, "if the bed starts a-rockin'—"

"Don't come a-knockin'," Autumn finished. "Do I look like I

was born yesterday? I might just put in earbuds. If I ain't getting any, I don't want to hear anyone else getting any."

As Carla and Christian climbed the stairs, Christian asked in a whisper, "Why is Autumn with Johnny?"

"That, *bebé*, is the $64,000 question," Carla said, putting the bag of muffins on the one open spot on the dresser and eagerly digging one out to eat. Bella was busy rubbing against Carla's legs, meowing her greeting, but for the moment, they both ignored her. "If any of us could see what she saw in him, we'd understand it better. But yeah…they've been together for years, and never have I seen two people be more mismatched in my life. She keeps attending our Early Spinster's Club meetings because she says she's never going to marry Johnny, so…"

Christian felt a hitch in his throat at the mention of marriage.

As strange as it was, they'd never actually talked about marriage. Raising kids and buying a house, sure. But marriage…

Carla was old-fashioned enough that she was probably waiting for him to ask her, or at least for him to be the one to bring it up.

Why the idea of buying a house with someone didn't scare him as much as marrying that person, he wasn't sure. If he was going to marry anyone in the world, it was Carla.

He just wasn't ready to tackle that conversation. Yet.

He side-stepped the topic and dove into why he was there. "So…" he said, sidling past her to sit on the end of the bed and pull Carla up between his legs, "I talked to my parents today."

Her hand stopped halfway to her mouth, a crumb dangling from her upper lip that was absolutely killing Christian to look at. He wanted to suck it off. Thinking with Carla Grahame around? Virtually impossible.

"Yeah?" she said cautiously. "And how did that go?"

He began stroking his hands up and down her glorious thighs and ass. If he couldn't kiss her, he could at least be feeling her up.

"I told 'em the good news. Told 'em you were pregnant. My mom cried."

"Happy tears or sad tears?" Carla asked instantly. Her tongue flicked out and picked up the stray crumb. *Dammit*.

"Happy," he said, working hard to keep his mind focused, despite the distraction that was Carla Grahame. "Honestly? I really believe my parents thought I was gay," he said with a low chuckle. "After all, I'm 38 and have never been married. To know that I really do like girls and all of their fun parts makes my pretty conservative parents *very* happy. Plus, our kids will have the Palacios last name, unlike all of my sister's kids. That sort of thing is damn important to my father."

Carla nodded slowly, but didn't say anything. He couldn't tell what she was thinking. He was dying to ask her, but also wanted to give her the *really* terrific news.

He decided to go for terrific first. Then he could figure out what was going on.

"After Mom cried her happy tears, I laid out the ultimatum. We will never bring our children around if my uncle is there, too. Period. My dad quickly said he'd talk to my uncle about this and straighten him out."

"Do you think that'll help?" Carla asked cautiously, a crease between her gracefully arched eyebrows.

"Not at all," Christian said cheerfully. "Fortunately for us, my mom wasn't born yesterday. When my dad said that he'd talk to his brother, my mom jumped all over him. Said that *she* was gonna talk to Nicolás and if he didn't straighten up, she was done with him. She wouldn't have him in her house 'no more.'"

Christian's smile broke into a laugh at the memory. "My mom is so sweet. You have to know, she doesn't *ever* talk to my dad that way. So when she started into this, he just sat there, his mouth opening and closing like a fish out of water. I swear I could see him gasping for breath. I think Mom's hated my uncle's drinking for a long time, and hasn't wanted him at their house, getting drunk all the time, but…"

He ran his hand through his hair distractedly. This was something he wasn't particularly proud of, and when it came to his kids, was not something he would stand for. Luckily, he was sure Carla was on the same page with him.

"You know how the traditional Hispanic culture is," he finally said. "My dad is the one in charge, so she goes along with whatever 'the man of the house' says. Younger Latinx aren't this way, but the older generation…"

He trailed off for a moment, and then decided that this wasn't the time to discuss women's rights in a very traditional household. "So here, she'd finally been handed her chance, and she grabbed it with both hands. She laid down the law; told my dad that *no one* was going to stand between her and her grandbaby. I really think my dad finally agreed just so my mom would stop spitting nails at him."

He laughed again. Honestly, the look on his father's face…
Priceless.

"Is…ummm…is your dad actually going to be okay with this?" Carla asked, not so much as even cracking a smile. She normally had an easy laugh, and the fact that she wasn't finding the humor in this like he was, caused a tiny splinter of worry to appear. "Do you think he's going to resent me for making him choose between his brother and his grandchild?"

And with that, the splinter grew into a small tree, and he sobered up. It was a damn good point, as much as Christian hated to admit it.

Still, he shrugged. "It'll be fine," he said confidently, not ready for anyone to rain on his parade. "My mom rarely puts her foot down like that, so he knows she means it when she does. He won't want to piss her off by fighting her on it. He wants sex again this century, sooo…"

He winked at Carla. She blushed and shook her head.

"Is sex the only thing that men think about?" she asked rhetorically.

"No, of course not!" Christian contested hotly. "We also think about how to get *more* sex. See? Totally different topic."

Carla threw back her head and laughed. "Of course," she said dryly, when she could finally talk again. "Excellent point. I don't know what I was thinking."

"But I bet you can guess what *I'm* thinking," Christian said with a naughty wiggle of his eyebrows, squeezing her plump ass with both hands. Oh, she had an ass to die for.

And after that, there was a lot more kissing and a lot less talking.

CHAPTER
THIRTY-ONE

CARLA

Look. Are you just fiddling around with me or what?
~Westley in *The Princess Bride*

CHRISTMAS EVE, 2020

CARLA PULLED THE FLOWERS out of the vase with a grumpy sigh and then started stabbing them back into place one at a time, trying to keep her mind on her work. Was it pregnancy hormones that were making it so hard for her to concentrate?

Sure. She'd blame it on that.

Except for the part where Christian was just...off. Weird. Not acting right.

He'd come over the night before and they'd looked at real estate listings together online – a hobby that was quickly developing into an obsession. She enjoyed looking at the listings and dreaming together with Christian about their life to come, but at the same time, it was heart-wrenching.

Everything was so expensive. Stupidly expensive. How were they ever going to afford these kinds of prices?

But last night, in the middle of the usual sighing and

daydreaming and discussions about things that mattered to them (kitchen layouts) and things that did not (having a formal dining room), Christian had been as fidgety as a three-year-old boy stuck listening to an overly long sermon at church.

After the fourth time of asking him if everything was okay, he'd abruptly announced that he had to head home, had given her a kiss on the forehead, and then had headed out.

She'd been left staring at the open doorway of her apartment, listening to him clatter down the stairs and out the door of the flower shop, wondering what on earth was wrong with him.

He hadn't texted her first thing that morning, either. Not even sweet nothings, telling her how sexy he thought her toes were (she *did* have fun with her last paint job) or suggesting godawful names for the baby (no, she was not going to name their baby International – she didn't care how much Christian loved the new Case International tractor that Stetson had bought for the Miller farm).

The radio silence was starting to kill her. Was he messing with her mind on purpose?

But...*why*? That just didn't seem right. Christian wouldn't do that. What was causing this, though, she could not begin to imagine.

With a groan, she stepped back and looked at the bouquet with a critical eye. Better. Not her best, but better than the first disaster she'd thrown together.

Was it so bad that she wanted Christian to propose to her? Yes, she knew she was an empowered woman who could propose just as well as Christian could.

"I am woman, hear me roar," she muttered under her breath as she wrapped the ribbon around the neck of the vase.

And yet...

She wanted the grand romance. Was that so much to ask?

She felt impatience and a bit of righteous indignation boil up inside of her. Dammit all, Christian should know she'd want this. It wasn't like she'd been hiding this fatal flaw of her personality from him.

She wanted a big proposal, and she wanted a house to live in that wasn't an oversized shoebox or an ugly tin can, and she wanted to be married in a dress with a skirt so big, she couldn't fit into her shoebox apartment, and she wanted...

She was snuffling now. *Dammit.* She really, really didn't want to be snuffling. This was ridiculous. It was Christmas Eve, for heaven's sake. She should be happy, and singing carols at the top of her lungs, and drinking way too much hot chocolate.

What if a customer came in and saw her makeup wrecked? She dabbed at the corner of her eyes with a tissue, trying to salvage the hard work she'd put in that morning while getting ready for work. She'd hoped...

Well, what she'd hoped hadn't come true, and it was time to stop being a crybaby.

She tapped her cell phone to check the time – 10:13 am. Maybe Christian was just having a busy day at work, getting ready for the snowstorm the weathermen were all predicting was going to hit that night. Just because every other morning since they'd started dating, he'd sent her a sweet text message, didn't mean that she should read anything into this morning's silence.

She made herself hum a few bars of *Let it Snow.* Tonight's snowstorm would mean a fresh layer of snow for Christmas Day. It really was going to be a picture-perfect Christmas, and she scolded herself for not throwing herself into the Christmas spirit this year like she normally did. She was going to keep the store open until two, just in case anyone wanted to do some *very* last-minute Christmas shopping, and then—

The landline for the business rang, startling her out of her internal pep talk. She reached over the counter and snatched the phone out of the cradle.

"Happy Petals," she answered, a very bright – and very fake – smile pasted on her face. Like anyone with any modicum of customer service training, Carla knew better than to answer the phone with anything less than a brilliant smile on her face.

"Carla Grahame!" Declan half yelled into the phone. She instinctively jerked the phone away from her ear to keep from going deaf.

What on earth…

Declan Miller, a strait-laced, salt-of-the-earth farmer, sounded like he was drunk and giddy as a school girl.

She heard his voice, tinny and distant, spilling out of the speaker, and she jerked the phone back up to her ear. "—bigger than Austin's! *Twice* as big as Austin's! I know Iris loves her blue irises, but this occasion calls for red roses, don't you think? Every red rose in your store. Oh, and Franklin, too!" he added as an afterthought. "I don't want a single red rose left in the Long Valley area after you're done making this bouquet!"

"What, uh, what's the occasion?" she asked as she stood on her tiptoes to grab a notepad, sliding her reading glasses into place and pulling a pen out of the messy bun on top of her head.

"Iris is gonna have a baby!" he crowed. "She's pregnant, can you believe it?! I want every Congratulations balloon in the store too. Everything you've got. Can you deliver? I can't pick them up. I'm on my way to Boise – stupid snowblower decided to kick up a fuss and with that storm coming in, I need to do a part's run, especially before everything closes down for Christmas. Charge it all to my card on file," he added, abruptly switching back to the ordering of flowers. "Just write *I love you, Cookie* on the card. Can you deliver it today? I know it's Christmas Eve, but Iris is over the moon and I hate leaving her and—"

"No problem," Carla broke in, trying to hide the laughter in her voice. If she lived to be a hundred, she'd never hear someone as happy as Declan was in that very moment. "It's getting close to noon, though, and I doubt the florist shop in

Franklin will be open much longer. Is it okay if we just use the red roses I have in stock?"

"What?" he asked, clearly forgetting that he'd ever asked her for something different. "Yes, of course! All the red roses you have. Thank you!"

After he hung up, Carla pulled the receiver away from her ear and stared at it, then began laughing to herself as she hung it up.

Iris is finally pregnant. Holy shit, she's pregnant!

Carla did a little jig, grinning like a fool.

When Carla'd found out back in October that she was pregnant, the guilt had hung over her like a black cloud as soon as the thought had crossed her mind: This was going to hurt Iris.

She'd avoided telling her friend the news. She knew Iris would smile and hug and congratulate her, and then cry herself to sleep that night, cursing her body once again for failing her.

But now...

How far along is she? She clapped her hands with delight. *Our babies will be best friends, or future lovers, I'm just sure of it.*

As Carla gathered up every red rose she had in the store, even going so far as to strip them out of the other pre-made bouquets with the mental note that she needed to replace them, she began planning the wedding of the as-yet unsexed babies.

Iris would have a red-headed baby girl with fair skin and big blue eyes, of course, and Carla would have a baby boy with Christian's caramel skin and chocolate brown eyes, and they'd be beautiful together, and Carla would throw them the biggest party ever held inside the city limits of Sawyer for their wedding.

She got out a monster vase – the size she rarely used, since so few people wanted to pay for a bouquet of that magnitude – and got to creating the most elaborate, the most gorgeous, the most over-the-top bouquet in the history of Happy Petals. Declan was gonna shit a brick when he got the credit card bill for it, but he might be so happy about Iris being pregnant, he might not even notice.

Maybe.

When she stepped outside of the shop, bundled up against the cold, the bouquet cradled safely in her arms, the bite of winter air made her gasp. No matter how long it'd been winter, she never got used to the cold. Every year, she just endured it until spring finally rolled around again.

She got the bouquet to her van mostly by feel, balloons bobbing along above her head, hoping against hope that she didn't fall into a pothole or trip over something on the way. Her normal carrying crate for her creations wasn't set to accommodate Fezzik-sized bouquets, so she had to fiddle with it to get everything strapped in and protected.

With it finally settled and just so, she let out a giant sigh of exhaustion mixed with pride. She didn't remember being so tired all the time before she got pregnant.

She patted her belly with one hand as she steered the van out into the street. "You, *bebé*, are gonna make me as big as a house soon," she said, stroking her stomach.

She'd been able to hide her pregnancy so far because, well, she wasn't stick thin to begin with. But she was just starting to get to that point when smart people would wonder if she was pregnant, but wouldn't ask.

It was the fools who'd open mouth, insert foot.

At Declan's place, she held her breath as she shuffled her way across the frozen gravel and ice and up to the front porch. She had to turn sideways to study the front door and finally spotted the doorbell, which she whacked with her elbow.

As strange as it was, this was actually the first time she'd delivered flowers to her friend. Before, she'd always made sure to have one of her high school kids deliver the flowers. That way, Iris could pretend that Carla didn't know every detail about her personal life, and Carla could happily join in that pretense with her. It was best for all involved.

But today? Today she got to actually give the flowers to her friend, along with a huge hug.

It was 5th grade Carla all over again.

She heard the creak of the door open and then a gasp of shock.

"Carla, is that you in there?" Iris asked, and then burst into tears. "I'm pregnant!" she hollered, and then, "Shit, it's cold out there! Come inside before you let all the heat out."

Carla crab-walked in, trying not to run into Iris (or anything else), and she could hear it in her voice when Iris switched from happy tears to laughter.

"Oh Carla!" she exclaimed, clapping her hands with delight. "Declan told me he was going to order a bouquet that was bigger than the one Austin had ordered for Ivy, but I didn't think it was possible."

"Where, uh, where do you want this?" Carla tried to keep her tone light and happy, and not show how much her arms were struggling under the strain. She was beginning to regret not at least trying to strap the vase to a dolly and carting it around that way.

"Here," Iris said, taking her by the arm with a soft hand and leading her forward. Together with a lot of patting and feeling of the granite counter, they got the vase down and Carla stood back to admire it with a huge grin.

"How much did that—"

"Don't ask," Carla advised her friend.

"Good plan," Iris admitted with a laugh. "Declan is just so happy…we're having a baby!" She said it with wonderment and glee, as if the concept hadn't quite settled in yet.

Carla pulled Iris into a huge hug, feeling how frail her body was now compared to what she remembered in high school. Iris had always been athletic and strong; now she was a frail piece of glass that needed to be protected at all costs.

A thought Carla would never, ever share with her friend.

She'd probably get whacked in the shins for saying something so blasphemous.

"I'm pregnant, too," she whispered into Iris' thick red hair.

"No way!" Iris gasped, pulling back, her blue eyes huge and sparkling. "Congratulations! When are you due?"

"Beginning of April," Carla said, grinning so hard, her cheeks hurt. For the moment, she was able to ignore everything that'd gotten her down just an hour earlier, and celebrate their good luck. "Do you know yet when you're due?"

Iris shook her head. "I have a doctor's appointment on Monday, but we're thinking somewhere towards the end of July."

"I've decided that our kids will either be best friends or marry each other," Carla said with a conspiratorial grin. "I made that decision while I was putting this bouquet together."

Iris let out a belly laugh. "I love how you think! Better yet, be best friends *who* marry each other!"

"Exactly!" Carla crowed. "We've got their lives all figured out. Now it's just time to get these babies out in the world. But! Not right now." She patted her stomach. "I still need to find a home for you first," she told her belly. "Plus, I think you still need to grow some good lungs and lots of other important body parts."

"Where does Christian live?" Iris asked as she turned back towards the kitchen counter, burying her nose in the bouquet and breathing in deep. Carla grinned to herself. She loved seeing someone enjoy her flowers; it made her heart so damn happy.

But at the same time, Iris' question was kicking over a hornet's nest, and her friend had no idea she was even doing it.

"Umm…" Carla said, stalling for time, trying to think of the best possible light to paint Christian's living situation in, that could still be considered the truth. "He's the foreman for Stetson, of course, and Stetson has some, uh, company housing he lives in."

Iris straightened up, nodding her understanding, and Carla could see it in her eyes – she *did* understand. She knew "company housing" was a euphemism for "ugly tin cans."

Clearly casting about for a different topic, Iris asked brightly, "So! Are you two getting married?"

Carla tried not to openly wince. If possible, this was an even worse topic than Christian's living situation.

"He hasn't...well, he hasn't asked yet." Like the pendulum on a clock, her emotions immediately veered from ecstatic to depressed. *Dammit!* She didn't used to be an emotional wreck. She was definitely blaming pregnancy hormones for this new delightful personality quirk. "I'm sure he's just trying to come up with the right words," she rushed on. "It's a lot, you know? Bucko here wasn't on purpose." She rubbed her stomach. "I don't know—"

Iris put her hand on Carla's arm, and she stopped her insane babbling.

"Christian's a good guy," Iris said softly. "You two will get it figured out, I'm sure. And," she said, brightening up, "with Christian working for Stetson, and Declan being Stetson's older – and he'd definitely say better-looking brother," she winked, "you're practically one of the sister-in-laws now. We'll invite you over for our commiserating parties, where we drink bottles of wine and complain to each other about how the Miller brothers never seem to manage to get their dirty socks into the hamper. And, none of them know how to cook worth a damn. Luckily for Jennifer, she has Carmelita so she doesn't have to cook either, but Abby and I..." She let out a long-suffering sigh. "It's damn good they're such good-lookin' guys. That's all I'm saying."

Carla laughed at that. She knew Iris was deeply and completely in love with Declan, dirty clothes on the floor or not.

"Well," Carla said with a regretful sigh, pushing away from the kitchen counter and heading for the door, "I need to go shut down the shop. Merry Christmas, my dear." They hugged, and then Carla opened up the front door, sucking in a lungful of freezing air that set off a round of coughing.

Winter in Idaho. Why do I live here again?

She crunched down the sidewalk and to her turquoise van, waving back towards the house one more time before sliding inside. She turned the key and sat waiting for a minute for the engine to warm up.

Almost noon. She'd told herself that she'd keep the shop open until two, but now…the two hours stretched bleakly out in front of her.

She shifted the van into gear and crunched forward over the frozen tracks of ice and snow that would cling to the streets of Sawyer until spring.

It was time to go back to the shop and while she counted down the two remaining hours, she'd figure out what to eat for dinner. Somehow, they'd overlooked discussing Christmas Eve before now, and after he'd practically ran out of her apartment last night like his ass was on fire, she wasn't particularly inclined to beg him for a dinner date.

But to spend Christmas Eve by herself? Her parents had invited her and Christian over, of course, but she'd turned them down, telling them that she and Christian had plans.

She didn't want to call them back and admit the truth.

When she got into the shop, she dropped onto the beat-up couch in the back room and began petting Leo, the dim afternoon lighting of a wintry day the only illumination.

Faith. She needed to have faith in Christian.

She snuffled a little, trying to hold back the tears.

Unfortunately, faith was a little scarce on the ground at the moment.

CHAPTER
THIRTY-TWO
CHRISTIAN

And as they reached for each other— Nah, it's kissing again.
You don't want to hear that.
~Grandfather in *The Princess Bride*

T HROW UP or let out a whoop of excitement.

Those were his options, and as far as he could tell, he was on a razor-thin blade between the two of them.

"Good luck!" Jennifer called down the hallway of the old Miller homestead as he headed for the front door, and he could've sworn he heard laughter in her voice. Somewhere in the depths of his soul – *way* deep down – he could vaguely appreciate how someone on the outside might consider what he was about to do to be cute. Adorable. Something to cheer about.

From his point of view, though…

He white-knuckled the steering wheel all the way back to town, and not just because of the icy roads. Hell. He'd lived in Sawyer, Idaho all his life. Icy roads didn't make him hold onto the steering wheel as if it was his only lifeline.

Breathe in. Breathe out.

It was going to be fine. Carla loved him. She loved their

baby. She wanted to be with him. Just because this baby wasn't planned didn't mean it wasn't wanted.

"Don't screw this up, big brother." It'd been the parting words of Yesenia last night. "She's the best thing that's ever happened to you."

As if that was news to him. He already knew Carla was so far out of his league, they might as well be in different galaxies, but somehow, she hadn't figured that out yet and from what he could tell, wasn't prone to thinking that way.

Which he considered to be nothing short of a minor miracle.

He crunched through the ice and snow to a stop in front of Happy Petals, relieved to see Autumn's little Toyota sitting there.

She'd remembered. Autumn had said she wouldn't miss this for the world, but still…Seeing her car there allowed Christian to suck in his first full breath in days.

Things were coming together…whether into a nuclear explosion or a fireworks display of happiness was still up for debate.

A coin toss, honestly.

He reached over into the passenger seat and grabbed the paperback copy of *As You Wish*, a behind-the-scenes book written by the guy who'd played Westley in *The Princess Bride*, and stuffed it into the console to hide it. He'd talk Yesenia into wrapping it up with a pretty bow for him tonight. His wrapping skills were…lacking, to say the least. He was crossing his fingers that Carla had never read the book; at least, he'd never seen a copy of the book anywhere and had never heard her refer to it. If she already owned five copies of it, he'd be shit outta luck.

He pulled open the front door to Happy Petals, the warmth and sweet floral smell filling his nostrils, calming him just a little.

He was home.

Carla looked up, her perfunctory greeting dying on her lips.

"*¡Bebé!*" she called out, the joy clear in her voice. She shoved the pen she'd been writing with into the bun on top of her head along with her reading glasses, and hurried over to him. "I didn't know if…"

She trailed off as she got within arm's reach of him, eyes huge and shadowed with worry as she nibbled uncertainly on her bottom lip. He gently tugged her forward, wrapping his arms around her waist and snuggling her curves against him.

Oh, she felt amazing. He closed his eyes and drew in a deep, steadying breath, feeling like a homeless man walking into a shelter after years of wandering out in the bitter cold. He wondered if he'd ever grow tired of pulling her against his body after a long day's work.

He couldn't see how.

"You didn't know if…?" he murmured huskily as he placed a trail of kisses at her temple and down her neck.

"You…you didn't text me this morning," she said in a breathy whisper as she tilted her neck further, begging without words for his touch. "After last night, I didn't know…"

He stopped for just a moment, the pain in his heart a searing jab that made him gasp for air.

He was such a bastard. He'd let Carla worry all night, and all of today just for some ill-conceived attempt to make what he was about to do more romantic.

He buried his face in the crook of her neck and let out a sigh. "You're worth ten of me, you know that?" he murmured against her skin. "I have a whole lifetime to learn how not to be quite such a douche canoe, but I'm afraid I've got—"

"A douche *what*?" Carla asked, pulling back and bursting out into laughter. Her hazel eyes, ever shifting between blue and green, were sparkling with light, the shadows he'd spotted when he'd first came in already fading away.

"Nieves taught me that one," he said dryly. "Apparently, calling someone a douche canoe is all the rage at Sawyer High School right now."

Her shoulders began to shake as she shook her head. "There isn't enough money in the world to make me agree to be a teenager again," she said baldly.

"Agreed." He looked past Carla and into the depths of the store. "Autumn, you got this?" he hollered.

Carla shot him a disapproving look, no doubt wondering where his manners were at, but Autumn appeared in the doorway to her closet-cum-office, curls bouncing as she shot him a go-get-'em grin. "Yuppers. I'll man the joint until two o'clock straight up, and then I'm heading to the Kingsley place. I'm spending the evening with Kimber, Rex, and their baby Iris. If I'm *real* lucky, I might get a goober kiss from Iris on the cheek."

"What about Johnny?" Carla asked, and Autumn shrugged.

"He's doing his own thing," she said cryptically.

Carla turned in Christian's arms to look back up at him. "Why, pray tell, is Autumn watching over the store for another hour? And when was anyone going to ask me what my thoughts were on the topic?"

"Right about never or so. You can't ask someone if they'd like to be surprised by you. It rather takes out the 'surprise' part of things."

Carla shot him a skeptical look, and then let out a long-suffering sigh. "I suppose…if you put it like that…" She turned back to Autumn. "Merry Christmas, my friend. Tell the Kingsley family a Merry Christmas to them too. Is Mike joining you guys?"

"Pshaw," she scoffed. "You think that man would miss his granddaughter's second Christmas Eve? I've never seen a man so thoroughly wrapped around the pinky of a little girl before. She just has to bat her baby blues, and he's jumping right to it."

As Christian helped Carla into her thick winter coat and scarf, he wondered for the hundredth time if they were going to have a little girl or a little boy. If his own family was anything to judge by, he was gonna be wrapped around the pinkies of a whole lot of little baby girls over the coming years.

That was, *if* everything went to plan, and the nuclear explosion didn't happen instead.

He swallowed hard. It'd be fine. Everything would be fine.

He gripped Carla's elbow tightly in his hand, his other arm around her waist, as they crossed over to his truck. He really needed to come spread more salt on the sidewalks. This ice and snow was *not* okay for his Carla to be walking on.

After he got her settled in, he hurried around and got the truck started, waiting for a moment for it to warm up. The skies were a dark, ominous gray, and Christian was sure the weather forecast was spot on for once. He could feel it in his bones – this was going to be a hell of a storm. He'd better get Carla out and back again before things got really nuts.

As he backed out into the street, Carla spoke up. "So, good news!" she said brightly. "Do you remember that time we were up in the mountains and I told you about the couple who couldn't get pregnant?"

"Oh, I remember that," Christian said with a lustful laugh. "I will *never* forget that."

"Not the part where we had sex," Carla said, laughing and slapping at his arm as he rolled to a stop, checked both ways, and turned right. They were out of town now, and well on their way to the Miller farm. If she kept talking, maybe she wouldn't notice where they were going, and that'd make up for him forgetting to find a blindfold for the drive.

"Well, anyway, she's pregnant!" she said triumphantly. "Her husband called me and asked me to deliver the biggest bouquet in the history of ever, so I drove it over this morning. I love that part of my job. More than anything else, sharing in that…" She sent him a joyful smile, so beautiful his heart hurt.

He reached over and squeezed her hand. "This is why you're everyone's favorite florist," he said, taking another right.

Almost there... "You genuinely care about other people. Do you know how rare that is?"

She shrugged, running her fingers up his arm idly as they talked. "It's not hard to do. I don't know how *not* to care," she said. "I'd have to be turned to stone."

Typical Carla. She'd acknowledge that she was unique – special and kind and amazing – right about the time she chopped off her nose. That was okay. He had the rest of his life to keep telling her.

They passed the main farmhouse but instead of continuing to the back of the property where the single-wide trailers were lined up, Christian took a right down a two-track dirt road, the ruts jerking the steering wheel out of his hands. He pulled his right hand away from Carla with a sigh and white-knuckled both hands on the steering wheel instead. *Job number one: Fix this damn road.*

"What are we..." she got out, half-shouting in an attempt to be heard as they bounced from one rut to another. "Where are we going?" He didn't blame her for asking. The view at the moment wasn't inspiring – icy and frozen; in the grip of winter. A few scattered pine trees added a dull green to the view, but it was otherwise only bare trunks and limbs of deciduous trees stark against the sky – a jungle of tans, browns, grays, and white as far as the eye could see.

"We're almost there," Christian called back over the rattling. This wasn't an answer to her question at all, of course, but he wasn't ready to tell her *quite* yet. "The road turns here..."

The ruts made a large grand swoop to the left, opening up the view to a meadow. It was beautiful here during the summertime – Christian had chased plenty of cows through it to know how green and lush and gorgeous it would be in about five months.

He pulled to a stop and put the truck into park, but didn't cut the engine. He wanted the heat running.

"Jennifer and Stetson are giving this to us," he said softly. "As our wedding present."

Carla whipped her head around so fast to stare at him, eyes huge with shock, she was probably going to need a visit to the chiropractor after this.

"Giving…wedding present…" she whispered.

He pulled the simple gold band out of the pocket of his shirt. "Carla Grahame, will you marry me?" he asked, his nerves on fire. Now was the nuclear explosion…

Or the fireworks display.

"Yes!" she shouted, launching herself across the console at him, raining kisses, tears streaming down her face. "Yes, I'll marry you," she sobbed, veering wildly between tears and laughter.

It took a moment – or maybe a year – for her words to register.

She said yes.

She said yes!

The fireworks exploding, he poured his heart into his kisses, trying to show her without words how much she meant to him. How much he loved her. How she completed him.

Slowly, he forced himself to pull back. He wanted to see it on her finger.

"Can I?" he whispered, holding the gold band between his thumb and forefinger. "It's not what you deserve – you should have a 10-carat diamond—"

"Shhhh…" she said, pressing her finger against his lips. "I love jewelry – you know I do. But we have so many important things to focus on right now. A gaudy ring that will just get caught on everything? *Not* at the top of that list. I couldn't wear a huge diamond ring at work anyway. Can you imagine the cleaning regimen? I'd have to scrub the prongs every night to get the dead and slimy leaves out of it."

He laughed even as his hands trembled, trying to slide the

ring onto her finger. She took pity on him and slid it the rest of the way onto her finger herself.

"I borrowed one of your rings," he admitted with a guilty twinge, digging the costume jewelry out of his pocket. It'd been a ring she'd worn often on their dates – although never while at work – so he'd known when he'd pocketed it that it was a ring that actually fit her.

"There it is!" she gasped, her eyes lighting up with relief. "I've been blaming Bella for knocking it underneath the bed or something. You owe Bella an apology," she scolded him. "I've been telling her what a bad kitty she is for weeks now."

He reached out and stroked his hand against her soft cheek. "I'll bring her a can of tuna to make up for it," he promised. "Are you ready to see Jennifer and Stetson's wedding present to us?"

"Oh!" she squealed. "I forgot! Someone," she tapped him on the chest, "proposed marriage to me, and I plain forgot about the rest."

"I'll take that as a compliment," he said with a weak laugh. Now that she'd said yes, his limbs felt rubbery, like he was trying to keep himself upright with muscles that hadn't been used in years. He turned the truck off. "Let's go for a little walk."

He helped her out of the truck and then pulled her against his side – a warmth he'd *never* get enough of spreading through him at the simple touch – as they followed a little deer trail through the center of the clearing.

"I know it's dead and brown right now," he said, his breath coming out in puffs that encircled his head, "but come spring, it's beautiful here. Stetson told me that he'd always thought this piece of property deserved to be sold off and enjoyed by someone, or maybe he'd build a summerhouse here, but it didn't make sense to spend a bunch of money to build a house less than a mile away from his own, and he was worried about selling it to someone who'd be a shitty neighbor. His grandfather bought this parcel years and years ago when it came up for sale so he could keep people from building a house out here."

They turned in a slow circle so Carla could take it in fully.

"Whoa," she whispered. "How much land is there?"

"A little over two acres. Most of it is overgrown and unaccessible, but we can build paths through it if we'd like."

"But…where are we going to *live*?" Carla asked. "I don't want to sound ungrateful!" she hurried on. "It's so sweet of them to give us this property, but there isn't a house—"

"I've talked to Georgia over at the credit union." He gave her a huge grin. If possible, this was the best part of his news. "If we own this land free and clear – and we will because Jennifer and Stetson will give it to us as our wedding present – then we can borrow against the equity in the land to build a house. It'll be a simple house – not any more fancy than this ring." He pulled her left hand up to his mouth and kissed it. His ring on her finger – there was a sight he'd never grow tired of. "But it'll be *ours*."

"Oh," she breathed. Her hazel eyes, gray out here against the white snow, filled with unshed tears. "I can't believe…" she whispered, and wiped at her eyes. "This is wonderful." Her voice was rough with emotions. "I never expected…"

"I didn't either." He pulled her against his chest, rubbing his hands up and down her back briskly. "I never expected anything like this."

Anything like you.

Did Carla know how wonderful she was? Did Carla understand how happy she made him?

Well, he had the rest of his life to show her this truth again and again.

EPILOGUE
CARLA

Mawage. Mawage is wot bwings us togeder today.
~The Impressive Clergyman in *The Princess Bride*

JUNE, 2021

THIS WAS IT.

How was it that this day had *finally* come? It'd somehow taken forever to arrive…and no time at all.

Six months of planning a wedding, and designing a house, and surviving another Valentine's Day (only just barely), and giving birth to a baby (even worse than V-Day, which she didn't think was possible), and moving into Christian's shitty single-wide (that had at least been cleaned up with new carpet and paint by Stetson and Jennifer before she moved in) to live in until the house was done…

Their wedding was some far-off dream that'd happen "someday." She'd dreamed about it between diaper changes and breastfeedings and hundreds of boutonnières for prom night and flowers for other people's weddings. She'd started out with some nutty idea that this would be the Wedding of the Century in Long Valley, and it'd be more romantic and more gorgeous and more insane than any other wedding in the history of ever.

Reality had quickly come knocking on her front door, though, and bluntly informed her that she had better shit to focus on. She couldn't believe she actually admitted this, but...

Reality was right. She *did* have more important things to focus on than whether or not she arrived at the church in a limousine.

One thing she didn't compromise on, though – her dress. She looked in the full-length mirror and sighed happily.

"Ding, ding, ding..." she whispered softly to her image as she swished the voluminous skirt back and forth. It was one of her favorite scenes from one of her favorite movies *not* named *The Princess Bride* – *Runaway Bride*.

"Admiring yourself?" Michelle asked, coming up behind her and giving her a light squeeze on the shoulders. "You look gorgeous, by the way. Christian's gonna have to scrape his jaw off the ground after he takes one look at you."

Carla smiled at her friend in the mirror. "Thanks," she said, trying not to tear up and ruin her makeup that she'd worked so hard on for so long. She fussed with the comb holding her veil in place, making sure it was secure, and then carefully pulled locks of her hair forward to cascade down and around her face and breasts. The high empire waist of the white satin gown emphasized Christian's avowed favorite feature: Her overly generous boobs. Between the cut of the gown and some heavy-duty undergarments that'd taken three of them to wrestle her into, Carla actually managed to look like she had a waist to speak of, even if drawing in a deep breath wasn't possible.

The way she figured it, breathing was overrated anyway.

"How is Rosie doing?" she asked anxiously, straightening a curl to lay just so. "She isn't fussing, is she?"

"Your mother-in-law has her coddled to within an inch of her life," Michelle said dryly. "*Rose Petal* is just fine."

Carla pursed her lips together, trying to hide her giggle from

Michelle. Yes, it was true that her daughter's name was Rose Petal Palacios, but of course, no one was actually supposed to call her that. She was to be known as Rosie to everyone...

Except Michelle, who never missed a chance to call her by her given name. Michelle, who thought that the name was completely bonkers. The only thing that Carla could get Michelle to – grudgingly – agree to was that *Rose Petal* was better than *Buttercup*, which'd been Carla's first choice. Sadly, Christian had vetoed it.

Which was fair enough. After all, she'd used her veto power to abolish Cassandra – a beautiful name that she might've agreed to, except Christian had made the mistake of revealing his plan to shorten it to "Case."

Yes, *Case*, not *Cass*. When she'd asked him archly if he wouldn't just like to call their daughter "Tractor" instead, he'd protested hotly that he had absolutely *no* idea what she was talking about.

"I'm glad *Rose Petal* is doing well," Carla said, pretending as if she was oblivious to Michelle's sarcasm. "Thank heavens you thought to have me feed her before we wrestled me into this dress. This doesn't exactly have an easy access panel for breastfeeding."

"A failing of the wedding dress industry, to be sure."

Carla was trying to decide if Michelle was being sarcastic or not – never a sure thing with her – when Keila opened the door. "Christian's up at the front," she whispered excitedly. Her friend had told her that she'd never been a bridesmaid before, and had taken to the role like fish to water. "You ready?"

Carla nodded, the butterflies going berserk in her belly. Despite the fact that there shouldn't be enough room inside of her support garments for an ant to do the conga, butterflies were somehow doing a hell of a lot more than that.

"Is Dad out there?"

"Sure am, dear," he said from the hallway. "Are you decent?"

"I am," she said with a light laugh. She was supposed to be walking down the aisle in just minutes. If she wasn't dressed by this point, she would've been in deep trouble. "You can come in."

Her dad peered cautiously around the door frame as if he somehow thought she might be lying about her state of undress, and then sucked in a quick breath. "You're beautiful," he whispered, and dabbed at the corners of his eyes with the sleeve of his suit as he came over and gave her a delicate hug, clearly afraid he was going to mess something up. "Well, my dear, are you ready?"

She nodded and slipped her hand inside the crook of his arm. Michelle, Autumn, and Keila got matched up with their escorts, and the processional music started. She watched her friends disappear through the open door and into the chapel with trembling lips. She'd always been one to cry at weddings, but she was beginning to realize that she was a hundred times worse at her own wedding.

She scooped up her bouquet from the side table – a giant draping concoction of every one of her favorite flowers – and together, they moved to the doorway into the chapel.

At the sight of her, the organist quit playing, the guests stood, and the haunting bars of *Storybook Love* began to play through the PA system.

> *Come, my love, I'll tell you a tale*
> *Of a boy and girl and their love story*

Willy DeVille's voice, singing the iconic theme song from *The Princess Bride*, rang through the chapel as Carla slowly moved up the aisle. Her dad was snuffling loudly now, as were most of the guests. Carla saw Iris, her brilliant red hair unmistakable, snuggled against Declan, her basketball of a stomach sticking out in front of her. She was due in a month, but looked ready to pop at any moment. She was rubbing her hands across her protruding stomach idly as she watched Carla. She looked up and caught Carla's eye, and for a moment, Carla was sure her friend was going to break down into tears of joy. Iris blew her a quick kiss and Carla gave her a tremulous smile, her lips quivering.

It was happening.

A movement to her right caught her eye and Carla looked over to see her mother-in-law, María, waving Rosie's chubby hand in the air. Carla's arms ached to hold her baby again – she didn't think she'd been away from her daughter for this long since her birth eight weeks ago – but she knew she was safe in the arms of María. True to her word, María had kicked her brother-in-law to the curb, and hadn't wavered in her pronouncement that he'd never step foot inside of their house again. Enraged, Nicolás had moved out of state, wanting to make his older brother pay by refusing to spend time in his company any longer.

Not a single fistfight had broken out at a Palacios dinner since then. Funny how that worked.

> *She said, "Don't you know that storybook loves*
> *Always have a happy ending?"*

And then she looked at the head of the aisle where Christian stood in his tux, his hair slicked back, looking more formal than he ever had before, and probably ever would again. Gone was her cowboy who could wrestle a calf into the dirt, give it a booster shot, and send it on its way quicker than Carla could decide which earrings to wear that day.

In his stead was a quiet, somber, beautiful man. His face was alight with a beaming smile that made Carla's heart take wing. How was it that this gorgeous being, inside and out, wanted to marry her?

She didn't know, but she'd stopped asking a long time ago, lest he start to question that fact also.

My love is like a storybook story
But it's as real as the feelings I feel

The last strains of the haunting music died away, and the Catholic priest cleared his throat. For just a moment, Carla thought he was going to say, "Mawage. Mawage is wot bwings us togeder today," but he didn't. She'd asked him months ago if he would, of course, but he'd refused.

Turned out, Catholic priests didn't think that a lifelong obsession with a movie was a reason for them to impersonate John Malkovich.

Life couldn't be perfect, she supposed.

After her father gave her away to Christian and Keila took her bouquet to hold during the ceremony, she moved to kneel next to Christian, hands clasped together as they listened to the priest read with total solemnity from the Old Testament.

She felt Christian give her hand a gentle squeeze, and she peeked at him out of the corner of her eye.

"Mawage," Christian mouthed. "Mawage is wot bwings us togeder today."

With a suppressed giggle, Carla looked forward again.

Maybe life could be perfect after all.

∪ ∪ ∪

Quick Author's Note

Wiping away a sniffly tear...

Bloom of Love took longer for me to write than any other book of mine, by a looonnngggg shot. Exactly 18 months passed between my last book (*Strummin' Up Love*) and the release of this one. It was never my intent to take this blasted long to write Carla and Christian's love story, but in my defense, 2020 was 12 of those 18 months, so... *shrug* Need I say more?

I begged, borrowed, and stole ideas from a plethora of

people in my life to bring Carla and Christian's love story to life, so please bear with me for just a moment as I give my little Oscar speech.

Thank you to Iris and Matt for showing me what true love was. Only that could entice a guy to get allergy shots so he could move in with his girlfriend…and all of her cats. 😉

Thank you to Cary Elwes for writing *As You Wish*, the fantastic true story and behind-the-scenes view of *The Princess Bride*. I've always loved and adored this movie (I rather think it's illegal not to!) and listening to him read his tell-all as an audiobook was a special treat for me.

Thank you to my own Great Pyrenees, Marshmallow, who is the sweetest, kindest, most loyal dog on the planet (and no, I'm not biased!) I've had people freak out a little when they met him because of his size, but he's always won them over with his sweet personality. (And yes, my Marshmallow is also an outside dog! He takes a special pride in patrolling the farm and protecting us – and the chickens! – from a pack of coyotes that roam nearby). Although he can't be my writing buddy like Jasmine the Writing Cat is – I write inside, so this does put a damper on that idea – he was certainly an inspiration in this book.

Speaking of, thank you to Jasmine the Writing Cat for all of your snuggles and plot ideas. Just for you, my writing partner in crime, there were *two* cats in this book and only one dog. #youarewelcome

Thank you to the many florists who shared their stories with me, and especially the florist who shared the story of how he got into the business. Carla's confession of being a flower thief on May Day – of stripping the neighbor of flowers in order to give paper baskets of flowers away to everyone on the street? Yeah, I stole that one wholesale. Delivering baskets to neighbors on May Day has sadly become a forgotten relic of the past, and so I especially enjoyed using this bit of nostalgia here.

Carla has always held a special place in my heart, with her

turquoise van and her rose-colored glasses. She loves everyone, but somehow, hadn't found someone to love her. I'm glad I finally found just the right guy. Speaking of…

I'd mentioned Christian in my very first book – *Accounting for Love*. You'd be forgiven if you don't remember him – Stetson only mentions him in passing when he has truly deep, contemplative thoughts like, "Christian will make sure that the men were doing what they needed to." Which, Christian being Christian, was totally true, but still, this does mean that Christian's introduction in the Long Valley world was both early on and completely forgettable.

It was actually Christian's younger sister, Yesenia, who gets more "screen time" in *Accounting for Love* – do you remember Yesenia coming to feed Nudges the calf, and Stetson talking to her when she arrives? She was only 16 at that point – young, and beautiful, and already showing that she's smart as a whip.

It took four years, but I finally worked my way back around to the Palacios family. Don't say I'm not dogged!

And yes, Yesenia will get her own book down the line. #duh She still has some growing up to do (and some college to attend!) but she'll get there.

In the meanwhile, be sure to check out the start of my Firefighters of Long Valley Romance series, *Flames of Love*, a book where you have the combustible combination of firefighters who are *also* cowboys. Yum! It is available at your favorite book retailer or local library, so be sure to find it there and enjoy.

Here's to many more years of loving Long Valley together,

Erin Wright

Be sure to find my books at your favorite bookstore, retailer, or library

Or, buy them directly from me at
https://ErinWright.net/My-Books

If you prefer, you can also scan this QR code with your phone:

ALSO BY ERIN WRIGHT

~ COWBOYS OF LONG VALLEY ROMANCE ~

Accounting for Love

Blizzard of Love

Arrested by Love

Returning for Love

Christmas of Love

Overdue for Love

Bundle of Love

Lessons in Love

Baked with Love

Bloom of Love

Broken by Love (TBA)

Holly and Love (TBA)

Banking on Love (TBA)

Sheltered by Love (TBA)

~ FIREFIGHTERS OF LONG VALLEY ROMANCE ~

Flames of Love

Inferno of Love

Fire and Love

Burned by Love

~ MUSICIANS OF LONG VALLEY ROMANCE ~

Strummin' Up Love
Melody of Love (TBA)
Rock 'N Love (TBA)
Rhapsody of Love (TBA)

~ SERVICEMEN OF LONG VALLEY ROMANCE ~

Thankful for Love (TBA)
Commanded to Love (TBA)
Salute to Love (TBA)
Harbored by Love (TBA)

About Erin Wright

USA TODAY BESTSELLING AUTHOR ERIN WRIGHT has worked every job under the sun, including library director, barista, teacher, website designer, and ranch hand helping brand cattle, before settling into the career she's always dreamed about: Author.

She still loves coffee, doesn't love the smell of cow flesh burning, and is currently living out her own love story in a tiny town in rural Idaho.

Wanna get in touch?
https://erinwright.net
erin@erinwright.net

Or reach out to Erin on your favorite social media platform:

- facebook.com/AuthorErinWright
- x.com/ErinWrightLV
- youtube.com/@ErinWrightLV
- pinterest.com/ErinWrightBooks
- goodreads.com/ErinWright
- bookbub.com/profile/Erin-Wright
- instagram.com/AuthorErinWright

Made in the USA
Las Vegas, NV
15 August 2025

26390946R00134